Throne of Ash and Dust

Lynn Howard

Throne of Ash and Dust

To get early news, win free stuff, and enter giveaways, make sure to subscribe to my newsletter. Don't worry, I promise not to spam your inbox!
www.lynnhowardbooks.com

<u>Reading Order</u>

Big River pack:
Gray's Wolf
Micah's Match
Emory's Mate
Reed's Girl
Tristan's Voice

Blackwater Clan:
Colton's Kitty
Noah's Fire
Carter's Devotion
Luke's Redemption

Ravenwood Pride:
Braxton's Warrior
Aron's Element
Daxon's Heart
Mason's Princess

Morse Pack:
Koda's Challenge
Auddi's Destiny
Zeke's Revelation

Shifter Council Executioners:
Shift in Priority
Shift in Focus

Other Titles by Lynn Howard:
Laken (Immortally Yours)
Zac (Immortally Yours)
Her Heart to Mend (A Contemporary Romance)

Chapter One

Prince Ahrkyn closed his eyes and lifted his face to the sky, letting the sun's rays warm his skin. It was quiet today. Birds chirped in a nearby tree, small animals scavenged through the underbrush, but the usual cacophony that deafened him was non-existent.

The only sounds not natural were the gentle footfalls of the Royal guard patrolling with him and the hooves squishing in the rain-soaked ground. He could stay out here until sunset if allowed.

It wasn't that he wasn't *allowed*; it wasn't smart to wander the woods alone once the sun disappeared past the trees. Nocturnal creatures didn't discern between Elf, human, or otherwise. They simply searched for someone or some*thing* to feast upon.

The perimeter checks of Ahdlai had increased since the bordering region of Mhahzin had attacked months prior. So many had been lost on both sides, but Ahdlai had come out the victor. Primarily because descendants of a resident Fae happened to be in search of her to get her out of harm's way. The chances of that particular Court coming to the aid of Ahdlai again was slim.

Although it had been months since Ahdlai had been attacked, he was still tired to his bones.

Ahrkyn usually hated quiet days like today. He liked action, liked running with the guard, loved going headlong into battle with their enemies. But now, he was particularly grateful for the silence, the simplicity of the day.

And after watching the way Jhelan and his mate, Valdis, constantly rushed back home to reunite after completing their duties, he had become lonely. Not that he would admit that to anyone, especially not his friends.

Ahdeben and Ihsander were both interested in finding a mate. They were interested in siring an heir.

That part didn't interest Ahrkyn. Or, at least, it *hadn't*. Originally, he had fought the urge to Claim a female and put a child in her belly, simply because his parents had been pushing him to choose a woman for so many years.

Then he began to wonder if he would be any good as a father or a mate. He preferred to be in the woods with his men, preferred to be free to come and go as he pleased. If he were to Claim a woman, she would be his responsibility until the day she gave birth. Then he would have a child to raise, albeit with the help of his family and the residents of his region.

But it was still more than he wanted to deal with on a daily basis, it was something he'd heard Jhelan complain about more than once when Valdis had come crashing into his life.

The resistant thoughts now sounded hollow in his head, the feelings forced and fake.

Yet none of the women who lived within the town of Ahdlai proper appealed to him; none had caught his eye or made him want for more than the life he currently lived and enjoyed.

"We should head back," Jhelan called from some distance.

"You just want to get back to your mate," Ahdeben teased.

Ahrkyn smiled to himself and shook his head. The four men had grown up together, had shared a wetnurse, had trained together as they had been brought up to be members of the guard.

They had grown to be as close as brothers, and Ahrkyn often thought of them as such.

They also busted each other's balls as often and as ruthlessly as brothers.

"Do you blame me?" Jhelan said.

Ahrkyn climbed atop his mare and aimed her in the direction of the others.

"I don't see Valdis as you do," Ahdeben grumbled. "It would be like finding a sister attractive."

Most of them had sisters and brothers but rarely grew up beside them. Since their race was long-lived and could only breed with humans, there were sure to be offspring of their parents scattered around the world.

Ahrkyn emerged through the brush where the rest of the guard waited. "I take it there was no trace of any trespassers?" he asked.

"None other than traces of humans and possibly some local Shape Shifters. Nothing of concern," Jhelan said.

He nudged his horse with the heel of his boot and turned toward town. Yeah. He definitely wanted to get back to his mate.

The Queen of Ahdlai was Ahrkyn's step-mother, but had raised him as her own since joining the family when he was barely a toddler. She was his mother in all ways that mattered. And his parents still appeared to have the constant need to touch each other, to be near each other. It was beyond simple love or affection. His parents were Fate Bonded, their mating blessed by Mother Universe. They were inseparable. If they were to choose to go their separate ways, the Universe would force them back into each other's arms.

A large part of Ahrkyn's reluctance to Claim a mate was because of his parents' connection. He didn't want to risk being tied for life to someone who might die long before him, nor did he want anything less than the Fated Bond.

It was maddening and confusing and something he simply chose to push to the back of his mind as often as possible.

Jhelan and Ahrkyn stayed in the front of the pack of horses with Ahdeben and Ihsander on the outside. The rest of the guard who united along the way fell into line, all ready to return home to warm food and, hopefully, a calm, relaxing evening.

There weren't often any disturbances in the region, but it felt as though everyone was constantly on edge after the attack, after their gates had been blown open by Fae magic, after an army of *Ihllr* Elves poured through the opening in the gate and attempted to slay the residents along with the King and Queen. Had it not been for Jhelan's mate, they might very well have succeeded.

The group engaged in small talk, complained about the lack of action, complained about the warming weather causing their leather battle gear to chafe. In other words, it was merely another day on duty.

Jhelan had been permitted to return to his duties as head of the guard because his mate was not human. She couldn't carry a child within her body, couldn't breed with Jhelan.

That wasn't a luxury others had. Yet another reason Ahrkyn was reluctant to Claim a woman, reluctant to plant his seed deep inside her belly – he didn't want to give up something he not only loved but had fought his parents to allow him to do once he had become of age.

It wasn't customary for the heir to the throne to act as a member of the guard. Should Ahrkyn fall, the throne would be up for grabs upon the death of the King and Queen.

Ruling the region wasn't something Ahrkyn often considered. Because of the long life of Elves, it could be centuries before his father was too old to hold the position any further, centuries before Mother Universe called him home.

Unless he was killed by someone hoping to usurp his crown. And after the actions of the Emperor of Mhahzin, it wasn't such an absurd possibility.

There had to be a way to put a stop to this nonsense. Why the hell did Emperor Ehmile have such a vendetta against those in Ahdlai? Ahrkyn's people, those under his parents' rule, simply wanted to live their lives. They wanted to grow their crops, raise their livestock, and produce healthy children who could become productive citizens of Ahdlai. Simple. Happy. Safe.

Since the massive attack, an outer wall had been built around the homes of the residents, ensuring they were as protected as the Royal Family. It was one more barrier against the enemy, whether Elven or otherwise.

"You're quiet today," Jhelan said, breaking into Ahrkyn's thoughts.

Ahrkyn's shoulders rose and fell. "Tired."

Not a lie. He was tired in his body, mind, and heart. Problem was, he wasn't sure what was causing the majority of it. There had been no action, no problems, and, as far as he knew, he was sleeping fine.

Yet there was this constant heaviness in his body. Perhaps it was the loneliness that had recently begun to plague him. It might be time to seek out someone to Claim, at least until his first heir was conceived and born.

But that thought was as palatable as slaking his needs with a nameless stranger. He wanted more, yet couldn't identify exactly what it was he sought. Over and over, he wondered whether it was a connection like his parents' he craved or dreaded. Over and over, he wondered whether Claiming a woman would dispel the sense of uneasiness that felt as though it had inhabited every cell in his body or whether it would simply add more stress to his already taxed mind.

"I'm starving," Ihsander blurted out.

"You're always hungry," Ahdeben said.

But Ahrkyn barely heard them. He barely noticed the others continuing to chat around him. His thoughts were scattered. His heart was both broken and empty, yet nothing had happened to cause either.

Brown eyes flashed through his mind when he blinked, there and gone so quickly he thought a bug must have flown past his face. When it happened on his next blink, a sense of excitement flittered through him.

Brown eyes. As he let his attention narrow to a laser focus on that particular vision, he felt lighter than he had in months. Years.

Lifting his head to the sky, he pled with Mother Universe that whoever she was sending his way would be for his betterment and the betterment of those he held dearest.

Ahrkyn didn't have the gift of precognition. There was no reason he would be foreseeing the future, yet he could see those brown eyes every time he blinked as though he was staring directly into them. He could see their shape, could see the dark lashes framing them, could see the flecks of green and gold in the irises.

The people of town were busy closing down their homes, locking up their animals, and preparing for the evening as Ahrkyn and the others rode through the first set of gates. A few waved or smiled, one female greeted the male she was currently mated to, her shirt clinging to the small bump of a growing child in her womb.

Ahrkyn peeled away from the rest of the guard as they put their horses away for the night and either headed to the Palace for a late dinner or to their own homes where they might or might not have someone waiting for them.

As the Prince and only son of King Nhaeem – he'd had only daughters before and after Ahrkyn was born before meeting Queen

Ahlmeda – he was the only member of the guard who lived within the Palace.

Unlike most nights when he arrived from patrolling duties, Ahrkyn didn't feel the usual contentment over dropping his battle leathers onto the bed and stepping into his shower. Today had been the first time in a long time where he would have preferred to linger in the fresh air, to lay upon the ground and stare up at the stars as the night air grew cooler.

But he couldn't. Not as long as the nocturnal creatures continued to prey upon any they could drain of blood.

The next few days were considered his down time. He hated downtime. Had always hated downtime. He liked to stay busy, liked to keep his mind occupied. Especially as of late since Jhelan had been Fate Bound to his mate.

It made Ahrkyn's loneliness rear its ugly head the moment his life grew quiet, the moment he had nothing else to occupy his thoughts.

As Ahrkyn turned the faucet and the spray pounded tile, he began to wonder why he couldn't simply climb atop his steed and wander the woods for no other reason than enjoyment.

And also began to wonder why he felt a pull toward that exact thing. It was more than the simple boredom – something was begging him to return to the woods over and over again until…

Until what?

From where did this need arise? It was far beyond his usual boredom, beyond his need to quell his loneliness. It was literally as though something was tied to his chest and tugging him toward the front door and into the woods.

Tomorrow. Tomorrow he would rise before the others and head out. There was something calling to him and he needed to discover what. Or who. Perhaps it was someone in need of help. Or someone who had become lost in the woods.

It could even be a remaining member of Jhelan's mate's Clan who they had all believed had been slaughtered in one fell swoop.

That was wishful thinking for Valdis. They had all come to love the woman as though she were a sister. The respect they held for her after she had kept the Queen from falling under the sword was felt by all in Ahdlai, and word of her efforts had traveled to the other towns in the region.

Valdis had been found in the woods after the guard had discovered the *Ihllr* attacking her Clan. The *Ihllr* had fallen at the *Vhtir's* hands, and then Valdis had been brought back to Ahdlai proper to heal. And she and Jhelan had discovered their happily-ever-after as though shit like that was common, as though they had somehow managed to live out their own romance novel like the ones the humans used to love before they destroyed civilization with their nuclear weapons.

As steam rose and filled the bathroom, Ahrkyn stepped under the spray and sighed as the heat relaxed his tense and sore muscles. It soaked his hair, straightening the jet-black strands until they hung to the middle of his back. The streams of water ran down his back, his pecs, and eased the aches he tended to ignore throughout the day so he could complete his duties.

He was sore from his week-long duties, yet was preparing to once again enter the woods. But this was for a completely different reason – this would be for enjoyment.

Or, at least, he hoped it would. There was nothing that gave him a sense of foreboding, nothing that sent anxiety burning through his veins.

No. When he considered disappearing into the thick press of brush and trees, excitement fluttered deep in his stomach and gave him an odd sense of hope. For what, he was unsure.

All he knew was his magic was demanding he head south. Not the best idea, especially when the border of Mhahzin was in that direction. But he would trust his gift, trust that his magic would alert him to any danger, trust that Mother Universe had something for him, something waiting for him, was guiding him to his future … or, perhaps, the future of Ahdlai.

Ahrkyn nearly sprung from his bed the moment the sun rose above the horizon. There was a chance others were up and moving about, readying for their day or tending to their crops or animals. But he didn't care. The need he'd felt last night was stronger, almost to the point of discomfort.

Pulling his undershirt and leather breaches on, he braided his hair back away from his face, then pulled on his battle vest. Just because he wasn't on a mission didn't mean he shouldn't protect himself in case he happened to run into the enemy.

After shoving his feet into his boots and lacing them, he grabbed his sword and rushed from his room. Like most Elves, his magic wasn't strong, but he had never experienced precognition the way Jhelan did. Ahrkyn's magic was more of a defensive tactic. He was able to push waves of energy from his body in a weak form of telekinesis. But it aided him in battle when he was outnumbered and needed to put space between himself and his foes.

So, if he didn't have the gift of precognition, why did he still see brown eyes each time he blinked? Why was he so adamant someone waited for him in the woods? Why was he willing to risk his safety to rush into the woods alone in search of the answer to this weird new mystery?

He didn't bother slowing to question the logic of his actions. He simply strapped his sword to his back, pulled his favorite steed from its stall, and kicked his sides, lifting a hand in thanks as first one then the other gate opened as he neared them at a full run.

No one stopped him, no one called out to ask where he was going, no one acted the least bit concerned that the Prince of Ahdlai was hurrying from the safety of the Palace alone.

For a brief second, Ahrkyn almost slowed his horse. The fact no one questioned his actions was odd.

But the sensation drawing him south grew stronger until there was a literal ache in the center of his chest.

His thighs gripping his horse, Ahrkyn lifted a hand and pressed the heel against his sternum, trying to massage the ache away. But it was deeper than skin deep. It was damned near soul deep.

The pull began to dissipate. Not disappear, but lessen as though he were growing closer to whatever Mother Universe was guiding him toward.

Pulling on the rein, he stopped his horse and dismounted, leaving her loose in case of an attack. He wanted his horse to be able to run home rather than become a snack if a predator decided either the Prince or his animal smelled like their next meal.

Leaves and twigs crackled under foot as he slowly made his way closer and closer to the border of Ahdlai, the same border that led into Mhahzin.

This was a bad idea. At any point, he could be captured and used as a bartering tool against his parents. His presence could be considered an act of war. And they had lost too many good fighters and good people during the last battle. They might not have enough guard members to win the next fight. And there was no guarantee they would receive any outside help from relatives of Valdis nor Brizio the ogre and his witch friends.

But as the sensation he'd been chasing grew and warmed him from the inside out, he realized he didn't care. He didn't care about the repercussions of his actions. He no longer questioned what the hell he was doing or why.

He no longer cared about anything but finding what it was pulling him in that direction. He no longer cared about anything but ending the ache pulling at his soul.

Chapter Two

What the hell was she doing? The second her stepfather noticed her absence, Freyda knew the entirety of his guard would be sent out in search for her.

Was it for her safety? Was it because he was concerned some member of the enemy might seek her out to punish her for his wrongdoings?

Nope.

It was control. If he could control Freyda, he controlled her mother. Emperor Ehmile might not have loved his mate, but she had successfully borne three sons for him since Claiming her when Freyda was barely three-years-old.

She should have taken a horse. Instead, she had snuck out the moment the eastern sky began to turn grey with the rising sun. Having no idea where she would go, she followed her gut and hoped Mother Universe would guide her in the right direction.

How long had she been running? The sun had peeked over the tops of the trees close to an hour ago, yet she continued to trek forward. The movement she made now couldn't quite be considered running. She was exhausted. Her legs felt as though they were full of lead and her muscles burned. Never had she used her body the way she had now. Never had she run so far in her life.

Yet she continued forward.

By the location of the sun and the moss growing on the trees, she guessed she was heading north. If she didn't stop soon, she might very well cross over the border into Ahdlai. She had been warned since she was a child the *Vhtir* Elves would kill her on sight if she were to cross the border. She was warned of their vicious tendencies, had been warned of their hatred of humans.

Slowing to a stop, she bent forward, bracing her hands on her knees, and sucked in breath after breath. She should be far enough she could rest. Maybe not nap, but at least allow her body a brief respite.

Birds flitted from branch to branch overhead. Small rodents and woodland creatures scampered through the brush looking for breakfast. It was peaceful out here. She had wondered at times why the humans and other paranormal beings would choose to live within the woods instead of the cities built near the capitols and Palaces of each region.

As her heart rate slowed and her adrenaline no longer burned through her veins, she began to understand.

There was no one out here to bark orders at her, to demand she wear a certain type of clothing or behave in a certain manner.

She was free out here.

And she wanted to stay that way.

Freyda's stomach grumbled as hunger pangs gnawed at her. Why hadn't she planned her escape a little better? She should have packed a satchel with food, even if only a snack. Instead, she would have to use her very limited knowledge of wild berries and plants to find any form of sustenance until she figured out her next step.

She had zero experience or knowledge of how to hunt any animal for food, so that was completely out of the question.

What was the chance she could find a human Clan? More importantly, what was the chance they would accept her for at least long enough to fill her belly and rest a few more hours?

As long as she'd thought about her escape, she hadn't bothered to put in any hours with training her body or increasing her knowledge of the woods that surrounded her home.

Not her home. Simply a place she'd been held prisoner most of her life.

She had been too young when her biological father had died to remember much about him. And the war that had changed all of human society had happened nearly a century before she had been conceived.

The most she knew of the time before and the events that had led up to those dark days was only what she'd learned from her stepfather's guards when she eavesdropped on their conversations.

This world, this life was all she knew, all she had ever known.

Actually, the world within the Palace was all she could remember. Which meant now she was officially in an alien world and had no idea how to survive.

"Damn it," she grumbled.

She put her back to a tree and slid down, wincing when the bark bit into her back. As long as she'd thought about her escape, she hadn't put much thought into the actual survival aspect.

Freyda now had two choices: Wing it in hopes of not succumbing to the elements or the creatures that hunted humans like her in the woods, or return home with some excuse as to why she was so far from home so early in the morning.

Soft footsteps made it to her ears. Leaves crunched and the birds overhead suddenly went silent. Predator? Were the birds afraid of whatever was coming their way?

She had no idea what kind of wild creatures wandered the woods, only that there were those who drained the blood of their victims or ate their flesh, or those like the *Vhtir* of Ahdlai who would sell her into slavery if they didn't kill her for simply existing.

Panic made her heart race as ice entered her veins. She couldn't fight, and there was no way she could outrun a predator, whether animal or humanoid.

Lifting her head, she stared up into the tree above her. It was either climb or stay where she was and hope the creature or person passed by her unaware of her presence.

The seconds she'd taken to decide on her next course of action wasn't enough. A man standing several inches over six feet with broad shoulders and hair braided down his back appeared through the brush. When his eyes landed on her, he looked as surprised to find her there as she was to see someone of his beauty walking through the wilderness.

And beautiful really was the only word she could think of to describe this man.

Lie. Beautiful, rugged, and intimidating. Those were the best words.

His eyes were an ethereal blue and the tips of his ears came to a point. He was an Elf. The emblem on his leather battle vest let her know she had officially come face to face with the enemy. This man was a member of the Ahdlai guard.

She was a goner. Even if she screamed for help, she was too far to be heard by anyone who could get to her in time.

Pushing to her feet, she squared her shoulders and prepared to bluff her way out of this situation. Perhaps if she alerted this man to her status in Mhahzin he would fear retaliation and leave her be.

"Hello," the man said, blinking rapidly as though shocked she hadn't faded into mist. He looked as though he'd seen a ghost, but was rather pleased instead of filled with fear.

Freyda couldn't find her voice. She was terrified of his presence yet confused as to his countenance and the fact he'd yet to threaten or harm her.

"I'm Ahrkyn."

It was her turn to blink a few times.

"Freyda," she replied.

He didn't know who she was. He might not even know she was human. She could possibly get out of this dire situation after all.

"You have brown eyes," he said.

"What?"

He took a step closer then stopped. "Your eyes. You have beautiful brown eyes."

Freyda frowned up at him. That was what confused him? Her eye color?

Elves didn't have brown eyes. The Fae didn't have brown eyes. He knew she was human.

A new wave of fear slammed into her heart, causing its cadence to beat painfully behind her breasts.

As he took another step closer, Freyda attempted to step away and bumped into the tree at her back.

"I thought I was losing my mind," he said.

There was a slight crease between his raven brows, but a small smile quirked up the corners of his lips as though he were both confused and pleased.

"You thought you were losing your mind?" she asked, repeating his words.

This was one of the oddest encounters she'd had to date, and she had been raised by one of the most ruthless men to have ever existed.

"I saw you," he said, but it sounded more like he was speaking to himself. "Every time I blinked, I saw your eyes."

When he took another step closer, Freyda tried to disappear into the bark of the tree but could not move any further. If she were to dart to the side to run away, he would catch her with ease. The *Vhtir* were excited by the chase. It was a game to them. The Emperor warned her that should she ever run into one of the Elves from Ahdlai that she should stay calm, she should hold her ground, because the second she showed fear, she would be treated like a rabbit pursued by a wolf.

She lifted her chin and stared at Ahrkyn, dared him to move closer while praying he would grow bored and leave her be.

"Freyda," he whispered, as though savoring the taste of her name on his tongue.

"Why are you here? You are close to the territory of Mhahzin." She tried to insert as much authority in her tone as possible but heard the tremor in her words.

"You are close to the territory of Ahdlai," he said with a tilt of his head. "Why are *you* here?"

"I—"

She couldn't tell him the truth. If he knew not only was she the stepdaughter of his enemy but had attempted to flee from the Palace, he could take her as prisoner and use her against the people of Mhahzin. Emperor Ehmile might have been a ruthless bastard, but the people of her home region were good, hard-working people. They did as they were told merely to survive, to protect their families from her stepfather's ire.

"I was checking the perimeter," she lied.

His lips twitched, then he threw his head back and laughed, the sound deep and full of both joy and humor.

"I might not be able to detect lies, but even I can tell that was false," he said.

Of course he wouldn't believe her. She stood nearly a foot shorter than he, wore no battle leathers, and was currently frocked in a dress with a hem that drug the ground and collected twigs and leaves with each step. She also carried no weapons and had no backup.

"Why are you out here? I at least gave an excuse. You've yet to offer one," she said, crossing her arms over her chest.

"I…I think I was looking for you."

That confused look was back on his ridiculously handsome face. He might have been the enemy, but even she could admit he was breathtakingly attractive.

"Why?"

She had done nothing. He might not have even known she existed. What reason would he have to seek her out?

"I don't know. You have brown eyes," he repeated.

It was her turn to smile in confusion.

"You've said that."

When he took another step closer, she found herself no longer fearing her imminent death. She held no gifts like the non-humans, was unable to detect dangers like some of the *Ihllr* Elves, but she was suddenly no longer afraid of this man.

In fact, she found herself wanting to know more about him. She wanted to know exactly what he'd meant about looking for her. She wanted to know why he believed he had seen her eyes in his visions.

She was real. Ahrkyn hadn't imagined her. He wasn't losing his mind.

Freyda. Her name was as beautiful as the eyes staring at him full of so many emotions, so much confusion. And, unfortunately, fear.

She had warned he was close to the border of Mhahzin. She must have been a resident of that area. She might have been taught to fear those in Ahdlai as those in his region had been warned to steer clear of the *Ihllr*.

As much as he wanted to reach forward and touch her to ensure himself she was real, he needed to keep his distance to avoid scaring her any further.

He needed her to stay right where she was so he could figure out exactly why he'd been pulled toward her, why he had been dragged from the Palace and so far into the woods to find her.

She obviously wasn't in any danger. She didn't appear to be injured.

So…why? What had Mother Universe found so urgent that he had to be right here at this very moment to find her?

Searching for a way to keep her there, searching for a reason to convince her to stay and talk to him, he pointed toward where he'd left his steed.

"Are you hungry? I packed a satchel in case I was out here too long."

She shook her head and opened her mouth, no doubt to decline, but her stomach grumbled loudly.

Freyda's cheeks instantly pinkened as she placed a hand over her belly. She was round in all the right places, soft and plush. He loved women in all their forms, but had always been partial to a woman with some…cushion to her body. A woman whose body resembled those who were painted in the earlier days of human civilization with round bellies, wide hips, and full breasts.

She was taller than he usually found himself attracted to, standing somewhere close to five feet seven, give or take an inch. But even that appealed to him.

When he turned to return to his horse, he realized he didn't hear her footfalls following behind. Glancing over his shoulder, he found her still watching him with an indiscernible expression on her face.

"If you'll wait there, I'll bring you the food. You have no reason to fear me, Freyda. I mean you no harm."

He dipped his head before hurrying to grab the satchel and forced his feet to walk at a fast clip rather than sprinting back to where she waited. There was a beat where he feared she would disappear in the short time he was absent. But she had waited for him, still under the shade of the tree.

"I'm sorry. I didn't bring a pelt or anything to sit upon. I would offer you my undershirt, but –"

"Then you would be bare chested."

"Exactly," he said with a grin.

It had felt like she'd come short of mentioning that it might be seen as inappropriate for the Prince to be bare chested, alone, with a woman. But he hadn't introduced his status among the region of Ahdlai. For now, she only saw him as a man rather than a position.

The only three people in his life who saw him as something other than Prince Ahrkyn of Ahdlai were his three closest friends, Jhelan, Ahdeben, and Ihsander. It was nice to not have someone bow to him, to not have someone dip their eyes in his presence, to not have someone insist upon doing things for him he was perfectly capable of doing himself.

"I can sit on the ground," she said, a shy smile on her face when his grin widened.

Ahrkyn nearly plopped onto his butt like a child and waited as she spread her skirt around her and lowered like a lady.

Watching her, his eyes narrowed briefly. Her gown was quite ornate, more ornate than the gowns worn by the women in the town of Ahdlai proper. But not having ventured into Mhahzin since the Emperor had declared Ahrkyn's family the enemy, he had absolutely no idea whether such frocks were usual for the women there.

The gown was also much less conservative than those worn by the women in Ahdlai, revealing quite a bit of her cleavage.

Ahrkyn opened the satchel and pulled various items out, offering her his meager selection. She wasn't picky. She eagerly accepted both the deer jerky and the apple he handed her. They broke their fast together in silence, occasionally sharing awkward glances.

When she got her fill, she set the apple core to the side and folded her hands on her lap.

"Thank you," she said, then quickly darted her gaze from his face.

"You truly have no reason to fear me, Freyda. I would rather cut my own throat than cause you any harm."

Her eyes returned to his face and narrowed. "But you are from Ahdlai."

"I am," he said with a nod.

"Then why are you being so kind? Why share your food? Is this the way your people ply your victims to come with you willingly?"

A frown pulled his brows together as anger hit him square in the middle of the chest.

"I would never hurt you. *We* would never hurt you."

"I am human. You've already pointed out my eyes, so I know you're aware of that fact."

"I know you're human."

Her shoulders rose and fell. "You hate humans. You kill them or take them as slaves."

His frown slowly smoothed until he found a sense of amusement at her words.

"Is that what they teach in Mhahzin? That the *Vhtir* of Ahdlai are monsters?"

She shrugged once more.

Ahrkyn chuckled softly and went back to his small meal with a shake of his head.

"Why is that funny?"

After swallowing, he took a small swig from his canteen and offered her a drink of water.

"We are taught the same thing about your region."

The laugh that escaped her petal pink lips was nothing short of musical and tightened his body in places he had no business noting.

It was his turn to ask, "What's funny about that?"

She waved a hand down her body. "I'm human. What could I possibly do to you or your kind?"

She had only meant to point out that she was harmless to his kind, but had merely drawn his attention back to her beautifully curvy body.

When his eyes lingered too long on her breasts that strained against the fabric of her gown, she cleared her throat and raised her arms to cross them over herself.

Damn it. He was doing his best to disarm her in hopes of learning why he was drawn into the woods and instead was making her uncomfortable with his leering.

Hooves hitting the ground hard and fast met his ears. She would not hear it yet, not with her weaker human senses. Someone was coming.

And they were not coming from his own region.

"We're getting company," he said, rising to his feet and offering her his hand.

Her brows puckered and she instantly slid her hand into his, allowing him to pull her to her feet.

"Am I in danger?" she asked with wide eyes.

"I suppose that depends on who is approaching. They're not my people. They come from your territory."

She was currently just over the border in Ahdlai territory. He could not be accused of trespassing. But he could be accused of many other things if the Emperor so decided.

"Damn it," she muttered.

Ahrkyn smiled at the curse coming from her sweet mouth.

As quickly as possible, Freyda smoothed her skirt and patted the braids in her hair.

Moments later, a large *Ihllr* guard appeared, shooting daggers from his eyes aimed directly at Ahrkyn.

"Princess Freyda," the man called.

Princess? This man, this *Ihllr* Elf guardsman from Mhahzin, had referred to Freyda as Princess. Meaning…

This woman was the stepdaughter of Emperor Ehmile.

He had been drawn to the woods, led by some unknown source, and directly to the adopted daughter of his family's enemy.

"You are Princess Freyda, daughter of Emperor Ehmile?" he asked, and was unable to keep the contempt and accusatory tone from his voice.

"I am."

"And this is Prince Arkyn, son of your father's enemy," the guard declared as he dismounted his horse.

Freyda's eyes turned to Ahrkyn, and he could practically see the wheels turning. She thought he had known who she was, thought he was luring her away.

How could she possibly believe that when he'd done nothing but offer her food and company? He'd asked her nothing but her name, had not asked her to leave with him, had not laid a single finger on her.

"What has happened, Princess? Did this bastard kidnap you?"

"What?" Freyda and Ahrkyn said in unison.

"Of course not," Freyda answered hastily. "I couldn't sleep. I decided on a walk and got lost. Ark—Prince Ahrkyn was aiding me in finding my way home but knew he was unable to escort me over the border. He offered me food and company while we awaited my rescue."

Her rescue?

Ahrkyn nearly had to bite his tongue to prevent from bursting out laughing.

"You should have asked for an escort before wandering from the Palace alone, Princess. Your father–"

"*Step*father," she quickly corrected.

"Is worried about you. He feared you had been taken by the *Vhtir*."

The tone in the guardsman's voice sounded more like he had spit the name rather than spoken it.

Freyda's wide eyes met Ahrkyn's. The accusation was still there, but so was panic.

Why was she out here alone? She had brought no revisions, no protection of any form, no chaperones. Was she attempting to escape, and this man was there to drag her back?

If she needed his sword, she had it. He would put himself between her and the guardsman. All she had to do was say the word.

"Will you be okay?" he whispered to her.

"Of course she will," the guardsman spoke. "I am tasked with her protection. I'm tasked with guarding her against men like yourself."

When the sardonic chuckle bubbled in Ahrkyn's chest, he didn't attempt to hold it back.

"Was it or was it not your men who attacked Ahdlai? I believe it was your Emperor and your guards who infiltrated our walls with the intent of slaying my parents and overthrowing our government. You slew many of my men and would have slain the residents of Ahdlai had you been given the opportunity."

"Rhamzin?" Freyda asked, turning to look into the face of the man who was glaring at Ahrkyn. "Is that true? Did my stepfather send you to slay an entire town of innocent people?"

How was the Princess so unaware of what her stepfather ordered, of the things he ordered of his guards?

"We need to get you back to the Palace before more of his kind arrive. Your father will not want us to allow any harm to come to you."

Rhamzin gently gripped Freyda by her bicep and began to lead her to a waiting horse. That small touch, the man's fingers wrapped around Freyda's arm, was enough to send a possessive rage coursing through Ahrkyn's system.

When he would have stepped forward to protest, to pull her away, to do…something, Princess Freyda looked him in the eye and shook her head in the slightest movement he was unsure Rhamzin noticed.

She was warning him off. But why?

She didn't appear afraid of the guardsman, but she did look reluctant to leave.

If Freyda truly was the Princess of Mhahzin, this might very well be the last Ahrkyn ever saw of her. So, what was the purpose of being drawn into the woods to meet her? Was it to watch over her? To keep her safe until her guardsmen found her?

None of those options rang true. Their meeting felt deeper, more profound, as though she was meant to be in his life in some capacity, although he couldn't figure out how any such thing could come to pass, not if she was the stepdaughter of the very Elf who had waged war on Ahrkyn's people.

Tamping down another wave of possessive urge as Rhamzin wrapped his hands around her waist, lifted her atop his horse, then climbed behind her, Ahrkyn watched Freyda closely for any sign that she needed his aid.

If she so much as gave him a look of panic, Ahrkyn would swing his sword free and lob the fucker's head off and bring the Princess back to Ahdlai.

By now, his own guard would have noticed he was missing and those who'd seen him riding off on his own would have pointed them in the right direction. She could be picked up and protected by his people.

"Thank you for your assistance, Prince Ahrkyn," she said with a dip of her chin.

Her words were polite and emotionless, but he swore he saw a touch of hurt in her eyes. She felt he had betrayed her by withholding his position within Ahdlai.

But she, too, had withheld the very same information.

He had not learned why she was so deep in the woods and had managed to wander into Ahdlai territory alone. He had not learned why he had seen her eyes in his mind before meeting her.

And he had not learned what had pulled him toward her or why he'd found the need to learn anything he could about her.

This woman, this Princess, would remain a mystery to him as would the visions he'd had of her…for now.

Chapter Three

"What the hell were you thinking?" Rhamzin asked from behind Freyda.

He kept the horse at a trot as he aimed it toward the Palace of Mhahzin. This region had been her home for the twenty-four years she had been alive. Compared to her stepfather and so many of the non-humans, twenty-four years was a blink of the eye. They were long lived, but not quite immortal, although the Emperor sometimes acted otherwise.

"I went for a walk," she muttered.

"Bull shit. You think I'm a fool? Do you think your father is a fool?"

"*Step*father," she said automatically.

She didn't remember her real father. Freyda had been too young when he was killed to recall those memories. Her mother had told her stories, but that was all her father was; a story, a ghost. It was no different than the characters in the books she adored about the princesses trapped in towers who were rescued by their knights in shining armor.

Of all the things that had been destroyed when the humans went to war with each other nearly a decade ago, books were her favorite things that had survived. She would lose herself for hours in their pages, pretend she was someone else, somewhere else, that she had a different life and someone would arrive to free her from her cage.

One wouldn't think living within a Palace would be a prison. That being the adopted Princess of the entire southern region of Mhahzin could be seen as a captivity. But she did not have a life of her own, was unable to make decisions of her own.

Every step she made was dictated by others. She was not to leave the Palace grounds without an escort, could not choose with whom she would mate, could not choose with whom she would grow a family.

Her stepfather had made it abundantly clear he would choose the man he felt was worthy of the honor of Claiming Freyda.

Like Rhamzin declared of himself, she was no fool. Emperor Ehmile would not wait until he found someone worthy, but rather someone who could help grow his empire and help him defeat the rulers of the northern region of Ahdlai so that he could rule over the expanse of land and all the people in it.

Freyda fought the urge to turn and look in the direction from where Rhamzin currently carried her away. That direction was freedom. It was the liberty to make her own choices.

The direction they were heading now…

She sighed and sagged in the saddle, careful not to lean back against Rhamzin. Of all the guards in her stepfather's employ, he was the only one she trusted. He treated her more like a sister than a charge or burden.

He never leered at her chest or made rude or inappropriate comments, but rather protected her from the rest of the guard and ensured she remained Untouched.

"Does my stepfather know I was gone?"

"I don't know," he said then went back to silently brooding. "You can't do that again, Princess. You can't trust the *Vhtir*."

"Prince Ahrkyn made it sound the other way."

And she had seen firsthand what her stepfather and his guard were capable of through the years.

"You've met him once and now you believe every word from his mouth?"

"I didn't say that," she said, crossing her arms and jutting her chin forward. It was hard to pout on top of a horse with the man's legs bracketing hers.

"Ahdlai is dangerous for humans."

"So is Mhahzin."

"Yet you traipsed through first one territory and directly into the other with no backup. You're lucky it was only me who noticed your absence and sought you out. By the way, if you're going to attempt to escape again you need to learn to cover your tracks better. It took me mere seconds to figure out which direction you were traveling."

Like she had any idea how to cover her tracks or anything about surviving the woods.

She and her mother were kept locked up like birds and treated like pawns in some sick game.

"Are you saying I should try again?"

Rhamzin pulled on the rein and stopped the horse. Freyda turned her upper half to look into his face.

"It is far too dangerous for a human woman to be alone in the wilderness. And I don't think you're going to find anything better outside of Mhahzin. There are monsters in every region, Freyda."

She preferred when he called her by her name instead of her title. It reminded her of their quiet friendship.

"I can't protect you if I can't find you. If you need to feed some rebellious spirit, let me know and I'll travel with you. But I wouldn't suggest running off on your own again. It's suicide. Especially if it's the Emperor's men who find you first."

She shuddered but nodded.

Her stepfather would order her death and blame it on the people of Ahdlai, giving them a reason to attack the northern territory.

Once again, Freyda sighed and turned toward the head of the horse.

Rhamzin nudged the horse forward with a heel in the beast's side. If Freyda had been permitted to learn to ride the animal without an escort, she would have found the fastest one in the stable and taken off. Sure, the hoof marks would have been tracked, but she would have been long gone. She could have put far more distance between herself and Mhahzin before anyone realized she was gone, could have passed through Ahdlai and found an uncharted area or maybe a Clan of humans with whom she could live. *They* wouldn't want her dead merely because she was human.

"What are you going to tell Ehmile?" Freyda asked after several moments of silence.

He huffed a laugh. The only time she used her stepfather's name was in front of Rhamzin, and that was only when they were alone.

"Hopefully, nothing. I see no point in bringing it up if no one else noticed your absence."

"And if someone did and alerted the Emperor?"

"Then we tell them you asked for an escort to pick wildflowers."

"Guess we should stop before we're close to the Palace to find some flowers," she said with a chuckle.

Rhamzin had been the head of the guard since long before Freyda and her mother had been brought to the Palace. He had known Freyda since she was a toddler, had watched over her, protected her, even spoiled her with extra treats when no one was watching her closely. If she had a single friend, it was him.

"What do you know of Prince Ahrkyn?" she asked after a stretch of silence.

The man had intrigued her. He was beyond handsome. Tall and lithe with crystalline blue eyes. His shoulders had been as broad as Rhamzin's, his chest and arms muscled. He also towered over her five-feet-seven frame by at least six inches.

Most of the non-human men were tall and strong. They were broad and intimidating.

But she hadn't felt intimidated by Ahrkyn's presence. Intrigued, curious, and mildly lust-filled, but not intimidated.

"Only that he is the Prince of Ahdlai."

"You know nothing more?"

"There is nothing more you need to know, Princess."

Back to the formalities.

"Have you never simply been curious of someone you met?"

"The way he looked at you was more than simple curiosity."

She turned and looked at him over her shoulder. "How did he look at me?"

"The way a man looks at a woman."

She raised her brows and waited for him to finish.

"He looked at you in a way he had no business looking."

"He didn't look at me the way your buddies in the guard do."

"They are not my buddies," Rhamzin ground out between clenched teeth.

"Still, the guard look at me…"

"In a way they shouldn't," he said quietly.

It was why Rhamzin stayed close to Freyda as much as possible. He despised a majority of the men her stepfather hired, and feared one of them would attempt to Claim her against her will, consequences be damned.

Her mind returned to Ahrkyn, to the way he approached her slowly, his hands held out in front of him as though showing her he was no threat. He'd fed her, had been prepared to protect her when he heard Rhamzin's approach.

What was the chance she would ever lay eyes on him again? More importantly, did she *want* to see him again?

As the silence grew between Freyda and her companion, she allowed her imagination to wander and pretend Prince Ahrkyn was a character from one of her beloved books. She pictured him riding through the gates of Mhahzin, a banner raised, as he declared he was there to rescue the Princess.

It was stupid. She knew such thoughts were stupid, but she didn't have much else to do as anything she had ever suggested was declared inappropriate for a Princess or for a woman.

She wanted a role in her own life. She wanted a purpose other than waiting for Emperor Ehmile to decide when it was time for her to move on and have children.

It wasn't that he feared any children from her would take over his throne; she wasn't his biological daughter and thus had no claim. But children from her would be more children who could be raised the way of the *Ihllr*, and would increase their numbers further.

"Why didn't Prince Ahrkyn kill me?"

Rhamzin stiffened behind her. "What? What would make you ask such a question?"

"I was told the *Vhtir* Elves kill humans on sight. Why did he not kill me? He fed me. He stayed a distance away from me. He barely even spoke to me other than to point out that I had brown eyes."

And that he'd had a vision of her. But she kept that part to herself.

"How do you know he wasn't preparing to do that very thing before hearing my arrival?"

"Because we were there for close to an hour. Why feed me? Are you trying to tell me he is like the witch in Hansel and Gretel?"

"Who?"

"Never mind. I don't think we have been taught correctly about the *Vhtir*. I don't believe they are the blood thirsty monsters my stepfather would have us believe."

The two regions had gone to war a few months back. But Rhamzin had been ordered to stay back with a contingency of guards to ensure the Palace inhabitants were safe in case there was an ambush. She was unsure whether he'd had any first-hand encounters with the Elves from the north.

She had been under the assumption that Ahdlai had started that war.

"You've met one *Vhtir* and are now an expert?"

She rolled her eyes, although he couldn't see her, and shook her head.

Then they went back to riding in silence until they were closer to the Palace.

"We should stop so you can gather flowers. I'm unaware whether you were seen, but it would be better to ensure we have our story covered in case you were."

Rhamzin stopped the horse and climbed off first, then helped Freyda slide out of the saddle, his hands on her shoulders until she was steady on her feet. The only time he touched her anywhere else was this day when he'd hoisted her onto the back of his horse by her hips.

As she moved away and lowered to her knees to gather a colorful bouquet, she went back to that moment. She had locked eyes with Ahrkyn when Rhamzin had climbed behind her. Had it been jealousy she'd seen in the Prince's eyes?

There was no reason for him to be jealous. He had no claim on her, never could. And Rhamzin didn't see Freyda in a sexual manner as other men did. He saw and treated her as a little sister or even daughter, although his appearance looked close to her age regardless of his physical years on the planet.

"Think this is enough?" she asked as she cradled her wildflowers.

He huffed a laugh and nodded. "It should be plenty. You woke me this morning and asked that I accompany you to pick wildflowers. That is all. That is the end of the story. You will never mention being alone, never mention being close to Ahdlai, and sure as hell will never mention meeting Prince Ahrkyn. Understood?"

She waved a hand in the air. "I'm not an idiot."

"Could have fooled me," he muttered under his breath as he folded his hands and waited for her to slide her foot in before pushing her high enough to throw a leg over the other side of his steed.

Freyda once again rolled her eyes as Rhamzin settled into the saddle behind her and urged the horse forward.

In a few minutes, she would discover whether anyone had noticed her absence.

If they hadn't…then what? Did that mean she could dare another adventure? And why not? Rhamzin wasn't angry with her, only worried about her. She could ask him to be her escort and she could explore the territory she called home, more than only the Palace grounds.

Surely, her stepfather would have no problem with that.

Or maybe she would simply keep her future plans to herself.

Ahrkyn wasn't sure how long he stood there staring in the direction in which Princess Freyda had disappeared.

Princess. She was the Princess of Mhahzin, stepdaughter of Emperor Ehmile, stepdaughter to his parents' enemy. Hell, the Emperor was enemy to anyone who dared stand against him or disagree with him.

Rumors had floated about for years of his previous mates, how he'd gone through several Empresses. He would kill them if they dared to disagree or speak against him in any manner.

But those were mere rumors. Ahrkyn had never met the man himself, had never been face to face with the ruler of the southern region of their shared continent.

It was unknown how many women, human and otherwise, had been taken and Claimed, their people slaughtered under the rule of Emperor Ehmile. It *was* known the *Ihllr* terrorized the vulnerable, specifically humans.

Had he mistreated his stepdaughter? She was well fed as evidenced by her delectable curves. The kind of curves he could run his hands along and get lost in for hours.

He needed to get Freyda out of his thoughts. Mother Universe might have had bigger plans for them than an accidental breakfast, but their families were lifelong enemies. Her stepfather was one of the biggest monsters on the planet even though he was of the same species.

Ahrkyn's magic flared. A *Vhtir* approached. Unlike Ahdeben, Ahrkyn didn't have offensive magic, only defensive. He was able to use minor telekinetic abilities to stop a sword or anything else that might be headed toward his neck. But if there were more than one assailant, he was unable to focus on them all.

Minor and not exactly useful in battle.

But the skills he'd honed over the past few decades were the only thing he relied on when fighting.

If a *Vhtir* was approaching, that could only mean his guardsmen were appraised of the Prince's whereabouts, or at least that he had raced away from the Palace grounds at dawn.

Turning from where he'd last seen Freyda, he climbed atop his horse, and aimed it in the direction of home, meeting Jhelan, his father's head of the Royal guard, on his way.

"What the hell is wrong with you? We don't have enough bull shit to deal with already that you thought you would take a morning stroll alone?"

Jhelan's mare was coal black and wasn't the friendliest beast, immediately nipping at Ahrkyn's horse's ankles.

"I'm a big boy. I can wander the grounds without an escort," Ahrkyn said, passing his friend and fellow guardsman.

"You weren't wandering the grounds. Do you realize how close to the border of Mhahzin you were?"

Yep. He did. Because that was how far he'd travelled until he had discovered Freyda. Honestly, he might very well have trespassed into the southern region if it would have meant finding her again.

And, though he would never tell Jhelan or anyone else, he planned on venturing out again if the Universe sent him another sign.

There was something about the human Princess, something that called to him in ways nothing else ever had. When he was near her, even in those fleeting moments, he'd felt a peace he didn't know was possible. He'd felt as though a hole he was unaware of had been filled during their silent meal.

"Does my father know of my absence?"

"If he is, he said nothing to me. A guard at the gate alerted my mate, who alerted me. Don't be so foolish again."

"And if I did?" the Prince asked, narrowing a look on Jhelan.

It was one thing for Jhelan to want to keep his friend safe, but it was another for him to forget he spoke to the Prince of Ahdlai, the next in line for the crown when King Nhaeem was no longer capable of ruling the territory himself.

"Don't pull rank on me. Your ass could have been killed. I'm responsible for your safety. If you run off without telling me or someone else, we won't know where to look if you're injured. We won't have a clue if you've been taken hostage by the *Ihllr* or someone else."

How the hell was Ahrkyn supposed to explain what drove him to rush into the woods alone without admitting that he was already obsessed with Freyda? And should he bother mentioning that not only was he planning on escaping into the woods again in the hopes of seeing her face, but that she was the Princess of Mhahzin?

No way would Jhelan or any of the rest of the guard let the Prince out of their sight if they discovered he'd developed a massive crush on the stepdaughter of Emperor Ehmile.

Was it a crush? Because if felt like far more. It felt…it felt like nothing he had ever experienced, deeper than anything he had ever experienced.

He wanted to know why the Universe had lured him into the woods, why she had given him a vision when that was not his particular magic. He wanted to know why the Princess had braved the wilds alone rather than stay within the safety of the Palace.

He wanted to know everything he could about Freyda.

Maybe it didn't make sense. Maybe the moment her beautiful brown eyes flashed through his mind he began to question every decision he'd ever made. Maybe hearing her voice made him question his resistance to Claiming a woman and siring an heir.

But he couldn't find the will to care nor question it.

No. He wouldn't tell anyone. Not Jhelan, not Ahdeben, not Ihsander, and definitely not his parents. Not yet. Not until the Mother revealed to him the purpose of his visions and his sole meeting with the Princess.

Chapter Four

"Absolutely not," Rhamzin whispered harshly, slashing his hand through the air. "Why would you ask me something so stupid?"

"If you don't ride with me, I'll find a way to go out alone again," Freyda promised.

It had been nearly a week since she'd first met Prince Ahrkyn. As far as she could tell, her stepfather and the rest of his Royal guard were completely unaware of her brief absence. If her mother noticed, she said nothing.

She usually said nothing. Empress Medora had been mentally broken by her mate years ago when Freyda was only a small child. Freyda wondered if her mother would notice her daughter's permanent absence or if she merely kept quiet to avoid her mate's wrath.

"Why the hell do you want to go out again?" he asked so low she had to lean forward and strain to hear his words.

Why did she want to go out again? Because she hadn't been able to stop thinking about Prince Ahrkyn since their one and only meeting.

But she had a feeling if she told Rhamzin the truth, he would nix the whole thing before she had the chance to actually talk to Ahrkyn to see if her newfound obsession was worth it or simple curiosity. She had never spoken to anyone from Ahdlai nor had any encounters with the *Vhtir*.

He wasn't the terrifying monster she'd believed his people would be. And he was kind and sweet. And incredibly handsome.

Or at least he was in her memories. She had also read a whole lot of books in the week since she'd met him, so maybe she was superimposing her fantasy dream man over the reality of who or what Ahrkyn really was.

What were the chances Ahrkyn would wander so far from the Palace again? When they'd met, she had wandered over the border line of Mhahzin and was officially in Ahdlai. She knew he wouldn't cross the border. And there was no guarantee he would be out again.

But she would never know if she didn't try.

Perhaps he was as intrigued by her as she was of him. Perhaps he'd had a hard time avoiding thinking about her as much as she had of him.

Or perhaps she was romanticizing the short time they'd had together and pretending he was her Prince Charming.

"I really want to learn to ride a horse better. And I'm tired of being cooped up all the time," she lied.

Half-lied. She was tired of being cooped up. And it couldn't hurt to learn to ride a horse better. But those two were simply excuses she thought Rhamzin might except.

"Do you realize what could happen if your father –" He threw his hand up when she opened her mouth to correct him as she always did. "*Step*father finds out that I accompanied you outside the safety of the walls?"

"I won't be alone. You'll be with me."

"Which would be fine if we don't happen to run into any enemies or someone looking to use the Princess as a bartering tool against the Emperor."

"Oh, please. Anyone who's met my stepfather knows he wouldn't pay a ransom to get me back. He wouldn't pay a ransom to get anyone from Mhahzin back, including his own mate or biological sons."

She'd only met her stepbrothers a couple times in the years she'd moved into the Palace. They'd come across as cold and detached as their father. If she had any stepsisters, she'd never met them and was unaware of their existence.

"That doesn't mean someone won't take you in hopes of that very thing," Rhamzin said.

"Shouldn't the risk be my choice to make? I'm tired of every move I make being dictated by everyone but me. I want to be in charge of my own life. I want to decide what I do each day, who I talk to. I want to decide whether or not I want to be Claimed and with whom I'll build a family."

His eyes narrowed and a muscle ticked in his cheek like he was clenching his jaw.

"Does this have anything to do with Prince Ahrkyn?"

"What? No," she said too loudly and too quickly to be convincing.

She'd always been terrible at lying. That was why she rarely broke the rules – she never got away with it. Had Rhamzin not come up with the story about picking wildflowers, Freyda would have been caught red-handed when she stumbled and stuttered through her lie.

He sucked his teeth and shook his head as a humorless smile quirked up one side of his mouth.

"I can't believe we're even having this conversation."

He looked behind him, checked the trees and shadows, making sure no one was eavesdropping.

"You realize he is the enemy of your stepfather. That makes him my enemy. *Your* enemy."

"Why does he have to be our enemy because his family and my family are at war. That has nothing to do with you or me. He's never done anything to me. He's never done anything to *you*. Had you met him before last week?"

"You know I haven't," he said with a huff of air.

"How can someone neither of us knows be our enemy?"

She smiled sweetly, attempting to look as innocent as possible.

"You're reaching."

Lifting a hand, he pushed his fingers through his hair and sighed. "Fine. One more time. That's it. We'll go riding. But say nothing to anyone," he said, holding a finger up with raised brows when she prepared to celebrate. "I'm serious. We'll have to find an excuse for your absence that will be more believable than picking wildflowers."

"We could always go before dawn. No one will see us leave."

"The guards positioned in the towers will."

She bit her bottom lip and looked away.

He groaned. "What are you up to now?"

With another forced innocent smile, she turned her eyes to his face. "I might know a way to get out of the walls without being seen."

"How often do you leave the safety of the walls?"

Freyda threw up both hands. "Only the once. I swear. That was it."

And she was telling the truth. She had found the tunnel underground, but had never been brave enough to actually exit the tunnel when she discovered where it led. Not until a week ago when she'd gotten it in her head that she would simply run away and start a new life somewhere else.

Rhamzin shook his head again then crossed his arms over his chest.

"Once. That's it. We'll go out once more."

"How can I learn to ride better after one time?"

Like he'd said, she was reaching. And she knew he could see through her, but she wasn't exaggerating when she'd said she wanted to make her own life's decisions. She wanted to have choices, wanted to be in control of her own destiny, whether she believed in such a thing or not.

"How about…three times? And if I haven't gotten any better at riding, we scratch the whole plan."

"You do know I know this isn't about simply riding a horse."

"No. It isn't *only* about riding a horse. That part was true. I do want to learn to ride better. And…if we happen to run into anyone while we're out…"

She shrugged and went back to smiling sweetly in hopes it still worked as it had when she was little.

"You're going to get me decapitated," he grumbled. "When are we doing this?"

"Tomorrow?"

Another groan. "Fine. Before first light. Where is this secret passage? It will look strange if someone sees me come to your room before dawn."

Freyda gave Rhamzin the location of the hidden tunnel and promised to meet him there before first light.

Now that she had a plan to head out of the walls again, and possibly see Ahrkyn again, she could barely contain her excitement.

She knew sleep would elude her, but the lack of sleep would so be worth the freedom she would have, even if only for a few hours.

Ahrkyn had wandered from the safety of the walls every day since his first meeting with Princess Freyda. Because the tower guards had alerted Jhelan of his first absence, Ahrkyn had had to get creative and duck out when the guards turned or were otherwise distracted.

It was growing precarious and tiresome.

And disheartening.

Surely, Mother Universe hadn't given him the vision of Freyda for a one-time meeting. What could something like that accomplish other than to drive him insane?

Once again, he was in the woods, only a few yards from the border leading into Mhahzin. Because he was out alone, he felt it safer to stay within his own territory. If the southern region patrolled the way the Royal guard of Ahdlai did, he could be discovered. That wouldn't go well for him or Ahdlai.

The *Ihllr* elves frequently crossed the border to hunt humans or other vulnerable groups to steal women for their sick needs. At any point, he could run into one of them or members of his own guard on patrol. He'd yet to come up with an excuse as to why he was out alone, but he would cross that bridge if or when he came to it.

For now, his sole focus was on seeing Freyda once more. He kept telling himself if he saw her again, he would know without a doubt whether his obsession was built in his mind or if she was nearly as sexy and intriguing as he remembered.

He'd had no more visions, had seen no more signs of what was to come. He'd had a feeling he'd have no more as that wasn't his particular gift. But he'd hoped for at least one more sign. One more glimpse of Freyda's eyes framed by long, dark lashes.

Although the real thing would be far better than a simple flash through his mind.

The sun was slowly rising above the trees, warming the air and filling the woods with thick humidity as the dew burned off the grass and young leaves on the trees.

Early summer had always been his favorite time of year. When the mornings were warm enough to take his coffee on the back patio but cool enough he wouldn't sweat, when the sun began to rise earlier and set later in the afternoon, and the gardens began to produce fruits and vegetables.

Early summer always felt as though it brought along a feeling of a fresh start, of new beginnings.

But as the sun rose earlier, so did the residents of Ahdlai. Meaning he would soon have to head back or risk his absence being discovered by Jhelan or another member of the guard.

With a sigh, he pushed to his feet and brushed the dirt and debris from his breaches. Another day past with no sight of the woman who had buried herself in Ahrkyn's every thought and invaded his dreams at night.

Even with the disappointment squeezing his heart, he knew, without a doubt, he would be right back out there the next morning. And the morning after, in hopes of finally getting another few moments with Princess Freyda of Mhahzin.

As he made his way through the brush, pushing branches out of his way, a tingling touched his senses. Moments later, a faint sound made its way to his ears.

Horse hooves hitting the ground from some distance away. How many? Straining, Ahrkyn focused on both the sound and the prickling of his magic.

Two horses. Two riders.

And his gift let him know his Princess was moving closer at a fast clip.

She'd returned. Almost a week later, Freyda had returned to the place where they had first met.

Ahrkyn turned from his steed and forced his feet to slow when he began to jog toward the border of Ahdlai. He had to remain in his own territory lest someone accuse him of trespassing or his presence as an act of war.

His heart began to race, threatening to burst through his ribs. She was coming. Freyda had returned. She'd returned to him, to see him. She had felt the same pull as Ahrkyn.

Within a minute or two, the horses and riders became visible. Freyda sat atop a smaller mare while the same guard he had seen that first day, Rhamzin, rode beside her.

Freyda's lips instantly stretched into a smile when her eyes found him, while Rhamzin looked…pissed. Pissed and worried.

Ahrkyn knew neither should be so far from the Palace, knew if the Emperor discovered Rhamzin had escorted the Princess to the border of Mhahzin, both the guard and Freyda would be punished. The guard might very well be executed.

Like a child on his birthday, Ahrkyn paced back and forth along the border as he waited for his Princess to grow near. His Princess. His.

There was no more denying. Not to himself, anyway.

He'd wondered if he saw her again whether he would feel the same excitement as the first time, whether the pull he'd felt as she'd ridden away and during her absence was imagined.

If anything, the pull was stronger. And his excitement was nearly bubbling over as he shifted his weight from one foot to the other in anticipation of hearing her voice again.

"Hi," she breathed with a wide smile as she slowed her horse along the border.

"No further, Princess," Rhamzin grumbled.

She made a sound of dismissal and climbed down from her horse as Rhamzin scrambled to drop from his and help her feet lower to the ground without stumbling.

"What are you doing?" the guard asked as she nearly jogged toward the border.

"Hello," Ahrkyn said, doing as she did and stopping with his toes barely touching the invisible line that separated their territories, their people, and their families.

"I didn't think you would come back," he admitted.

"It's difficult to sneak away. And Rhamzin demanded I not come out alone again."

"I agree. It's too dangerous for you to wander out alone. Both because you're a woman and because your stepfather is the Emperor of Mhahzin. Both would fetch someone a lot of money."

Ahrkyn moved as though to step closer, but her eyes dropped to the border and she held a hand out.

"I promised Rhamzin we would stay within our own territories. That is the only way I could get him to allow me to come this far."

Ahrkyn glanced up at the hulking guard and nodded a silent thank you for escorting her to Ahrkyn. Whether he was aware of the Princess's goal beforehand didn't matter. She was here now, so close all the Prince had to do was reach out a hand and he could touch her porcelain pale skin.

His fingers itched with the need to touch her, but he would refrain. At least for now. At least while there was an ever so vigilant guard watching their every move.

Not that he would do anything untoward had they been in private. But she seemed as pleased by his presence as he was of hers. Seemed as inclined to reach forward and wrap her arms around his waist as he was to pull her close to his body.

After a few moments of simply drinking each other in, the guard, Rhamzin, retrieved a pelt and laid it on the forest floor for his Princess. When she lowered, spreading her gown around her in an obviously practiced maneuver, Ahrkyn lowered with her, his eyes staying glued to her face as though he feared she would vanish if he looked away for even the briefest moment.

"I couldn't stop thinking about you," Ahrkyn uttered without thought.

Her cheeks flushed a bright pink as she ducked her gaze and smiled.

Rhamzin grunted and shook his head but said nothing. The man might have been guard to Mhahzin's Royal family, but Ahrkyn was still the Prince of Ahdlai and required and demanded respect.

"I felt the same," Freyda said.

"I came out here every day hoping you would return."

She looked up at him through her thick lashes. "Really? You've come out every day?"

"Yes. I…I told you about my vision. About seeing you in my mind before we met. I needed to know why, what the vision meant."

"Your gift is not that of precognition?"

He shook his head. "No."

As much as he wanted to know everything about her, he would rather not disclose his own magical gift in front of the guardsman until he knew that he could be trusted absolutely.

"I wanted to come earlier. But had to ensure I would not be seen leaving the walls. I couldn't risk my stepfather's men following me to the border or reporting to the Emperor that I was sneaking away to visit his enemy's son."

"Is that what you're doing? Sneaking away to meet me?"

Her brows dropped in confusion. "Why else would I be out here?"

"To learn to ride. That is the only story you will ever tell, Princess," Rhamzin said as he turned in a slow circle as though checking the area for intruders.

She rolled her eyes but smiled at Ahrkyn. "And learning to ride my horse. For my own safety, of course." She winked at Ahrkyn, and his body instantly hardened.

It was a teasing wink, not a flirtatious one, but apparently his body had a hard time discerning the difference when it came to this beautifully curvaceous woman.

The gown she wore was a soft purple, much like the color of the lavender flowers growing in the herb garden, and hugged her from her breasts down to her hips. It also pushed her breasts up until quite a bit of cleavage was visible and made it difficult for Ahrkyn to keep his eyes on her face as she spoke.

Every cell in his body wanted to reach across the distance separating them, pull her to his body, and bury his face in her ample flesh until he could no longer breathe. He might suffocate but what a way to meet Mother Universe in person!

Ahrkyn and Freyda gradually fell into an easy conversation, filled constantly with stories of their families, their territories, filled with their favorite foods and books, filled with their hopes and dreams. There were no awkward silences, no moments where they looked around as though seeking a topic to discuss or checking the time for when they could finally go their separate ways.

In fact, as the sun continued to rise and the morning grew late, they both eyed the sky with dismay. They would have to part. She would have to return to her home in the Palace and he would have to return to his duties with the Royal guard. He was mildly surprised Jhelan or another of his friends had yet to seek him in the woods.

If he thought no one was aware of his daily wanderings into the woods he was only fooling himself. There was a damn good chance someone with the guard followed him at a distance he wouldn't detect but near enough to close in should the Prince be ambushed by an enemy.

"I should go before my absence is noticed," the Princess said with a sigh similar to the sound that had come from his own mouth every day that he had ventured out without catching sight of Freyda.

"I don't suppose I can see you again? Perhaps in a few days' time? We don't want anyone growing suspicious."

Rhamzin turned a glare on Ahrkyn. "This one trip alone could raise suspicions. Do you have any idea the risks she took to be here?"

"Of course I do," Ahrkyn said.

He rose to his feet and offered a hand to the Princess, closing his fingers over hers and pulling her to her feet.

"I'm aware of the reputation of her stepfather. I wish no harm to come to her." And still he wondered if he'd been correct that first day they'd met and she had, indeed, been attempting to flee the territory. "I can keep her safe should she wish to remain within Ahdlai. She would be welcomed in by my parents, the guard, and the residents of my home. She would be treated –"

"No," Rhamzin said, slashing a hand through the air.

"Shouldn't that be my decision to make?" Freyda said, slowly turning to face the guard who had risked his own life to escort her into the woods for a clandestine meeting with the Prince.

"Of course it should. But you are not the only one at risk, Princess. I, too, will be punished should we be caught. My head will be removed from my shoulders should I return to the Palace without you."

"You could always sneak back in the way we went out."

He made a sound in the back of his throat that let Ahrkyn know he would not be returning without his charge.

The Prince had no idea how long Rhamzin had worked for the Royal family, how long he had known Princess Freyda, but it was obvious his loyalty laid with the Princess more so than the Emperor. Why else would he have willingly travelled with her to the border of Mhahzin?

"I will not leave you here with the *Vhtir*." Rhamzin turned his back on the pair, both ending the conversation and giving them an air of privacy.

He would not leave his charge in his enemy's hands. And, honestly, Ahrkyn didn't expect Freyda to be willing to leave her mother and any friends she might have back in Mhahzin so easily, even if she had originally sought to flee.

"I'll try to come back. I don't know when," she said.

"One week. Why don't we wait one week to the day? That way, we'll both know whether anyone has noticed our odd behavior or our absences. That will also give us time to come up with, uh…better stories." It was his turn to wink.

Rhamzin snorted.

"One week," she said with a nod and a sweet smile.

Her eyes dipped to his lips and his heartrate increased once more. Oh, how he wanted to taste her lips, to close the space between them and press his mouth to hers.

It would be her decision and on her time. If she wanted to kiss him –

Princess Freyda quickly glanced over her shoulder, then practically lunged at Ahrkyn, throwing her arms around his neck and closing her mouth over his in a move so quick their teeth bumped.

Neither deepened the kiss, but nor did they pull away. They simply stayed that way, their arms around each other, breathing each other in, until Rhamzin cleared his throat.

Freyda pulled away so fast Ahrkyn nearly stumbled. A dopey smile lit his face as he watched her through lust drunk eyes as she walked backward, a matching smile on her sweet face.

"One week," she said before allowing Rhamzin to help her atop her horse.

"One week from today," he called after her. "I'll be right here waiting."

Her smile never left her face, even as her horse turned to follow the guardsman. She turned to watch him for as long as she could, that smile never dropping from her soft, petal pink lips.

He'd kissed her. He'd officially tasted her lips.

Technically, *she'd* kissed *him*. She had thrown her arms around his neck and kissed him.

And now, he had a full fucking week before he could see her again. Seven days he would have to wait.

And then he would be right there, right at the border separating their territories, waiting to see her beautiful face.

Four more days. Freyda only had to wait four more days. In the three days that had passed since she and Ahrkyn made their plans for the following week, Rhamzin had done everything in his power to dissuade the Princess from wandering into the woods again.

He had bartered with her, warned her, attempted to scare her, even begged her.

Nope. She would not be deterred. She had to see the Prince again, had to hear Ahrkyn's voice again, had to feel his lips again.

She had thought when she'd thrown herself at him, he would have slid his tongue into her mouth or at least tangled his fingers in her hair. Yet, all he'd done was wrap his arms around her back and hold her tightly to his body.

What was it about this particular man, this particular Elf, that drove her so crazy? She was nearly insane with want from the moment he'd come into view. Maybe not insane, but her body had warmed in places she'd never experienced. He made her feel…hopeful. Hopeful about a different future, hopeful about her life. About her future.

The problem was she was human and he was an elf. A *Vhtir* elf. He would live centuries while she would be lucky if she lived another fifty, maybe sixty years. And that was if she wasn't killed or died during childbirth.

Not many humans survived childbirth, not when carrying the offspring to one of the non-humans. And if she were to give birth and survive, would Ahrkyn have the child taken away and raised by strangers the way they did in Mhahzin?

She was getting ahead of herself. Already, she was picturing her life and future with Ahrkyn when she wasn't sure they would survive the next meeting or that he would want her for anything more than solving the mystery of his visions.

Hopefully, he felt this weird…energy between them, the same sparks she felt when he was near, the same pull. It was like a magnet reaching for its other half, or like she was tethered to him, and the strap grew tight and uncomfortable around her chest the longer they were apart.

Rounding the corner to the dining room, Freyda nearly groaned. Her stepfather sat at the head of the table, her mother to his right, a plate set in front of the empty seat to his left.

The Emperor had deemed her worthy to join him and his mate for dinner. Actually, he had deemed both Freyda *and* her mother worthy. He rarely ate with any company unless he was entertaining a leader from another territory, and that was rare.

Why today? If he'd found out about her meeting with Ahrkyn, wouldn't he have said something before now?

Or was he biding his time, gaining ammunition before putting her in front of the firing squad?

"Your Highness," Freyda said with a curtsy. "Mother."

"She is your mother, but still the Empress," her stepfather said without looking up front his plate.

"Yes, Your Highness." She nearly gagged on her words.

Rhamzin pulled out her chair, settled her in, then left the room with a deep bow of the waist, pulling the heavy wooden doors closed behind him.

She would have preferred he stayed in the room. He might not raise a hand to the Emperor, but she always felt safer when he was near, and had since she was a child.

"I haven't spoken to you in a while. I thought we should catch up before things get too busy."

"Busy for who?" Freyda asked, keeping her eyes from his face and on the plate in front of her.

He huffed a sardonic laugh. "You, my dearest stepdaughter. I've decided it's time for you to be Claimed. It's time for you to carry an heir for our family."

"How would my child be an heir for your family?" she asked, feeling the fear and anxiety begin to rise within her chest. "I'm not your biological family, therefore, the child would be nothing to you."

Emperor Ehmile slowly set his fork down and turned a glare on his stepdaughter.

"You are my stepdaughter. Your mother is my mate. You are mine. She is mine. Anything that comes from either of your bodies belongs to me. Anything within my territory, any*one* in my territory belongs to me."

Bile churned in her stomach and rose into her throat. This couldn't be happening. She had finally taken steps to work toward building her own life and, if possible, earning her freedom.

She should have taken Ahrkyn up on staying within Ahdlai. Then she wouldn't be having this conversation while her mother sat silently picking at the food on her plate. Empress Medora had yet to raise her eyes to her daughter, hadn't bothered offering an argument on her daughter's behalf.

Freyda still had time to change things. Surely, the Emperor couldn't expect to find a male to Claim his stepdaughter overnight. Unless, of course, he had begun making plans long before mentioning them to Freyda.

"When will this happen?" she asked, forcing her voice to sound strong and calm. She didn't want him to know she was beginning to make plans to disappear before the date of her virtual imprisonment.

"In one month's time. I have sent out word to surrounding territories, have invited the rulers to send their sons. I will not accept anything lower than a head guard. But would prefer you mate with a Prince. It's imperative we keep the lines pure, after all."

How pure could they possibly be? She was human. Full Elves and Fae were rare, even with their long lives. Since the nuclear war spawned by the humans, all life left behind had been affected, and that included the fertility of the non-humans.

One month. She had one month to learn to ride as fast as the guard, to learn to fight and survive in the woods, and find somewhere to go where her stepfather either couldn't find her or wouldn't dare come near. Like Ahdlai.

But that was only one option she should consider. She and Ahrkyn barely knew each other, were only just beginning to explore this strange attraction and attachment. She didn't want to put all her proverbial eggs in one basket.

Freyda knew Rhamzin would help her. Even if he wouldn't leave with her, there was no way her only friend would play a part in her being sold off and bred like cattle. It was obvious by the way her stepfather spoke that she would have no say in who her future mate would be, and she already knew her child would be taken away from her at birth.

As her heart raced behind her breasts, she forced her expression to remain neutral and calmly lifted food onto her fork and brought it to her mouth. She couldn't let the Emperor catch on to her plans, couldn't let him know she was anything but compliant. She had to behave like the well-trained Princess he thought she was.

There were plans set to meet the Prince of Ahdlai in four more days. At that time, she would alert Ahrkyn of her stepfather's plans. If the Emperor planned to send invites to all territories, perhaps Ahrkyn would also receive the same invitation, not that she expected her stepfather to accept the union. But it might allow another moment for Freyda to slip away with Ahrkyn and his guards as protection.

Her thoughts swirled as she choked down her meal, gently setting the fork atop the plate and dabbing at her lips with the linen napkin folded in her lap.

"May I be excused?" she asked.

Emperor Ehmile cocked his head to the side. "You're not the least bit curious as to what I have planned?"

Forcing a smile, she looked at him. "I trust you will do what you believe is in my best interest."

The lie tasted bitter in her mouth. His own forced smile sent anger through her veins. She had to resist the urge to lift her hand and smack the smirk right off his lips. That would only ensure the rest of her life would be miserable, not only during her Claiming with whatever stranger he chose, although she knew that time would be pure torture. Her father would choose someone as diabolical and cruel as himself to ensure she stayed in line and did as she was told.

"You're becoming as obedient and loyal as your mother."

Her mother who had never looked up, who had never argued with her mate, who had never stood up for her only daughter. Her mother who brought her only daughter into the Palace of Mhahzin and popped out a few sons for her mate and watched in silence as each was yanked from her arms directly after birthing them.

Her mother who held no light or life in her eyes as she stared at her plate as though she were in a vegetative state.

If Freyda could get them both out successfully, she would do it without question. But the Empress had long since given up on any idea of freedom and did as she was told without a word. She had had the spirit beaten out of her over a decade ago and had never regained her strength.

Perhaps there would come a time when she could send someone for Medora. She could send a group of soldiers or fighters to retrieve her mother and deliver her somewhere safe where she could one day find herself once more.

For now, she would have to focus on getting herself as far from the Palace and Mhahzin as possible before the time was up and she was forced to carry the spawn of a complete stranger.

It had been the longest week in his life. Ahrkyn struggled to pretend all was well and normal. But he didn't miss the sideways glances he received from Jhelan, Ahdeben, and Ihsander on occasion. They knew something was up, whether they voiced as much or not.

"You're eager to turn in tonight," Jhelan said as he followed the Prince to the stalls.

"As you are every night."

Jhelan had become Fate Bonded to a Fae woman a few months back. They had found her in the woods after her Clan had been slaughtered. Ahrkyn had put her in Jhelan's care, trusting the head of the guard to keep her safe as she healed from her severe wounds. He'd had no idea Jhelan would fall so hard for the woman.

Of the group of four, Ihsander was desperate to sire an heir and Ahdeben was currently seeking a woman to Claim. Which was why Ahrkyn hadn't placed Valdis with either of them. It was one of those situations where Mother Universe had her own plans and didn't care how the participants felt about them.

Was it his turn? Was he correct in what the Mother had in store for him? Had he waited long enough for Mother Universe to send him who he should spend his life with instead of picking an available human to Claim?

The fact she was human was both a blessing and a curse. She could carry his children, could birth him an heir, but she would also die and leave him alone for centuries.

He should step away. Meet with her in the morning, thank her for meeting him, and let her go. She needed to find her freedom far from the Elves, and Fae, and all the other creatures. She could find a human Clan, fall in love with someone of her species, and spend her life with him.

But even as he thought the words, possessive rage burned his veins and turned his stomach.

He wanted her. He wanted her more than he wanted his next fucking breath. If she would have him, he would do anything and everything to make her presence in his life possible.

"I have a mate waiting for me. You have…well, I guess you have Mommy and Daddy."

"Asshole," Ahrkyn muttered.

The men released their horses into the appropriate stalls and closed the gates. He had patrolled with the guard every day since Freyda had disappeared over the horizon, her beautiful face and voice haunting his every waking moment and invading his dreams at night. He had gone out every day in hopes she would wander out again before their scheduled meeting.

As much as he wanted to see her again, he would prefer she not wander so far from the safety of her own territory's walls. There were far worse dangers in Mhahzin than in Ahdlai. Both had to worry about the nocturnal creatures that would feast on their flesh and blood, but the *Ihllr* elves held no honor and would take Freyda without a single thought as to her position within the Royal family.

"Are you eating in the Palace tonight?" Ahrkyn asked as the group left the stables.

"I am," Ahdeben said.

"Absolutely. I'm starving," Ihsander said.

"Not me. Valdis said she wanted to make me something special tonight," Jhelan said, and was answered with a series of catcalls and teasing.

They could tease Jhelan all they wanted, but at least he'd found someone who called to his soul. Not merely a woman to Claim. Not merely a woman to carry his heir, although Jhelan would never have children with Valdis since she was a Fae halfling. But he'd found someone for his heart to call home.

And for the first time in his life, Ahrkyn found himself envying his friend.

Tomorrow. Less than twenty-four hours and he would see the face of the woman he craved, hear the sweetest voice to ever tease his ears, lay eyes on the body that had kept his body hard from the moment they had first met.

But he had to eat and act as though it was a normal night before rushing to bed. He couldn't wait to get to sleep simply so he could wake to a new morning. The morning he would finally see her again.

One week, yet it felt like a month or more had passed. He had never felt so damn impatient in his life.

He still had the whole routine to follow to avoid anyone catching on. He had to behave as though this were any other day, as though he were famished after a long day of patrolling and eating nothing but the nonperishables they carried in their satchels.

Of course, he really was famished, but that discomfort took a backseat to the pressure in his chest that had only grown in the time he had spent apart from Freyda.

He wanted her. He needed her. But he couldn't force her to make a decision. Wouldn't force her. All he could do was hope she felt the same pull.

The worse part – other than the fact she was human and he would lose her far too soon – was that she would have to walk away from her family, away from her friends, and reside in Ahdlai if they were to be together.

Would she be willing to turn her back on everything for him? He would never expect it from her, but could only hope. And promise her he would make every day worth that sacrifice.

Jhelan peeled off from the group when they grew near the grouping of houses, heading for the home he shared with his mate. Ihsander and Ahdeben walked with Ahrkyn back to the Palace where the King and Queen would share a meal with the higher up guards while the lower ranking and those in training would eat either in their own homes or in the staff quarters.

As they walked, he continued to feel the glances and sideways looks from his friends. They knew something was amiss, but he still wasn't ready to discuss it. He wasn't ready to tell anyone he craved the stepdaughter of the greatest enemy and threat to their home and territory. They would think him mad, and would most certainly alert his parents.

A brief excitement skittered through him. These clandestine meetings sent a sense of naughtiness through him, something he hadn't felt since he and Jhelan were merely boys causing mischief.

Only this time, the mischief could end in someone's death.

"Do you plan on letting us know what you're up to, or shall we simply follow you into the woods tomorrow?" Ahdeben asked before they crossed the lawn of the Palace.

Ahrkyn slowed to a stop. They knew. They knew he had wandered into the woods at least twice and knew he planned to do it again in the morning.

"Jhelan open his fucking mouth?"

"That and you've been acting strangely for days. Not to mention you returned home with the scent of a woman clinging to you last week. Who is she? Why do you meet her so far from home?"

The Prince sighed and pushed stray hair that had come loose from his braid from his face. If he told them the truth, they might try to stop him. They might tell his father of his plans.

Or they might simply demand they accompany him at dawn.

"She is the stepdaughter of Emperor Ehmile," he said barely above a whisper before looking around to ensure there was still no one within hearing distance.

Ahdeben cursed under his breath. Ihsander whistled low and shook his head.

"Not a good idea, brother," Ihsander said.

"I had no choice. Mother Universe sent me a vision of her. I had to follow my instincts to discover what she was trying to tell me. I believe her to be…I believe Princess Freyda to be my mate. I believe her to be Fated to me by the Universe."

Both men stood with their brows to their hairline, eyes wide, lips parted as they gaped at him silently.

"How can you be sure? Does she carry your mark?" Ihsander asked, his eyes dipping to Ahrkyn's blank arms.

"Neither of us carry brands. But why would the Mother send me visions when that is not my gift? Why show me this woman if she is not meant to be in my life?"

"As a warning?" Ahdeben offered. "Although by the scent, I can only imagine she wasn't trying to fight you."

Ahrkyn couldn't refrain from rolling his eyes as he shook his head at his friend and fellow guard member.

"No. She wasn't fighting me."

"You didn't…does she remain Untouched?" Ihsander asked.

"You know better," Ahrkyn said.

He was no prude. And definitely not a virgin. But he had only slaked his needs with Elven women through the years, and only because there was no risk of them carrying his heir. Elven women could not get pregnant, just like the rest of the non-humans, save the Shape Shifters.

"You have not laid with her yet you're willing to risk your father's wrath – her stepfather's wrath – for a simple meeting?" Ahdeben asked.

The man had sought an available woman to Claim for some time. He, of all people, should know the difficulties of finding the person whom one could spend more than a few minutes with, the person who made the day feel all that much brighter.

What the hell was wrong with him? Freyda made his day brighter? He was a man possessed. Because those thoughts sure as hell couldn't have come from his own damn mind.

It was Freyda. Or perhaps the Mother.

Or perhaps the Mother was telling him she had plans for him. And those plans revolved around a human woman whom he wanted to sink into until he didn't know where he ended and she began.

Chapter Six

Freyda should have been excited. It was the morning she'd been looking forward to for a week.

Instead, all she felt was dread. She would have to bring him the news that her stepfather intended to offer her womanhood and hand to anyone who wanted it.

That wasn't necessarily true. He would send out the invite, but would be the one who chose who would Claim and breed her.

Perhaps Freyda didn't know Ahrkyn well, but he would be the one she chose. At least he was kind. He was sweet and handsome and admirable. He cared for the people in his territory, respected Freyda by keeping his distance, had even waited for her to make the first move, had waited for her to choose whether she wanted to move their relationship – if that was what they were attempting – any further.

Instead, she would have to tell him goodbye.

"Have you heard who your father intends to invite to the games?" Rhamzin asked as they trotted toward the border of Mhahzin before the sun rose.

"I was unaware there would be games," she said.

She had not been able to conjure a smile since the Emperor had declared his intentions.

"He's planned an array of games and courses to choose the victor."

"The victor meaning the person who gets to deflower the Princess and fill my belly with his seed."

Her stomach had been sour from the moment her stepfather had announced his plans. She'd been unable to eat more than a few bites at a time. Had barely slept.

Now, she couldn't find the excitement she'd felt the first days of last week, the same butterflies of anticipation in her belly over getting the opportunity to see Ahrkyn again.

Not that she didn't want to see him again. But this time felt as though she were going to tell him goodbye. Because there was no way the Emperor would choose his enemy's son as her mate.

"Should I participate in the games?" Rhamzin asked softly.

Freyda turned in her saddle and frowned at the guard.

"You know I wouldn't force myself on you. We would sleep in the same bed so my scent would be on you. When you didn't become pregnant with a child, your stepfather would assume the fault was on me."

"And then he would choose another. But thanks for the offer."

For a brief moment, she'd wondered if her only friend had actually considered mating with Freyda. From what she'd been able to tell through the years, he saw her as a child. Maybe not a child, but definitely a daughter of sorts. Or younger sister. He watched over her, allowed her to confide in him, and now, was escorting her to the border of Mhahzin for the second time.

The last time.

Her heart ached at the thought. This was supposed to be the beginning of something, not the end. This secret meeting was supposed to be a way for her to get to know Ahrkyn better, a way for them to explore the emotions and feelings that had blossomed between them since that first morning.

"Do you know what you'll tell him?" Rhamzin asked after a long stretch of silence.

"I haven't a clue," she admitted.

Rhamzin had turned his back and given them a moment of privacy the last time she'd visited with Ahrkyn. The first and only time she'd kissed him. But whether he'd turned his back or not, he could tell there was something between the Prince and Princess, could tell she was smitten with Ahrkyn, could tell there was something akin to affection between them.

He also knew what she'd already deduced – her stepfather would rather gift Freyda to a member of his guard than the Prince of Ahdlai.

"You must tell him goodbye."

"I'm aware," Freyda said, filled with the deepest sense of melancholy.

It was more than melancholy. It was grief. She was grieving something that had felt real, something that felt as though it would be life changing. Something she could never have.

The last time she'd taken this trip, she had kicked her horse and urged her to race through the woods. This time, however, she was in less of a hurry. She would rather not go at all.

Not true. She wanted to see Ahrkyn's face. She wanted to feel his arms around her one last time. To feel his lips one last time.

But she knew her heart would shatter into a thousand pieces when she had to walk away.

The sun would rise soon. Regardless of her reluctance, they needed to hurry so they could get back before someone sought Freyda in her chambers and alerted the Palace to her absence.

Nudging her heel into her mare's side, she clenched her thighs the way Rhamzin had taught her and held on as her horse took off at a sprint, sending Freyda's hair to flow behind her in long waves. She hadn't bothered to braid it back, nor had she donned her favorite gown. She had dressed for comfort and invisibility.

There was no reason to be as pleasing to the eye as possible. It no longer mattered. She no longer had any reason to appeal to Ahrkyn if she couldn't have him.

As she topped the next hill, Prince Ahrkyn came into view. His smile both warmed and broke her heart. He was happy to see her.

But he appeared to notice something in her countenance. His smile faltered then fell and his dark brows knitted together.

He took a step forward, as though to cross the border, but glanced down quickly and stopped himself.

The frown stayed on his face until she stopped her horse and allowed Rhamzin to help her to the ground, holding his forearms as he steadied her.

"Princess Freyda?" Ahrkyn called out, his tone unsure.

"Prince Ahrkyn," she said, dipping her head in respect.

"What is it? What's happened?"

No matter how hard she fought, no matter how much she blinked, she couldn't keep the tears from welling in her eyes and falling over her lashes.

"I cannot return here again."

He reached for her but dropped his hand to his side when she didn't step closer.

"What has happened? Was your absence last time discovered?"

"No," she said then swallowed hard.

A lump rose in her throat, choking off her words as her bottom lip quivered.

"Her fa—stepfather has arranged games to win her hand," Rhamzin said.

"He's holding a competition to earn the right to breed his only fucking daughter?"

"*Step*daughter," Freyda corrected on impulse.

"Yes," Rhamzin confirmed.

Ahrkyn's entire countenance changed and suddenly matched Freyda's. At least for a moment. Then his sorrow changed to fury, and he began to pace along the border between their territories.

"He can't do that. He can't use you as some twisted prize."

"He can. And he will," Rhamzin replied.

Freyda turned to look up at him, and was shocked to find the guard watching Ahrkyn with something akin to pleading in his blazing blue eyes.

A glance back at Ahrkyn confirmed his eyes were also glowing bright, although the Prince's glow was closer to silver from his icy blue irises.

"How can I help? How can I get you out of this?"

Another tear rolled down Freyda's cheek. "There is nothing you can do, Prince Ahrkyn."

She nearly gasped when he took a deliberate step toward her, completely ignoring the borderline. His hand reached forward and he cupped her cheek. "I'll enter the games." The last word sounded as though it tasted bad in his mouth. "I'll win your honor. I will win your freedom."

"There is no way my stepfather would choose you. You know that. And unless you plan on bringing the entirety of your guard and leaving your territory unprotected, your presence in Mhahzin could be dangerous. Fatal. And I can't live with that. I can't live without knowing you're out there alive and well and happy."

"Happy? The first time I've felt anything close to that sensation was when I discovered you were real and not a figment of my imagination."

The air caught in her lungs and she choked back a sob. That was exactly the same moment she'd felt anything close to happiness – the day she'd met Ahrkyn.

And now she would have to tell him goodbye and walk away. Even if she were able to find a way out of mating with a stranger, she could never run into Ahrkyn's arms. Such would bring danger to his region, to his family, and to his people. He might tell her it was worth it, but the cost was entirely too high.

Rhamzin sauntered off a few steps, far enough as to give them a few minutes of privacy while they embraced their last time.

"I'm so sorry, Ahrkyn. I truly wanted…I don't know. I wanted to at least get to know you better. I planned to find freedom so that we could be friends."

"I don't want to be friends. I want more than friendship. I want you," Ahrkyn admitted, tears glimmering in his lovely eyes.

Freyda had never seen a man cry before, had never seen any emotion other than fear or anger from a single man in her life.

But there was obvious emotion in Ahrkyn's eyes and all over his ruggedly beautiful face.

"I'm sorry," she choked out. "Even if I could find a way to escape Mhahzin, there is no way I would bring my stepfather's wrath to your door."

His mouth parted, his lips moved though nothing came out, then he reached forward, cupped the back of her head, and slanted his mouth over hers.

Unlike a week ago when she'd raised onto her toes and pressed her lips to his, this one was desperate, hungry, full of everything they couldn't say and would never experience. His tongue touched the seam of her lips and she opened immediately, letting him in, savoring the velvety sweetness of his mouth.

Tears began to flow unbidden and hot down her cheeks as she threw her arms around his neck and pressed her body as closely to his as she could get without wrapping her legs around his waist.

Ahrkyn tilted his head and deepened the kiss further, a sorrow filled growl rattling from his chest as his other arm snaked around to her back and pressed her closer to his chest, to his body, until she was fully lined with his form, her breasts mashed against his hard chest, his erection straining through his breeches and trapped against her stomach.

She should drag him further into the woods. She could raise her dress, free his erection, and lower herself onto him. If she laid with him, her stepfather could no longer declare his stepdaughter Untouched and valuable. She would be like any other woman who had allowed a man to enter her, like any woman who had already birthed children for non-humans. She would no longer be worth the games, worth the power he could gain from the right familial connection.

Once again, that wouldn't be fair to Ahrkyn. It would be no different than the men who forced themselves on women. And the Emperor might use it as another excuse to attack Ahdlai. Not that he ever needed a reason to attack a region. As long as they had something he wanted, he would come up with some excuse or another.

As Freyda pulled away, a tingling, burning sensation started in her chest and radiated down her left arm until it settled in her fingers. She gasped and yanked her hand up, expecting to see a burn or insect bite or sting.

Before her eyes, brands, dark henna-colored marks began to snake their way from her fingertips, up her arm, where they disappeared under her dark sleeve.

Ahrkyn's wide eyes were on his own arm, his breath coming in short gasps.

When he finally settled his gaze on her, all he could do was shake his head back and forth slowly.

"I had assumed. But I wasn't sure. I'm so sorry. I'm so sorry," he repeated as he kept shaking his head.

Freyda's brows furrowed deeply as she went from studying her own arm to his then back.

"What is this? What does this mean?" she asked, lifting her hand between them.

"You've got to be fucking kidding me," Rhamzin barked out.

His footfalls were heavy as he stomped toward the couple, who stood silent and wide-eyed.

"What did you do? I was only gone for a few minutes," Rhamzin said, gripping Freyda by the wrist and yanking her arm up.

"Nothing. We did nothing. I was kissing him goodbye. That's all," Freyda said. "What is this? What does this mean?"

She had only seen similar marks a handful of times in her life, but never on anyone in Mhahzin. They were either guests or simply passing through, and she'd never had the opportunity to question the meaning.

"They're Bonding brands. It's the mark of a Fated Bond," Ahrkyn said, his tone hushed and unbelieving. "We didn't do anything," he muttered, turning his hand and wrist this way and that, studying his own brands that looked identical to Freyda's.

"How the hell is she supposed to hide this from her stepfather? From the rest of the guard? If anyone spots them, they will alert the Emperor. Do you have any idea what you've done?" Rhamzin nearly bellowed at Ahrkyn.

"We only kissed. We did nothing more," Ahrkyn said, but his voice was still low, still full of confusion. "We only kissed."

"Bull shit. Since when does a Bond mark appear so quickly and so easily?"

"The Mother showed me a vision of Freyda. A couple days before I found her in the woods. The Mother was trying to warn me, trying to tell me…I'm so sorry," Ahrkyn said again.

"You have the gift of precognition?" Rhamzin asked with narrowed eyes.

"No. I don't. I have…I don't have precognition. But the Mother felt it was important enough to guide me to the Princess. And she now carries the Fated Bond marks. We're branded by Mother Universe. It's irreversible."

"What does this mean?" Freyda asked, holding her arm up, her voice growing shrill.

Ahrkyn reached forward and pushed hair from her face with a gentle hand. "It means, *khaere*, that your stepfather will have no choice now. We are Fate Bound. Even he has to hold the judgement of the Mother above his own."

Rhamzin snorted. "You don't know him. He won't give two shits about those marks. He'll use them, use your bond to her, to punish her and attack your people. This is a bad, bad thing, Prince Ahrkyn."

Ahrkyn looked from Rhamzin, to Freyda, and back. "What can I do to help?"

No. He couldn't allow this to happen. Ahrkyn had only just found Freyda. She now carried the matching brands blessed to them by the Mother. Ahrkyn could not lose Freyda to some stranger.

"There is nothing you can do," she said, heartbreak and resignation plain on her face. She was resigned to her future, resigned to unhappiness, resigned to the fact any form of control over her own life was effectively and permanently being taken out of her hands.

She could say no all she wanted, but there had to be something he could do to protect her, to get her away from Emperor Ehmile, to avoid her being forced into a Claiming she didn't want.

Perhaps it was time to speak to his father. His parents might be able to help. They had to help. They would understand his need to have her in his life, his need to have her near.

"Come to my Palace. Speak with my parents. Please. We can help."

"She can't go into Ahdlai. We've been gone far too long as it is. The sun will soon be high enough and the rest of the Palace in Mhahzin will be awake and tending to the area. Which means the guards will be active. If we don't leave now, she will be seen sneaking back into the walls. Surely, you wouldn't want her punished for your own selfish needs."

"Do you know what will happen to her if she isn't allowed to be with me? This bond isn't like falling in love or being infatuated. It's a soul deep connection. We will both feel the separation as though someone ripped us in two," Ahrkyn said.

Though the guard had raised his voice multiple times, Ahrkyn kept his voice low and steady. It was the only way he could keep himself under control rather than raging against the atrocity that would befall his mate if she were to leave his side and fulfill her stepfather's wishes.

And she *was* his mate. Had he any doubts before, the matching brands on their arm solidified the fact.

She. Was. His.

He could not stand by and allow another to lay a finger on her. He could not stay safely in his territory and allow another male to take her into his bed and fill her with his seed.

"We have to return. Rhamzin is correct. If I stay much longer, my absence will be noted. The consequences are far too high for myself, for Rhamzin, and for you."

Tears glimmered in her chocolate brown eyes as she blinked rapidly. Another tear trailed down her cheek as several others had done since she'd arrived and told him the devastating news.

His every instinct was to wrap her in his arms, toss her onto his horse, and race back to the Palace with her. Ahrkyn needed to protect her, to care for her, to be near her.

But she was right. If the Emperor noted her absence, he could lash out and she would be his victim.

"What will you do about the brands? If someone notices them…" He shook his head, unwilling to voice the obvious.

"I'll find a way to hide them. I'll find a way to keep myself intact and out of the hands of any man my stepfather chooses. I am not up for sale, and I am not a reward for some fucked up games."

Both Rhamzin and Ahrkyn blinked and gaped at Freyda. It was rare to hear a female of any species curse, but even rarer to hear that type of language from a Princess.

And it was kind of sexy. He knew he was odd, but he couldn't help himself. Everything about Freyda set his blood on fire.

"Stay safe. I'll speak to my parents. We'll find a way to get you out of this, to get you safely to Ahdlai. I swear on my life and my position as Prince of Ahdlai, I will earn your freedom," Ahrkyn said as his heart felt as though it had officially crumbled to pieces and was now in her hands.

Her body shook as a sob hitched in her chest. Stepping forward, she wrapped her arms around his waist and pressed her cheek to his chest. "I'm sorry," she whispered.

Ahrkyn wrapped his own arms around her and rested his cheek on the top of her head, inhaling her scent and praying it wouldn't be the last time he would have her in his arms.

Chapter Seven

"What the hell were you thinking?" Ahrkyn's father, King Nhaeem, bellowed, reminding Ahrkyn of Jhelan when he discovered where the Prince had been.

"I wasn't thinking. Or rather, I was simply following what the Mother was showing me. I wanted to know why I was having visions. Those visions led me into the woods and to Princess Freyda."

"She is the daughter of Emperor Ehmile. The daughter of the same asshole who sent his guard, Unseelie Fae, and Shape Shifters to attack our people," King Nhaeem said.

"Technically, the Shape Shifters only–"

The King sliced his hand through the air. "Do not argue with me, boy. You might be an adult, and you might be my son, but I am still your King."

"Yes, Your Highness," Ahrkyn said, fighting the smirk that tried to pull up one side of his mouth.

His father rarely pulled rank on Ahrkyn. But even Ahrkyn had to admit this was the perfect time for it. A union with Freyda, the Blessed Bond with the Princess, could cause a war between the two territories.

But his father was Bonded. His union to Queen Ahlmeda was Blessed by the Mother. He knew the discomfort, the *torture* Ahrkyn would endure if he wasn't able to not only complete the Bond with Freyda but to have her near, to touch her, to hold her every night.

Ahrkyn inhaled and blew it out in a rush, then rolled the sleeve of his under shirt up high enough for his parents to see the marks covering his arm. They would appear as faint silver lines to their eyes, much as theirs did to his, but any in the Elf world knew exactly what those marks meant.

The Queen gasped lightly as her eyes widened. A light flashed through his father's irises as he released a low growl of frustration.

"How far have you gone?"

"We have not completed the Bond. The brands appeared when she was telling me goodbye. Or attempting to tell me goodbye."

"That is a strong Bond," his mother said softly.

"I told you I saw her before I knew she existed. The Mother led me to her. She guided us to each other."

"I still don't understand why she was in the woods that first day," his father said.

"I believe she was attempting to flee Mhahzin. But the guard, Rhamzin, located her and escorted her back."

"Did she appear afraid of this guard member?" King Nhaeem asked.

Ahrkyn shook his head. "She did not. He treated her as a sister or even daughter rather than the Princess. He escorted her to the woods to where I waited, aided her in escaping the walls and into the woods for our visit. Neither of us knew…she only found out days ago what her stepfather had planned for her future."

Ahrkyn dropped his head as emotion threatened to close his throat and tears burned the backs of his eyes. He could not show that kind of emotion. His parents would not see him as weak, but he was the Prince and a member of the Royal guard. He couldn't let anyone see tears in his eyes. Rather, he wouldn't *allow* them to see his tears.

"We cannot let this happen. I'm begging you to intervene. Or at least allow me to enter these…games. Allow me to attempt to win the Princess's hand."

"You know Emperor Ehmile will never choose you. Your mere appearance in Mhahzin could incite violence. You would require a large group of the guard to accompany you to ensure you weren't executed on sight, but that would leave the territory with less protection."

"Have you received an invitation to this spectacle?" Ahrkyn asked his father.

The King shook his head. "I have not. I would have told you."

"You said she only learned of these plans days ago?" his mother asked.

"Yes."

"Perhaps the invitations have yet to be sent. When is this supposed to occur?" his mother asked.

"Princess Freyda was told in a month's time."

His parents looked to each other, holding some silent conversation before his mother nodded.

"If we have yet to receive word from Mhahzin or any invitation to whatever it is they have planned by the third week, we will come up with our own plan to free the Princess," King Nhaeem said.

Ahrkyn nearly sagged with relief.

"But you must stay away until then. If the Emperor gets the slightest idea that you are interested in his daughter or observes the marks on her arm…" The King shook his head.

The words didn't need to be spoken. If the Emperor knew of Prince Ahrkyn's interest, he would use it against him and against Ahdlai. If the Emperor spotted the marks and knew the pair were Fate Bound, there was no way he would allow them to be together and would use the Bond as some kind of bartering tool or weapon against the Royal Family of Ahdlai and all its people.

He must stay away. Those words were easier spoken than the action fulfilled. Staying away from the woman his heart called home would be like ripping a piece from his soul.

"Have you told anyone else of your…idiocy?" his father asked.

Ahrkyn could merely snort at his father's choice of words.

"Jhelan knew of the first meeting. Ahdeben and Ihsander know something is brewing but don't know the details. I haven't told anyone of the brands or the Bond."

His father nodded slowly, his eyes moving to the side as though deep in thought.

"Keep this between us for now. Do your best to hide the marks, although I assume Jhelan will eventually notice them. The boy is quite perceptive—"

"He's not a boy anymore, love," Queen Ahlmeda said with an affectionate smile.

"Perhaps you might let Jhelan know the details, take him in to your confidence, ensure he will mention it to no one else. Keep the marks hidden to the best of your ability. We will await an invitation. In the meantime, you, Jhelan, and I will come up with an alternative solution in case we, indeed, are left out of these games."

His father seemed as repulsed by the idea of pawning one's daughter off as a prize as both Ahrkyn and Rhamzin had.

"The guard, Rhamzin. He might be of some assistance should we have to help her escape. He appears to genuinely care for Freyda's wellbeing," Ahrkyn said. And hated to admit it.

He wanted to be the one to care for Freyda, to protect her, to keep her wrapped securely in his arms. But she was a world away in the enemy's territory and in their claws. If Ahrkyn wanted to get her out safely, he would have to utilize any and every form of help he could find.

"What about the ogre? Has anyone heard from Brizio or his witch friends since they came to our aid last time?"

"I'll send out word," King Nhaeem said. "Tell him we wish to speak with him. If he agrees to a meeting, only then will we discuss the possibility of either attending the games or infiltrating the walls of the Palace of Mhahzin on this…suicide mission to rescue your Princess."

Queen Ahlmeda smiled wistfully at her mate. "Are you saying you wouldn't have climbed the tower to save me?"

The King raised Ahlmeda's hand to his lips and feathered a kiss across her knuckles.

"I'm pretty sure you could have not only saved yourself from any tower but kicked the ass of any who attempted to hold you."

"This is true," the Queen said with a haughty smile and a chuckle.

Ahrkyn's adopted mother was more than capable of defending herself. She and the King had held off those who'd attacked Ahdlai months before and had nearly sacrificed their own lives to keep their residents safe before Jhelan's mate was able to make it to their side and even the odds.

"For now, stay away from Princess Freyda, keep those marks hidden, and behave as though nothing has changed. We don't want any word getting out about your union with Emperor's Ehmile's stepdaughter. I don't believe anyone in this territory would dare betray us, but it's better to be safe than sorry."

"I hate that saying," the Queen said with a wrinkle of the nose.

Ahrkyn nodded and turned.

"Will you be joining us for dinner?" his mother asked.

"Yes. I need to shower and remove Freyda's scent from my body. Ahdeben noticed it before. I don't want anyone else to catch on."

"Probably a good idea," the King muttered as Ahrkyn left the room.

In reality, the last thing Ahrkyn wanted to do was remove her scent from his flesh. He wanted to wrap himself in it, wallow in it, memorize it and seal it in his every pore. But if he were to behave as though it were simply another day, he couldn't carry the scent of a woman lest others ask questions he could not yet answer.

His legs felt heavy as he trudged through the Palace, down the halls, around the corners, until he was finally before his bedroom door. The guard members all resided in their own homes while Ahrkyn lived in the Palace with his parents.

When he was able to free Freyda and bring her to be with him, would she stay with him in his room or would they have their own home?

Or would she prefer to live separately since she'd yet to have her own privacy or a single choice of her own?

He would support her either way, although he could see himself sleeping on her damn porch every night, as long as he could be near her and keep her safe.

Ahrkyn was getting ahead of himself. He needed to focus on keeping all eyes averted from the marks on his arm. Then, he had to find a way to get word to Freyda that he would find a way to get her out of the Palace before it was too late.

Yes, he had promised his father he would stay away from the Princess. That didn't mean he couldn't send a messenger to her, give her a reason to hold on, to fight, something to look forward to rather than dreading the future her stepfather was trying to force on her.

But how? How could he send word to her without anyone spotting the messenger? Any member of his guard would be easily detected. He couldn't send any member of the town without them learning of the union between the Prince and Princess.

Valdis. Jhelan's mate was fairly unknown to Mhahzin. While she had been paramount to the success during the battle with Mhahzin, those who had fought against Ahdlai had been slaughtered.

Well. Not all. Some had retreated. But what was the chance they had truly thought to heed a small female's presence?

She would not be seen as a threat due to her size. But she could be a target because she was a woman.

And no way would Jhelan willingly allow his mate to walk into the enemy's lair.

"Damn it," Ahrkyn muttered as he shuffled across the cool wood floor of his bedroom.

The bathroom connected to his space was large enough for ten people as were all bathrooms in the Palace. The Royal Family lived in luxury, but so did the people of Ahdlai, whether in Ahdlai proper or one of the towns on the outskirts. Their spaces and homes might not be as large, but they wanted for nothing.

Those who refused to live under the rule of the King and Queen suffered hunger, disease, and the hunting of their people by the *Ihllr* Elves and other predators. But it was their choice whether they lived in the forest or the caves. King Nhaeem would never force anyone to bend a knee to his rule.

What could he do in the meantime? A month was a long fucking time to wait. A long fucking time to be without his mate. A long fucking time to discover whether or not his mate had been dragged away by some sick, twisted bastard who would force himself on her and sire an heir that she would never know.

Freyda paced the length of her quarters, tugging at her sleeve and wishing she could make it longer. The marks on her forearm, bicep, and shoulder were covered, but there was nothing she could do about the back of her hand.

Rhamzin said they were barely visible, merely soft, silvery lines. But to her eyes, they were the color of henna, bright orange-red and, well, beautiful, whether she knew what each design or swirl meant or not. All she knew was they meant she was tied to Ahrkyn in a way that couldn't be defined or described.

And since those marks had appeared, she could have sworn she could feel his emotions, could feel him inside her heart, could feel his location like a beacon in the dark. It was as if she could close her eyes and find her way to his side without a single misstep or stumble.

That also meant she could feel his anger and fear. At times, she wasn't sure whether it was her own emotions or Ahrkyn's, and it made her feel as though she were losing her mind.

Or perhaps it was the separation causing the feeling of insanity.

She missed him. It had only been days since she'd last seen Ahrkyn, yet her heart ached as though it had been weeks, months. She barely knew the Prince, yet craved his touch, craved the feeling and taste of his lips.

Was this how it felt to love? How it felt to *fall* in love? Or was it something more primal, something chemical and fate driven?

All she knew was she didn't have the urge to dance through the hallways of the Palace singing. Instead, she had become more withdrawn in hopes of avoiding her stepfather and keeping the brands on her arms hidden from any guard loyal to him.

Rhamzin watched her closely, ensured no others came too close to her or her room. When she walked through the halls, he always stayed on her left side to block the view of her arm.

But she would eventually be called to the dining table to join her stepfather and mother for a meal. How could she hide the brands at that point? No doubt the Emperor's eyes would zero in and she refused to think about what he would do or how he would react to the news she was Fate Bound to his enemy.

If she wore the matching brands of the Bond, did that then mean she was Claimed? She and Ahrkyn had done nothing more than kiss and embrace. Wasn't there more to the Claiming? Weren't they to share a bed? She remained Untouched and preferred to stay that way, at least until she could be free of the ruler of Mhahzin. And would only willingly give her heart and body to Ahrkyn.

Who was she kidding? Already, he held her heart in his big, strong hands. And as another beat filled her head, she realized she held his, as well.

How could she go along with this ruse of her stepfather's? There was no way she would willingly leave with some stranger and allow him to violate her body, to fill her with his seed, to force her to grow a child inside her womb only to have that child taken away and raised by strangers.

Stopping her pacing near the window, she pulled the curtain back and peered onto the large expanse of lawn stretching along the back of the Palace. Tents and tables were being set up in anticipation of the upcoming games. She had only weeks before she was handed over to the winner.

Freyda was literally being gifted to some stranger by her stepfather. He was rewarding a man who bested the others by allowing them to breed his stepdaughter. Emperor Ehmile never ceased to amaze her with his depraved ways.

And her mother…

Still her mother had yet to say a single word to Freyda about any of it. Had the female servants not educated Freyda on the duties of a Claimed and mated woman, she would have no idea what to expect. She also wouldn't carry the fear in her heart over being Claimed by someone who could possibly be as sick and twisted as the Emperor.

Tears burned the backs of her eyes as a couple guard members glanced up and spotted her in the window, their neutral expressions turning into sneers and smirks as one said something to the other that made him throw his head back and laugh. They were making fun of her, of her situation. They were two of the guards most loyal to Emperor Ehmile, and mainly because he ensured they always had first choice at slaves or women stolen from other territories.

At least Rhamzin couldn't be bought. She had to believe there were others like him in her stepfather's employ, but he was the only one she truly felt she could trust with both her safety and her secrets.

The fact he had snuck her into the woods to meet with Ahrkyn was a risk to himself. There was no reason for him to put himself in danger other than his compassion and love he held for her.

Could there be a chance she could convince her stepfather to allow Rhamzin to enter the games? He had already offered, but she had figured it would be a long shot. She knew the man would never force himself on her.

But there would come a time when the Emperor would question why she was not yet carrying a child, why she had yet to become pregnant, and then it would start all over again. He would seek someone of power to mate with the only female member of his screwed up family and produce heirs that would bring him more power.

There had to be something she could do to escape her fate. Some way she could get away, find her freedom, and build a life, preferably with Ahrkyn at her side.

A sliver of her heart and mind warned her not to grow so attached to someone she hardly knew. But it was literally only a sliver, a tiny fraction that she chose to ignore. She didn't know Ahrkyn, not really, but she trusted Mother Universe to pair her with the person who was meant to awaken her soul and complete her heart in a way no other could.

Tugging at her sleeve once more, she pushed away from the window and looked to her closed bedroom door. She knew should she open it, Rhamzin would be positioned in a chair outside her room, his feet crossed at the ankles as he was any time he was on duty. He despised leaving other guards to watch over her when she slept, fearing they would sneak in and violate her when she was most vulnerable.

What would her stepfather do if one of his guards took her status of Untouched? Would he punish them if they impregnated her, or simply pat them on the back and reward them with more slaves, more women, more of what they requested?

She hated to think she was nothing to anyone in the Palace. Hated to think her own mother either couldn't or wouldn't protect her only daughter. Hated that the only person who cared about her physical and mental well-being was hired by the man intent on making her life a living hell.

No. She wouldn't live like this. She would no longer wait patiently as her future was planned for her. She would no longer abide by rules that enslaved women. She would no longer bend the knee to a dictator who treated all below him as nothing more than dirt on his shoes.

The sun had risen hours ago. It would be nearly impossible for her to slip away unnoticed. *Nearly* impossible. But not completely.

Looking around her room, she contemplated grabbing supplies to carry with her but feared anything else would only slow her down. She had clothes on her back. Rhamzin had taught her to ride her horse. He had taught her how to follow the trees and brush for direction and warned her against poisonous plants and berries.

She could do this. She could survive away from the Palace.

But she had to get out first. She had to slip through the walls without any of the guard noticing her and get far enough away before someone noted and reported her absence.

There were a lot of people milling around in the gardens and property surrounding the Palace, but they were all within the walls. If she could sneak into the cellars and use the same underground tunnel she'd used before, she might very well be able to make it.

Or she could be smart and wait until nightfall when the rest of the town was asleep and the area was cloaked in darkness.

With a deep breath, she pulled the door open slowly and peered out, sighing when Rhamzin's face was the only she spotted.

"I can't stay here," she whispered barely above a breath.

His brows shot high and his head whipped around to check for any who would overhear their conversation and report it to another.

"Now is not the time," he whispered back.

"Tonight. I can't stay. You know I can't."

His nostrils flared with a deep breath, but he nodded once.

"My duty is over at sunset. I won't be the guard at your door."

That could pose a problem. Another guard member would demand they escort her if she said she was merely taking a stroll through the grounds of the Palace or even a trip to the kitchen for a late-night snack.

"When do you return?"

"Not until sunrise," he whispered.

They would have to wait until then. No others would be complacent to let her wander off alone and they surely wouldn't aid her in an escape.

"I have to go, Rhamzin. I cannot stay. You know I cannot."

"You still have a few weeks."

"Of what? Waiting for my stepfather to make more comments about my…womanhood? Waiting for the men to arrive so they can check me over and leer at my…" She waved a hand at the cleavage revealed by her low-cut gown.

His eyes dipped to her chest then quickly raised to her face as pink rushed his cheeks.

"If we are caught, you will be locked away and I will be executed."

"You've reminded me of that fact already. It's worth the risk to me. But I will not be executed. You may choose to stay here. Stay outside my room so no one suspects anything. I'll leave the window open, maybe even make a…a rope of some sort to make it look like I climbed out while you were unaware."

"Do you really think that will make it any easier for me?"

They continued to whisper, but Rhamzin's tone grew harder, harsher. While it was obvious he didn't relish the thought of having his head removed from his shoulders, he was more afraid for Freyda's future if she was caught attempting to escape Mhahzin and the fate her stepfather had planned for her.

"I won't let you traverse the wilds alone. Please remember the *Ihllr* of Mhahzin are not the only predators outside these walls."

He had attempted to teach her of the many carnivorous creatures, both wild and non-human, that lived in the woods. He tried to teach her of the vampires, the Strigoi, even the Shape Shifters. But their lessons were always rushed and short. All she knew was there were a lot of beings that would feast on her flesh, drain her of her blood, or use her body for their own depraved needs. None of which sounded appealing.

But how different would it be if the mate her stepfather forced upon her used her body? Even if the man her stepfather chose was kind, it wouldn't be Ahrkyn. He was all she wanted. He was…well, he was the missing piece of her heart and soul.

Mind made up, she raised her chin and squared her shoulders. "I'll wait until sunrise. I would prefer you join me but would never demand you risk your life or freedom for mine. I thank you for all the years you watched over me. Please know that I love you. You are my best…my only friend, Rhamzin. If you choose to stay, that won't change. You will always be an important part of my life whether I ever see you again or not."

Pushing to his feet, he stretched to his full height, towering over her by close to a foot, and looked down his nose at her.

"Pack only what you'll require. We'll need to push the horses faster than you've yet to ride. We need to put as much distance between ourselves and Mhahzin as possible. If you change your mind before morning, tap the door twice when you hear the changing of the guard outside your door."

Tears welled anew, but this time was from relief. If they were anywhere but in the hallway of the Palace, she would have thrown her arms around him and buried her face in his neck. She would have thanked him profusely.

For now, all she could was smile and nod her head before ducking back into her room.

It was time to make her plans. Time to decide whether she would take any of her personal belongings with her or leave it all behind. Nothing inside her room held any form of emotional sentimentality.

There were no photographs of her father, no letters from him left before he was killed. She'd never owned many toys as a child and had nothing that she would miss when she walked away.

Perhaps she should bring along changes of clothing. But all she owned were gowns and the like. Those wouldn't be realistic if she was unable to get to Ahrkyn right away. They hadn't made plans to meet again, so she might have to stay along the border of Ahdlai until either he wandered in her direction or the Royal guard of the northern territory located her and brought her before the King and Queen.

Yet, as she made her plans, as she wondered how long it would be before she would find Ahrkyn again, she felt him in her heart, felt his concern for her, felt his anticipation of her arrival.

He knew she was coming. He would be waiting for her.

She just had to get to him without getting caught.

Chapter Eight

Ahrkyn felt unsettled. For a moment, he couldn't pinpoint the sensation. Nothing seemed out of place within the Palace, no alarms had been sounded by those stationed in the towers, the guards walking the halls appeared relaxed as the Prince peered through the window and onto the lawn in front of the Palace.

Nothing was out of the ordinary.

Yet, his heart raced and anxiety turned his stomach and burned as it seared through his veins.

Focusing on his emotions and the feeling fluttering deep inside, he traced it until he was almost looking through Freyda's eyes.

He felt her. Felt her emotions. Felt her fear and something else. Determination.

While he couldn't literally see through her eyes, he could feel a conversation between herself and Rhamzin, felt the moment she decided to leave the Palace and walls of Mhahzin, felt the moment she decided to seek her freedom.

He also felt the moment she wondered how she would find Ahrkyn, then felt the moment she felt his presence in her heart and mind.

"I'll find you, *khaere*," he whispered into the dark of his bedroom.

She was going to risk leaving the grounds, rushing toward the border where she would seek her freedom within Ahdlai.

And Ahrkyn was determined to ensure she was safely behind the walls and inside the Palace before any sounded the alarm and sent a search party after her.

She would leave in the morning. How the hell he knew that he wasn't sure. There was some connection between them, a form of unspoken communication. Perhaps he should seek council with his father or even Jhelan. Both men were Fate Bound to their mates, both carried the brands gifted by the Mother for a Blessed union. Their brands were gifted by the mother only by those whose union was anointed.

If he spoke with either of them, they would know he planned to leave at first light to seek the Princess at the border separating Ahdlai from Mhahzin. They would demand he bring members of the guard with him.

But if he did not and there was an issue, it would be more difficult to protect Princess Freyda should any of the Mhahzin guard catch up to her as she fled.

It would be safer for Freyda if there was backup. As much as he would like to be solely responsible for her happiness and safety, he wasn't naïve enough nor stupid enough to believe he could take on large numbers alone, not if he wanted to keep her from being dragged back to Mhahzin.

Hours. He had only hours to prepare a number of his guard, alert his father and adopted mother of the Princess's arrival, and make a space for her in his bedroom. If she wanted the room to herself, he would find a spare room or sleep on the floor on the other side of the door, as long as he could be near her.

Hurrying from his chambers, he sought his parents and startled them when he burst through their bedroom door. Luckily – for both him and them – they were fully dressed and simply sitting up in bed, both reading a book they each held in their hands by the light of the candles and oil lamps scattered throughout the room.

"What is wrong with you?! Why did you not knock before bursting into our chambers? What if I was making love to your mother?" his father said, his face mottled with both anger and surprise.

"Then we would have been in a very uncomfortable situation. I have to speak with you. Now," Ahrkyn said, moving into the room and swinging the door shut.

Without halting, he told his parents of what he believed was to come at first light, that he believed his mate, the woman the Mother chose for him, would be fleeing her territory and heading straight for Ahdlai, and of his need to ensure she crossed the border safely.

By the time he was finished, he was nearly breathless, and both parents sat straight up in bed wearing matching expressions of surprise. Although, his mother bared a wistful smile as she pressed a hand to her chest.

It had been her dream to have grandchildren, to see her adopted son finally Claim a woman and sire an heir. While Ahrkyn had been resistant his entire life, everything had changed the moment he'd seen those brown eyes flash through his mind's eye.

He hadn't Claimed her, yet she carried the brands blessed by the Mother. It was truly a sanctified union, meaning there would never be another for Ahrkyn. He would never feel the need to seek the attention or affection of another woman, would never feel the need to slake his needs with another.

His life, from the moment his lips had touched Freyda's, became all about her, about having her in his life, about giving her the life she wanted, needed, the life of which she dreamed.

And that started with ensuring she crossed the border into Ahdlai unmolested.

The King threw the blankets away from his body and climbed to his feet. He was rattling off orders to the guard, who stood dumbfounded in the hallway, to retrieve the head guard, Jhelan, his feet never slowing as he hurried to the living area where he and Ahrkyn would derive a plan.

"Are you certain she will arrive in the morning?" the King asked, impatiently glancing at the front door of the Palace.

"I'm certain. I can feel her, Father. Here," Ahrkyn said, pointing to the middle of his chest.

The King's serious expression softened as he nodded. "I remember those days, how confusing it would be not knowing whether it was your mother's or my own emotions coursing through my veins."

"Will it stop? Will the sensation lessen?"

His father shook his head as he leaned back against the cushions and finally relaxed.

"No. While it only intensifies after you've completed the Bond, you will grow more accustomed to feeling her with you at all times, as she will you. It will simply feel as though you have a second heart beating within your chest."

"Will I be able to find her? Should she ever become lost or if she is ever taken by the enemy, will I be able to find her?"

"No matter where she is in the world, you will always find her," his father said.

Such an unnerving yet peaceful thought. On one hand, he mildly felt as though his mind was splitting, as though there was a second person living within his skin. But on the other, he could always get to her should she ever become a victim to kidnapping or should her stepfather decide to attempt to steal her away from Ahrkyn.

"We need to discuss another matter," the King said.

"Which is?"

"War."

"I've already considered the possibility that Emperor Ehmile will accuse me of stealing his prized possession."

"I wouldn't put it past him. Once he discovers where she is being…kept, he might very well call for retribution. Are you prepared to enter into another battle? Are you prepared to ask Ahdlai and your fellow guards to enter into another war with Mhahzin?"

"Would you? If Mother were being held by the enemy, would you be willing to go to war?"

"I would burn the planet to ash to bring your mother home," the King admitted.

While the Queen wasn't Ahrkyn's biological mother, she was all he had ever known. His earliest memories contained her presence. And he would like to think he'd learned how to love, how to treat women, how to show the respect women deserved by watching his parents' interactions and relationship through the years.

Soft padding of bare feet came from the hallway where the Queen emerged from around the corner moments later. She was wrapped in a vibrant purple dressing gown, her hair hanging loose over her shoulders and down her back. Ahrkyn had only seen his mother so casual in a handful of occasions and none of the guard had witnessed her so.

But Jhelan would the moment he stepped through the door to confer with the Royal family about the arrival of Princess Freyda and the possibility of upcoming trouble.

"How will she hide her brands before she arrives?" the Queen asked.

Ahrkyn shook his head. "I don't know. I can only assume she has done so successfully since we parted. I have felt no fear from her, only anger and determination."

His mother sighed and settled beside her mate. "Ah, the start of a Blessed bond. I remember those days as if they were yesterday."

The King raised a brow at his Queen and gave her a sideways glance. "You no longer feel me in your heart?"

Nudging him with her shoulder, Queen Ahlmeda rolled her eyes. "You know very well of what I speak."

"As much as I appreciate your romanticizing my newfound union, we have far more pressing matters than emotions and brands," Ahrkyn said, though he couldn't hold back the smile. "This is an extremely delicate matter."

The front door burst open. Jhelan hurried inside, Valdis on his heels. Both wore what they had donned before bed, only hastily slipping on their battle vest over their bed clothes.

"What is it? I was told you required my immediate assistance," Jhelan said.

Valdis held a sword in her hand while Jhelan's was strapped to his back.

Ahrkyn jerked his head toward an empty love seat and waited for the couple to settle before relaying every detail he'd already told the King to the head of the guard.

"You've got to be fucking kidding me."

Valdis turned wide eyes to her mate.

Jhelan immediately dipped his head toward the King and Queen. "My apologies, Your Highnesses. But…what the hell were you thinking, Ahrkyn?"

No one bothered to correct Jhelan's casual use of the Prince's name. They were friends; brothers by name if not blood.

"You, of all people, should know I had no choice in the matter. She was sent to me by the Mother, just as your mate was sent to you. She will require our protection. We will need to increase the patrols of the border to prevent anyone from sneaking over to take her from me."

"And you're sure she's coming here for you and not simply to find her freedom?" Jhelan asked.

Valdis turned a skeptical eye on her mate. "If I were to leave, would you simply sit by and watch me go?"

"This is about the Prince and Princess. Not us." His reluctance to answer was an answer in itself.

"How will she travel?" Valdis asked.

"What do you mean?"

"Will she come by carriage? Will she have any belongings?"

"I doubt it," Ahrkyn said. "From what I felt, she will be in a hurry. A carriage will only slow her down. She will be on foot or on horseback."

"Alone?" Valdis asked, her brows high.

"I don't know that. But I truly hope not," Ahrkyn said.

"If she isn't bringing a carriage, she will have nothing when she arrives. I'll make sure the staff provides her with any clothing or toiletries she requires. I'll also have a room prepared for her should she wish for her own space while she settles," the Queen said.

When Ahrkyn opened his mouth to argue that she would stay in his room, his mother raised a hand to stop him.

"She has lived under the rule of a dictator her whole life. She will need time to decompress and to learn to trust us. I'm sure she has been told horror stories of the *Vhtir* much as our kind is told stories of the *Ihllr*."

"Except the stories of the *Ihllr* are true," Valdis said, her eyes growing dark with anger and sorrow over memories of her Clan who was slaughtered by the *Ihllr* elves of Mhahzin.

Ahrkyn watched and listened as his parents and his closest friend made plans for Princess Freyda's arrival. Not just for her safety, but her comfort. They wanted to make sure the Princess received the same luxuries and amenities to which she was accustomed.

Perhaps the fact they were making sure there was space for Freyda in the Palace, ensuring there were gowns and other items in which she could indulge, seemed alien to Valdis or those who lived on the outskirts of the towns surrounding Ahdlai, Mhahzin, or any other regions' capitals. But it was how Freyda had been brought up, how she had been raised.

Throwing her into one of the smaller houses and demanding she work the gardens or work inside the Palace to earn her keep would be as alien to her as wearing gowns had been to Valdis.

As his heart raced, as the excitement of having her near grew, as the fear of the unknowns of her travel sent adrenaline coursing through his system, Ahrkyn couldn't help but picture her sitting beside him on the very couch where he reclined. He couldn't help but picture her in the halls of the Palace, couldn't help but picture her among his people.

And a new wave of terror hit him. This one was his own. What if she wasn't happy here? What if she didn't feel as though she could fit in? What if she felt as though they were taking her from one gilded cage only to lock her in another?

He decided then and there any and everything that happened while she was there with him would be her choice. She would choose whether she wore the gowns similar to the Queen or the tunics and breeches like the women of the town. She would choose whether they would live together in his room, in the Palace, or whether she would have a home of her own among the villagers.

And she would choose whether they ever completed the Bond. She would choose whether she would ever carry his child in her belly. She would choose the kind of future she would have with Ahrkyn.

She could do this. She just had to keep repeating those words to herself. Over and over, even as fear turned her stomach sour and made her head swim.

The times Freyda had gone to see Ahrkyn, excitement had been her motivating factor. The second time, of course, sorrow had been stronger than anything else.

This time was different, though. She wasn't simply running off for a secret meeting with a man on whom she'd developed a crush. This man, Prince Ahrkyn, was her mate, the Bond blessed by Mother Universe.

And she wasn't running to see him, to hold him, to kiss him. She was running away from her home, from Mhahzin, from the Emperor, from a future dictated by her stepfather.

This had to work. She could not be captured. If anyone spotted her, if they dragged her back, she would never again have even a modicum of independence or freedom. She would literally become like the Princesses in the fairy tales she adored and be locked in her room or, worse, a cell in the basement that was nothing more than a damp, dark cellar.

Rhamzin had yet to arrive outside her room. She had changed into the only pair of breeches she owned and donned a gown over it. She had no blouses similar to the ones the servants or town's people wore. It would have to do. If she had to run, she could only hike up the front of her skirt and pray she didn't trip over the hem.

Sunrise would arrive soon. Why was the guard change taking so long? There was no way anyone had caught on to her plans. No way Rhamzin had mentioned it to anyone, no way he had alerted the Emperor or any others that she planned to escape and run directly into the arms of the enemy.

Pacing from one end of the room, she stopped each time she neared her bedroom door and pressed her ear to the wood, listening intently for the sounds of footsteps leaving or arriving. The moment Rhamzin was settled outside her room and the first guard was on his way to his own quarters, Freyda would slip from her room and the odd pair would escape into the same basement she feared and disappear through a hidden tunnel.

How had no one discovered the tunnel in the long history of Ehmile's rule? How had no one thought to seek entry into such a heavily guarded castle?

Honestly, she didn't care about the whys or hows. The fact she appeared to be the only one with knowledge – beside Rhamzin – of the tunnel was of benefit to her. It was her path to freedom. It was her path to a new future.

It was her path to Ahrkyn.

Come on, Rhamzin. Hurry up.

Three more trips from the door to the window and back and she finally heard the heavy footfalls of her only friend and confidant.

Patience. She needed to be patient and wait until the former guard was well on his way to his chambers and wouldn't hear Freyda and Rhamzin hurrying through the hallway. She would have to trust Rhamzin's acute senses to detect whether anyone was in the hall or coming around any corners. They had made their excuses should they be caught roaming the Palace. She was simply having a hard time sleeping and needed something to fill her belly. And, of course, she wouldn't be allowed to travel the Palace alone, especially at night.

Their alibi was solid. But that didn't mean she wanted to use it. She would much rather they not see a soul as they moved throughout the large castle to the basement.

And she prayed they could get past the tower guards without being seen running from the walls and into the woods. Because the moment the alarm was sounded, dozens of armed guards would be racing after them on horses. Rhamzin had taught her to ride, but she still wasn't nearly as steady at a full run as those who had trained their whole lives.

She couldn't think about the risks. Couldn't think about whether or not anyone would see her. Because if she dwelled too long, she would lose her nerve.

As she pressed her ear to the door once more, a feeling hit her directly in the chest. As she focused on that feeling, it was as though she were looking through Ahrkyn's eyes.

He was out there. He was waiting for her. He knew she was coming. He was waiting to escort her over the border and safely into the town of Ahdlai. As long as she could keep enough distance between herself and anyone who might catch on to her escape, she would be in his arms within a few hours.

A few hours. It felt like a lifetime as she stood there waiting for the light tap on the door from Rhamzin indicating it was safe to leave her room and be on her way.

In the time she waited, she took a few moments to look around her room. Memorizing every inch of the place she had called home for the last twenty years, she took a deep breath and pushed down any ounce of sentimentality she held for the Palace and her bedroom.

She would miss her mother. There might not have been a relationship, they might not have been close, but she was the only family Freyda had, the only person other than Rhamzin who might actually care for her.

Not true. She had Ahrkyn. They might not have known each other well, but she could feel the affection he felt for her through their strange universal connection granted them by the Mother.

There was nothing for her to bring, nothing she would miss when she was gone. This was never her home. It was simply a place where she was held against her will, whether it took her over twenty years to discover or not.

Freyda would leave this place with nothing but the clothing on her back and the small dagger Rhamzin had snuck to her before he'd changed his post and the next guard took his place.

And that was all she needed. If she had to traverse the wilderness completely naked, it would be worth it to finally be free of the shackles around her ankles since arriving in the capital of Mhahzin proper.

And it would be worth it to finally discover and explore what was building between herself and Ahrkyn.

From the first meeting, he'd felt as though he would become a large part of her life, like their meeting had been destined since the beginning of time.

Now that she wore the matching brands of the Fated Bond, the brands blessed only by those brought together by the Mother, she knew their meeting truly had been destined, fated, blessed, and sanctified by the creator of all.

As she sank into her thoughts, the light tapping on the door startled her and caused her to jump. Holding in the squeal of surprise, she hurried and pulled the door open enough to peer outside. Rhamzin stood with his back to her, his shoulders squared, and only spared her a glance and a nod.

It was time.

Heart racing painfully behind her breasts, she stepped into the hallway and followed him down the hall, around corners, through the living area, the kitchen, then finally down the stairs that would take them to the cellar and the hidden tunnel.

No steps sounded nearby. No shouts of surprise alerted others to the movement through the Palace. Just a little further. She was so close. So close to freedom. So close to Ahrkyn.

Perhaps not close to Ahrkyn, but closer than she would ever be again if her stepfather got his way and she was forced to mate with a stranger of his choosing.

Cool, damp air caused chill bumps to rise across her exposed skin, but she ignored it, ignored the scampering sounds of rodents hurrying out of the way as Freyda followed Rhamzin through the tunnel. She tried not to think about the other creatures and critters that might have been occupying the same space like she did the last time she snuck through the secret passageway. The thought of spiders burrowing in her hair was almost as terrifying as being discovered.

A hand clamped around Freyda's shoulder, and she choked on a scream. Only Rhamzin. It was only Rhamzin hurrying her forward as they neared the mouth of the tunnel.

He only hesitated a moment, looking side to side then checking the towers before yanking her outside after him and darting into the woods with Freyda's legs struggling to keep up with his long ones.

The horses would be in the stable some distance from the walls of the Palace. Freyda always thought it was silly to keep their animals away from the protection awarded the Royal family, but this time, it worked to her benefit.

Rhamzin slowed and pressed Freyda behind him, wedging her against the thick trunk of a tree. His nostrils flared as he scented the air, then he tilted his head and listened. If there was anyone near the stables, the guard member should be able to detect him before Freyda was found.

All clear signaled, Rhamzin once again grabbed Freyda by the wrist and dragged her after him. They each secured their horses and burst through the open stable gate without a backward glance.

This was it. There was no turning back now. The last time, they led the horses away slowly, keeping their steps as quiet as possible. But time was of the essence. They needed to be moving and far from the Palace before the entirety of the guard was awake and on the move.

One hundred yards. Two hundred. They were in the clear. By Mother they were going to make it. She was going to make it. She was going to earn her freedom.

Four hundred yards. That was how far they made it before the distant clang of the alarm bells echoed through the woods and sent a fresh wave of terror and adrenaline coursing through Freyda's system and threatened to seize her heart.

"Kick her harder," Rhamzin order. "Use your heel. Lean forward like I showed you and hang on."

He could have gone ahead of her. He could have raced away from her and left her to fend for herself. But he was keeping pace, watching over her, and encouraging her.

She had to trust in the animal below her, had to trust in the short time she'd been trained, and trust Rhamzin would come back for her if she fell from the back of her mare.

Shoving her heel into the beast's ribs, she leaned forward the way Rhamzin ordered, clenched her thighs around its sides, and held on for dear life as her hair was blown from her face and tears welled in her eyes.

This was it. This was it. This was it.

She repeated the words over and over in her head, created her own mantra, used the words for support.

This was it. This was when she earned her freedom.

This was when she was finally able to build a life she'd always dreamed. And that started with throwing herself into Ahrkyn's arms the moment he came into view.

Chapter Nine

Ahrkyn's eyes were gritty and his thoughts sluggish. He hadn't slept a moment since discovering his mate would flee her territory and head to his. He couldn't. He couldn't rest until she was safely behind the walls of Ahdlai proper.

Groups of guards stood behind him, Jhelan, Ihsander, and Ahdeben on either side of him. They were all prepared for battle, all ready for the unknown.

It was the Prince's hopes that she would slip out unnoticed and make it to his side peacefully. He'd felt her rise in adrenaline, had noted the moment she had begun her escape, and now all he could do was wait.

"You are sure she's to arrive today?" Ahdeben asked.

"I'm sure," Ahrkyn said, his eyes on the horizon as the sky brightened to gray then lavender.

The horses sensed the anxiety of their riders and shifted their weight, periodically huffing with impatience. They were war horses, trained to rush their riders into violence. Standing idle was unnatural to the two dozen beasts lining the border.

Birds chirped and flitted from limb to limb overhead. Woodland creatures scampered through the underbrush in search of breakfast. A breeze blew loose strands of Ahrkyn's hair across his face, carrying the scents of dead leaves, pollen, and drought-ridden soil.

They were the scents he carried on him every time he returned from a patrol, the scents he washed from his flesh after each round of duty.

Now, they were the scents that would forever stay embedded in his mind as the scents of happiness, of his future.

The steed below him shifted again, stamping his front foot. He sensed something that had yet to touch upon Ahrkyn's ears or magic.

She was coming. The horses could already hear the approach of the riders, of Freyda and her guard, Rhamzin.

Nudging his heel into his horse's side, he urged him forward a few steps and narrowed his eyes to see through the trees, the morning fog, and the distance that separated him from his destiny.

She was coming. Freyda was coming. His Fated Mate was coming to be by his side, to build a life with him.

As he waited, the sounds of horse hooves hitting the ground finally met his ears.

And then he realized there were more than two horses traveling at a high rate in his direction.

"Fuck," Jhelan muttered, moving forward until he and his beast were several feet ahead of the Prince. "Move back, Ahrkyn."

Any other time, Jhelan might have used the formality of Prince in front of the guard flanking them on all sides. But from the sounds moving closer, they were about to be thrown into a battle with the guard of Mhahzin. The time for formalities was over.

When Ahrkyn nudged his horse forward again, Jhelan reached out and grabbed the reins, pulling the horse and the Prince to a stop.

"What are you doing?"

"Do not cross the border," Jhelan ordered.

Ahrkyn wanted to argue. He wanted to pull rank, to remind his friend he was the Prince and, therefore, his word was law.

But Jhelan was the head of the guard and hired and tasked by the King and Queen to protect all of Ahdlai, especially the Royal family. That included Prince Ahrkyn. While he wanted to rush forward and personally escort the Princess over the border into Ahdlai, he had to remember Jhelan would also rush forward, bringing the entirety of the guard with him, to protect the Prince.

That would be a call to war.

They needed to get Freyda over the border safely, and that would be more difficult if they were engaged in battle.

"There she is," someone called out. "Two hundred yards ahead."

Ahrkyn stood in the stirrups and craned his neck, searching for his mate, for his destiny, for the other piece of his soul.

Her long hair was loose as it flowed behind her, her body leaned forward, her face a mask of fear as she held onto her horse and pushed it forward. Rhamzin rode directly beside her, anger and concern etched into every line of his face.

"Come on, *khaere*. Just a little further," he muttered, fighting the urge to race forward, sling her onto his own horse, and race through the walls with her.

As she grew near, a large number of *Ihllr* guard appeared over the horizon, chasing after her.

"Shit," Jhelan muttered.

They had brought their own number of guard members, but the *Ihllr* guard of Mhahzin were double the number of *Vhtir* guard. If a fight ensued, there was a chance lives would be lost on both sides, especially from Ahdlai.

Freyda locked eyes with Ahrkyn. His heart felt as though it would burst from his chest as she practically pled for help with that simple look.

Rhamzin was obviously lagging back to keep pace with his Princess, his charge. His friend. He could easily outrun the guard, could easily disappear into the wilderness and safety, but he wouldn't leave Princess Freyda.

Ahrkyn might not have liked the fact the man had been solely responsible for Freyda's safety up to that point, but the fact Rhamzin was more than willing to risk his own life to keep the Princess safe earned him a hell of a lot of respect from Ahrkyn.

As Jhelan kept a death grip on the rein of Ahrkyn's horse, a decision was made before Ahrkyn had a chance to really consider it.

Thrusting his heels backward, he kicked his horse hard in the side and released something that could only be described as a battle cry. He had to get to Freyda. He had to get her over the border of Ahdlai. And the guard from Mhahzin were closing in on her and would reach her before she was safely in Ahrkyn's arms.

"Damn it, Ahrkyn," Jhelan bellowed after him, followed by the sounds of dozens of hooves hitting the ground hard as they chased after him.

Fifty yards. She was almost there. Ahrkyn caught up to her and flanked her vulnerable side, Rhamzin on the other.

"Keep going. Kick your mare harder. We won't let you fall," Ahrkyn called over the sounds of beasts running and chuffing and the *Ihllr* guard yelling orders to return the Princess.

They hadn't stolen her. There was no returning her. And she sure as hell had no desire to return to her cage, to the prison her stepfather had built around her, to a life as breeding stock, no better than cattle.

Jhelan, Ihsander, and Ahdeben circled around to protect her back as they escorted her forward. Ahrkyn's horse reached over and nipped at the legs of Freyda's, as though telling her to move faster, to push harder.

Her mare threw her head back but continued running.

Twenty yards.

Ten yards.

Almost there.

The guards who hadn't joined Ahrkyn in surrounding Freyda waited at the ready, swords in hand, luminescence glowing from their irises as they prepared for battle.

As though choreographed, the front line of the *Vhtir* guard separated, creating two long walls of beasts and men.

Ahrkyn waited for Freyda to enter first, then followed closely behind.

"Get her behind the walls!" Jhelan called out, his voice deep and full of rage.

There was no time to look back, no time to check on his guard. Ahrkyn needed to get his mate to safety, needed to have her behind the safety of the walls of the Palace.

He would have to trust the ability and skill of his friends, of his guard. He would have to trust they had trained the younger generation of guard members well enough to handle what was coming their way.

And he prayed to the Mother the *Ihllr* weren't foolish enough to cross into Ahdlai to chase after Freyda. Or perhaps he needed to pray they were ordered to stay within their own territory. Because another battle with the number the *Ihllr* had amassed would result in a number of casualties Ahrkyn didn't want on his conscience.

She was going to pass out. Or vomit. Maybe both.

Freyda's heart raced painfully behind her chest, feeling with every beat as though it would burst from her ribs at any moment.

She wasn't sure she had ever felt this amount of fear, this amount of terror in her life. Even when her stepfather presented his plans to sell her off, she'd maintained a level of calm she wasn't aware she possessed.

But this? Now? Not only had she been seen leaving the walls, but it appeared as if the entirety of the Emperor's guard had been sent after her.

When the *Vhtir* men from Ahdlai came into view, she had a moment, the smallest moment where she thought things were looking up. Ahrkyn was there at the front of the line with several rows of well-trained and well-armed men at his back.

Not enough. There weren't nearly enough men to combat the number chasing after her and closing in quickly.

She wasn't going to make it. They were going to yank her from her horse and race back to Mhahzin and she would never see Ahrkyn again, would never have the chance to earn her freedom again. There was no way her stepfather would allow her any semblance of freedom after today.

And then Ahrkyn broke rank and bolted ahead of his group, rounding Rhamzin and sidling Freyda on her exposed side. One by one, three other men raced forward and closed in behind her, effectively blocking her rear and preventing anyone from getting close enough to get their hands on her.

Ahrkyn ordered her to push her horse harder, to kick her heels into the mare's ribs. When she'd first begun to learn, she hated the thought of causing the animal any discomfort. Now, all she could think was what might happen to her beautiful mare if she was captured, whether the Emperor would dispose of the animal to spite Freyda.

Why in the world was she worrying about the future and well-being of her horse? If she didn't make it across the border…

She refused to entertain the consequences and possible punishments her stepfather would conjure for her traitorous behavior.

Dozens of men sat atop horses, their eyes on the guard chasing Freyda. In unison, they parted, forming two long walls for Freyda and Ahrkyn to pass through.

"Get her behind the walls," a man ordered.

Rhamzin stayed on Freyda's right, Ahrkyn on her left. He reached down and grabbed the rein from her hands, pulled it over her mare's head, and forced her animal to race faster, to keep pace with his own animal.

The trees began to thin, the underbrush became less clustered. There was an opening and about fifty yards past that was a wall as tall as the trees made of brick, stone, and foraged metals. It was a literal fortress and looked almost impenetrable.

At least she prayed it was impenetrable.

The sounds of bellowing men and horse hooves slamming into the ground faded into the background the further they moved from the border separating the territories. Were they engaged in battle? Were Ahrkyn's men, his friends, locked sword to sword with the *Ihllr* guard of Mhahzin?

And would they all hate her for putting them in this position?

The gates swung inward, several guard members flooded forth, their hands fisted around the hilts of their swords, their lips peeled back from their teeth in matching masks of rage.

They were as ready for battle as the men left behind to deal with those who'd tracked Freyda.

"Keep going," Ahrkyn growled out, pulling her horse alongside his.

All Freyda could do was continue to hold on to her animal for dear life. At least here, if she happened to fall from the saddle, she had people around her to help. She wouldn't be outnumbered. She wouldn't be yanked from the ground and dragged back to the walls of Mhahzin.

Houses flew past Freyda, barely registering in her periphery, as her focus remained on staying in the saddle and on top of her horse. Not much further. She was safely behind the border of Ahdlai, but it was obvious by the fervency of Ahrkyn's words that he didn't feel she would be safe until she was well behind the walls of his home.

She was mildly surprised to find homes behind a wall at all. Emperor Ehmile didn't bother to guard the people of Mhahzin, only those within the Palace. But since the Prince had yet to stop pulling her along beside him, she could only assume there was yet another barricade he wanted her behind before he felt safe enough for them to stop running.

Shouts of confusion, anger, and fear echoed around her. People ran in different directions, some ducking into their houses, those garbed in similar gear as Ahrkyn running toward the gate Freyda and the Prince had just ridden through.

Moments later, another tall gate appeared, the wall as formidable in appearance as the first. The gate swung inward and Ahrkyn finally slowed both horses as they crossed through the opening and trotted to the steps of the Palace.

Her breath whooshed from her lungs when he pulled her roughly from the saddle and crushed her body against his own, his arms becoming vices around her as he hugged her tightly. Almost too tightly.

"Can't breathe," she squeezed out.

Ahrkyn instantly released his hold, but cupped her face in both hands, bending at the waist to look her directly in the eye.

"Are you okay? Were you hurt?"

She shook her head, but lifted her hands to grip his wrists, preventing him from pulling away from her. She needed his touch, needed it to remain grounded. Because the world felt as though it were spinning around her, and her stomach dipped and rolled with nerves.

"Get her inside," someone called out.

Freyda turned only her eyes and gasped. The King and Queen of Ahdlai stood on the stoop, no crowns on their heads, but they were definitely dressed like royalty. The Queen's grown flowed and flittered in the wind, her beautiful golden hair was braided away from her face, the loose strands lifting in the breeze.

Her beauty was nothing short of ethereal.

The King…he was intimidating, but didn't hold the same coldness in his eyes as her stepfather. Instead, there was warmth and concern as he waved Freyda forward, stepping out of the way for the Princess and his son.

There was a moment, a beat of her heart where she feared this was a trap. There were several other guard members inside the Palace, their eyes glowing, swords strapped to their backs. They watched her closely, tensing as she neared like they were prepared for an attack.

An attack from her? Did they not know she was a mere human? That she held no magic and had not been trained in battle the way they had? What harm could she possibly do to anyone?

"Did any *Ihllr* follow you?" a man in black leather battle gear asked.

"I was unaware of anyone following. But I was focused on getting her to safety," Ahrkyn said.

He wrapped a hand around hers and pulled her to his side, the gesture familiar yet so new. While her heart felt as though it had known the Prince her whole life, her brain knew better. He was a virtual stranger, and she was now reliant on him and his people for not only her safety, but her well-being, as well.

What had she done? Yes, she'd wanted her freedom, but she had nothing to offer these people, no skills to donate to the running of their town.

A new wave of fear rushed through her system. What would they demand of her in return for staying in their territory?

"Princess Freyda, I am Queen Ahlmeda. This is my mate, King Nhaeem. And, obviously, you already know our son."

Freyda's brows pinched together. Why was the Queen addressing her first? And why wasn't the King reprimanding her or glaring holes into the side of her head?

"I assume you were unable to bring any belongings with you, but we will provide anything you need. I have already had my staff set out a few changes of clothing for you and they've cleaned a spare bedroom should you desire a space of your own."

The Queen raised one brow at her son. Ahrkyn said nothing.

"I don't have anything to give you. I don't...I can't garden or hunt or anything," Freyda blurted out. Might as well get that out in the open now. They would find out eventually, anyway.

The Queen looked first to the King then to Ahrkyn with a confused frown marring her beautiful face.

"I don't understand."

"I have no way to pay for the clothing. I have no way to earn–"

The Queen raised a hand, cutting off anything further Freyda planned to say.

"You are important to my son. Therefore, you are important to my mate and me. You are a guest in our home. Even the residents that reside here permanently aren't required to earn their place in our community. We each contribute what we can to keep our home running smoothly. For now, let's get you situated in your private space. You may bathe or simply rest if you please. I'll send either Ahrkyn or another of my staff when it's time for lunch. Does that sound acceptable to you?"

"Yes, Your Highness," Freyda said with a highly practiced curtsy.

The Queen dipped her head. "Would you prefer my son show you to your room or a female member of my staff?"

Staff, not servant. Were the people who worked for the Royal family actually free, or did the *Vhtir* simply use different terms than the *Ihllr* of her region?

Looking around at the three Royals watching her closely, she wasn't sure what the right answer would be. Should she ask the only person with whom she was familiar to show her to her quarters, or would she feel more comfortable with a woman in an enclosed space?

She was a stranger in this land. A guest, as the Queen referred to her.

"If it is allowed, I would prefer the Prince to show me to my sleeping quarters," Freyda said with another curtsy.

"When we are alone in our home, there is no need for such formalities," the King said.

Freyda looked to the guard standing sentry around the room.

The King waved his hand dismissively. "They will not intervene nor will they betray my confidence and speak of what occurs in my home. Every member of my guard can be trusted. I assure you, Princess Freyda, you are completely safe here."

"What of the guard in the woods? Will they be safe? What if the *Ihllr* are able to break through your defenses?"

A woman entered the room, garbed in a similar fashion to the guard but several inches shorter than Freyda. Her hair was a similar color of gold to the Queen's, but she didn't appear as a member of the Royal family.

"That's where I come in. I'm Valdis," she said, her hand outstretched as she approached Freyda. Her hand closed around Freyda's. "I'm mate to the head of the guard and the personal guard to Her Highness, Queen Ahlmeda."

Freyda didn't miss the roll of the eyes or slight smile on the Queen's lips.

"My mate just tried to assure her there is no need for such formalities within our home. Perhaps you could drop the charade while we are alone?"

Valdis's smile stretched. "Fine. I'm Ahlma's personal guard and will make sure no one lays a finger on you while you're a guest of the Royal family. And from what I've heard from my own mate, Ahrkyn won't allow anyone near you, either."

Ahlma? And the female guard just referred to the Prince by his first name. What kind of kingdom did these people run?

"Did you want me to take you to your room?" Valdis asked.

Freyda's heart began to race again. This was all so…different. So different than everything she'd known, so different from how she'd been raised, from what she'd been taught. These people weren't monsters. Not a single person had looked at her with malice or hate in their eyes. Not a single person had approached her or demanded a single thing from her.

She'd also only been within the territory for mere minutes. Less than thirty. Surely, they would let her get comfortable and coerce her into things she would never do…right?

"Prince Ahrkyn, please," Freyda said, unable to change her upbringing and training so quickly.

It would take days, maybe weeks before she would learn to treat these people the way they treated each other. If she was allowed to stay that long.

Ahrkyn had only offered her solace and protection while she escaped her stepfather.

He'd also stolen her heart and half her soul with a single touch and bonded them to each other with a touch of his lips. Or had it been she who had sealed their fate when she'd thrown herself at him and slanted her mouth over his?

She blinked. Then blinked again. Was she supposed to wait to be excused? Wait for the Queen or King to permit her to leave the room?

"Are you ill?" the Queen asked.

"What? No."

"You're extremely pale. Would you prefer to eat before bathing or resting?"

"I…"

Freyda looked around at the faces watching her expectantly.

"I have no idea what the correct answer is," she admitted.

The King huffed a laugh and attempted to cover it with a cough. The Queen elbowed him in the side but couldn't hide her own smile. Valdis didn't bother to hide her amusement as she raised her brows at Ahrkyn.

"See? I'm not the only one who feels like a fish out of water here," she said to the Prince.

"There is no correct answer, Princess. You may speak freely. You, too, are royalty. And you're not only a guest of the Royal family, but my Fated mate. You are just as much a part of this family now as I am."

The Queen leaned over and muttered, "I've always wanted a daughter," in the King's ear.

A daughter? The Queen wanted to be her mother? Freyda wasn't sure how a loving relationship between mother and daughter would feel. She could vaguely remember her mother holding her in her arms when she would cry as a toddler when they'd first travelled through the Palace walls.

"She's either going to puke, cry, or pass out," Valdis said.

Blinking rapidly, she cleared the tears that had, indeed, begun to well in her eyes. Only they weren't tears of sorrow. She was simply overwhelmed and unsure of what to believe. Her heart told her everything they said was true. Her heart and soul told her that Ahrkyn was the person who'd found her when she didn't know she was lost.

But her brain was still loaded with all the nonsense her stepfather had filled it with over the years.

Wrapping his hand around Freyda's, Ahrkyn led her from the room and down a hall. A door stood open, the room empty of anyone but full of wooden furniture and lavish, thick rugs and heavy drapes that would afford her plenty of privacy should she close them completely.

Privacy. That was something she had never had. There was always a guard outside her door, always someone following her around the grounds. The first time she'd escaped through the hidden tunnel was a fluke. She'd waited until she'd heard footsteps – Rhamzin's footsteps – moving away from her door. Then she'd taken the chance and darted out of her room and straight to the basement.

One time. One time in the twenty years that she'd resided within the Palace walls had she been left to her own resources long enough to slip away. Perhaps that was why the Emperor always assigned her with a shadow, to ensure she could never escape thus could be used to increase his power through promise of using her womb to sire heirs to complete strangers.

When Ahrkyn released his hold on her hand and stepped away, she took a moment to study her surroundings. It was large like her home in Mhahzin, but felt homier somehow, warmer. There were no personal pictures on any walls, yet it felt as though the room already belonged to someone.

"Is this your room?" she asked, turning her eyes to the Prince in the briefest glance.

"It is. I'll be staying in another room. Unless you would prefer I stay nearby. I can sleep on the floor. Or outside your room, if that would make you feel safer."

A frown pulled her brows together.

"Why would you sleep on the floor in your own room?"

A pink hue washed over his face, making the dark stubble peppering his cheeks and chin appear darker.

"I want to be near you. I've hated…" He inhaled deeply and blew it out in a rush. "I know this is all a lot to accept. I've never Claimed a woman, never mated with a woman. I have no heirs. All of this," he said, waving a hand in the air between them, "is as new to me as my territory is to you. The days apart felt like someone was trying to rip my heart from my chest."

She'd felt the same way. Although it made no sense. But from what she'd been told, the thought of Elves living among humans made no sense before the nuclear war had brought all the non-humans out of hiding to run the world and clean up the mess left behind from the human governments. There was no longer any such thing as normal or average.

"It's overwhelming. And…are your guard members going to hate me?"

His head snapped back a little as he frowned. "Why would they hate you?" He looked genuinely confused by her question.

"They could be out there fighting while I'm in here hiding. Your mother told me to bathe and rest. I can't do that knowing your men could be dying. Because of me."

"My men won't die. And they would do it for anyone who needed help. You're my mate. The entire group might not know that, but Jhelan does. And he's the head of the guard. He will do anything to keep you safe."

"I don't want anyone sacrificing themselves for me, Ahrkyn," she said as tears burned the backs of her eyes.

Ahrkyn closed the space between them and cupped her cheek in one hand. "You're safe here, Freyda. I promise you. The guard hired by my father are good men. They willingly put their lives on the line to keep our residents and those who live outside the towns safe from the *Ihllr* and any other predators who might cause them harm."

The *Ihllr*. The same Elves she'd grown up with her whole life. The same Elves she'd been raised to believe were the good guys. And it was the enemy who were out there putting themselves in harm's way simply to earn her freedom from enslavement by her stepfather and a mate forced upon her.

Ahrkyn carried the brands matching hers, carried the exact same marks that snaked from the back of her left hand, up her arm, and over her shoulder. Yet he had volunteered his room for her comfort and offered to sleep elsewhere until she was comfortable.

Throwing caution to the wind and allowing herself to do as she'd wanted since setting eyes on Ahrkyn from atop her horse, Freyda closed the space between them and wrapped her arms around his waist, resting her cheek on his chest.

His heart thumped rapidly against her ear as his arms closed around her and he leaned his head against the top of her head.

"You're safe. You're part of the family now. I'll never let anything happen to you, nor do I expect anything from you that you don't offer willingly. All I want from you is your trust. And this," he said, squeezing her tighter. "I wouldn't mind having you in my arms more often."

She chuckled softly. She loved the feeling of his body pressed against hers, loved the feeling of his strong arms holding her tightly like a cocoon of warmth and safety.

With a soft exhale, she let her body relax against him and her mind to slow. She was safe. She was with the mate given to her by the Mother.

Now, it was time to make the Palace and the territory of Ahdlai her home.

Chapter Ten

Ahrkyn leaned back against the cushion of the couch. Then sat forward and rested his elbows on his knees. He couldn't get comfortable, couldn't sit still.

"Were you that cute in the beginning?" Valdis asked Jhelan.

There had been no battle, no losses after Ahrkyn and Rhamzin had rushed Freyda away from the border. There had been plenty of threats issued from both sides, but the *Ihllr* hadn't attempted to cross the border to chase after the Princess.

Ahrkyn assumed it was only a matter of time before they received word from the Emperor with demands or intimidation tactics, some kind of order to return the Princess.

Not going to happen. She didn't want to be there and there was no way Ahrkyn could stomach the thought of some asshole breeding her against her will.

He couldn't stomach the thought of another man touching her at all.

"He was annoying," Ahdeben said. And it sure as hell sounded like he was jealous.

Both Ahdeben and Ihsander were interested in Claiming a mate and producing an heir, but neither had found a woman they wanted to spend more than a few hours with. Or perhaps they were hoping for what Jhelan and Ahrkyn had found. The bond both men were blessed with was rare, and the fact there were now three Fate Mated men in one town was extremely rare to the point of being strange.

"Do you want me to check on her?" Valdis offered.

Ahrkyn had left Freyda close to an hour ago, telling her to get comfortable, familiarize herself with the bedroom, bathe if she chose, and to rest if she needed.

An hour wasn't quite long enough for a bath and a nap. He needed to be patient.

"No. I want her to take her time. She'll come out when she's ready."

"She's going to miss lunch," Ihsander said. The man was always hungry.

"Then I'll have someone on the staff make her something fresh when she's hungry."

The King and Queen sat quietly by on a couch across from Ahrkyn, occasionally sharing glances and smiles. They were overjoyed that Ahrkyn had found someone, that he might finally sire an heir.

But just because the Mother had sent him his mate didn't mean she was amenable to carrying his child.

And while he might not know her well yet, he knew she would not accept her child being raised by anyone but herself.

That was fine with him. Since he wanted no one but Freyda, he would fight tooth and nail to ensure any child they might have in the future was raised by the two of them. And, if the child happened to be a boy and wanted to join the guard as he had, he would support his son's choice and ensure he received the best training available.

If he ever had a daughter…

Fear burned his stomach. There were so many threats in this world for females of every species. At least any daughter he fathered would be a halfling and would be of no use to any fucker looking to breed.

If he ever had a daughter, he would protect her as though she were the Queen, as though she were the most precious, fragile creature on the planet. Much the way he planned on treating his mate.

Once again, Ahrkyn leaned against the cushions, raising his left ankle to cross over his right knee.

"Be patient, son. Let her come to you. Show her she is not a prisoner here," the Queen said.

Ahrkyn couldn't contain the eye roll nor the way his head flopped back against the cushion. While the Queen might not have been his biological mother, she had raised him since he was barely a toddler. And had loved him as much as his birth mother might have had she been given the chance to raise him.

By now, his biological mother would be dead. At over eighty years old, he would outlive any human relative by decades.

Sorrow hit him square in the chest. Freyda was human. Meaning he would outlive her by decades, as well. He would have to live long after she passed, mourn her far longer than he would actually have her in his life.

He couldn't dwell on that. Couldn't allow that to affect the time he would have with her. Instead, he would simply celebrate every moment they had together.

First, he had to earn her trust and pray she would allow him in her bed. Sooner rather than later.

It wasn't merely the fact he wanted to feel her body below his, to feel her curves under his hands. He wanted to spoon behind her while she slept, molding his body to hers as he listened to her slow, steady breaths. He wanted to be there to comfort her if she woke from a nightmare, for her face to be the first he saw when he woke each morning.

Turning to glance at the large clock hanging over the fireplace, Ahrkyn bit back a groan. It had literally been seven minutes since the last time he'd looked. He couldn't sit here and wait. He would drive himself insane waiting.

"Why don't you boys go play? Valdis and I will wait for Princess Freyda. We'll make her feel at home, give her a little tour, and maybe have lunch on the patio," his mother said.

"Please don't embarrass me."

The King raised a hand and covered the smile he couldn't hold back.

The people in the room now were the only ones who truly saw the familial relationship between the Royal family, the only ones who ever truly saw them relax and simply be people instead of the rulers of the northern region.

"I promise not to tell her how long it took to potty train you," his mother said.

Ihsander barked out a laugh. Ahdeben grinned. Jhelan pointed a finger at Ahrkyn and snickered.

"Go somewhere else," Valdis said, jabbing her mate in the ribs with her small elbow. "There's far too much testosterone in here. We're trying to make her comfortable. I'm pretty sure walking out to you idiots cackling like hyenas will do the exact opposite."

But she, too, was chuckling and shaking her head.

It would be a while before Ahrkyn lived this one down.

"Thanks, Mother," Ahrkyn said as he pushed to his feet.

His friends stood and followed him onto the lawn stretching along the front of the Palace for nearly an acre before being cut off by the first wall. There were at least two more acres outside that wall that were encased by another line of defense that had been suggested by Valdis when she'd joined Ahdlai and then had been personally requested by the Queen to act as her guard.

"How does she feel about being your mate?" Jhelan asked.

Of Ahrkyn's three friends, the head of the guard was the only one who knew how it felt to be Fated and his union blessed by the Mother.

"We haven't had much time to talk about it. She knows what it means, but I have no idea how she feels about it," Ahrkyn said.

He lifted a hand and scratched the stubble he'd ignored over the past few days. The last thing he was concerned with was shaving. His thoughts had been solely occupied by Freyda, about when he would see her again, then the grief he'd felt when she'd told him of her stepfather's plans.

"I'm more curious as to why the hell you never bothered mentioning any of this to us," Ihsander said.

"He didn't exactly reveal anything to me, either. I just happened to catch him returning after his first visit with the Princess," Jhelan said with a sideways look in Ahrkyn's directions.

"You realize how idiotic that was, right?" Ahdeben said. "You should have at least taken one of us with you. It would have been far too easy for an *Ihllr* to be out there, hiding in wait to take you out."

His friend was right. Ahrkyn knew he was right. And, in hindsight, he would have lost his ever-loving mind if any other member of the guard had done something so stupid. But from the moment he'd seen Freyda's eyes in his mind, all rational thought had fled his body and he had one sole goal – to find the woman who had possessed him, mind, body, and soul.

"There was no plan. Not originally. I just knew…I'd had a premonition. Or a vision. I'm unsure of which. But I had seen her eyes in my mind. Curiosity and a strange pull dragged me into the woods that morning. I can't explain it."

Jhelan raised his brows and nodded. He, of all people, understood the lengths to which a man possessed would go to for the other half of his soul.

"You don't have the gift of precognition," Ihsander said with a smile.

"Yes. I'm aware. Yet, it happened."

Ahdeben walked along quietly beside the others, his eyes downcast, but it was obvious he was in deep thought.

"I'm surprised you're not still intent on verbally bashing me for riding off on my own," Ahrkyn said, glancing at him briefly.

They stopped near the garden and lowered to the ground, resting in the shade of a large tree.

Ihsander dropped onto his back, his hand over his stomach. "I'm starving."

The others ignored him. Ahrkyn sat with his knees bent, his elbows resting upon them. Ahdeben leaned against the trunk of the large oak, and Jhelan stretched his legs in front of him and leaned his weight back on his hands.

"The Emperor will eventually attack," Ahdeben said after a few moments of silence.

"He'll take this as an act of war on your part. He'll accuse you, at least in public, of kidnapping his stepdaughter," Jhelan said.

"What about the guard who came with her? Will he return to Mhahzin?" Ihsander asked.

Ahrkyn shook his head. "No. It appears they developed a…friendship over the years."

Green fog slithered through his belly as he struggled to keep the jealousy at bay. Rhamzin didn't appear to be attracted to Freyda, and she saw him only as a guardian and friend. But the guard member was a male who had protected her and demanded he continue protecting her, even within the borders of Ahdlai. It was Ahrkyn's job, and he couldn't refrain from taking it as a personal slight.

"Will he be a problem? Shall I assign one of our guards to shadow him?"

Ahrkyn shook his head. "I don't believe so. He appears to be loyal to Princess Freyda. I don't believe he would do anything that might result in any harm."

He also might be another soldier on their side if Mhahzin did attack. But both sides had incurred losses during the last battle. Should the Emperor enlist the aid of the Unseelie Fae again, Ahdlai would be lost. They'd heard nothing from Brizio the ogre in months, and didn't want to depend on his help and the help of his witch friends. Although, Ahrkyn knew the ogre wouldn't hesitate to offer his aid. He was a good man and a loyal friend to the region, regardless of the fact he was from the other side of the world.

"We need to come up with a plan of defense. I would rather be prepared for no reason than to be caught with our pants down," Jhelan said.

"Tell me," Ihsander said, a chuckle in his voice, "how long *did* it take for the Queen to potty train you?"

Ahrkyn snarled at him then shook his head. Nope. He wouldn't live that one down for a long damn time.

Princess Freyda stood in front of the tall mirror and examined herself from every angle. The clothing left for her was much more…conservative than she was used to wearing in Mhahzin. Her cleavage didn't spill out, the bodice didn't restrict her breathing, and she wouldn't trip over the hem simply walking across a room.

If the clothing was more comfortable, why did she then feel like a fish out of water? A servant – no, they referred to the workers here as staff – had quietly entered and offered to help with Freyda's hair. She had twisted and braided it into a rather appealing style, but was once again different than how the women wore their hair in her home region.

And the face creams. There were so many colors laid out when Elabeth first began that Freyda had feared she would resemble an exotic bird. But the older woman had merely smeared a pink cream on her cheeks and lips and said her beauty would shine through naturally.

Beauty wasn't something Freyda had often heard used to describe herself. She was round in all the right places; her stepfather had made sure of that. But she had always found her face…plain. Her eyes weren't the vibrant hues of the Elven women but a brown the shade of mud. Freckles dotted her nose and cheeks, her bottom lip was fuller than her top, and her nose was a little thin at the bridge, turning up at the tip.

Ahrkyn was beautiful. His mother was beautiful. In fact, she had yet to meet a single member of the Elven race who wouldn't be considered beautiful.

Yet Ahrkyn had chosen Freyda. They were bonded and their union blessed by Mother Universe. They carried the matching marks of the Bond.

He'd called her eyes beautiful. He'd told her as much when they'd first met. And he'd kissed her with a fervor of a man who truly wanted a woman, not a man simply looking to bury himself in her warmth.

As thoughts of his lips against hers, his body molded against hers, played in her mind, another warmth began to unfurl within her, starting from low in her belly and spreading to her limbs.

Ahrkyn. As she focused on those kisses, as she focused on the mark on her arm, she swore she could feel him, feel his emotions, feel his uncertainty and fear.

Fear of what? Fear of their union? Fear of being mated to the Princess of his enemy? Or fear for her future?

He had promised to keep her safe. Had promised his people would keep her safe. And whether it made sense or not, she trusted him to keep his word.

The more she focused on those feelings, on what Ahrkyn felt, the more she swore she could see his location.

Such a heady and terrifying sensation.

"You cannot remain within this room forever," she whispered to her reflection.

If nothing else, she needed to join the King and Queen for the midafternoon meal. It would be rude to do otherwise.

With a deep, calming breath, she smoothed her hands down the front of the gown, lifted her head, and squared her shoulders. She would maintain her role as Princess, remember her lifelong training, and behave the part she had been forced into as a child.

Even here, even with the man who held her heart before she truly knew him, she would be the Princess, the only mate to the oldest heir of the King.

But she doubted she would ever rule at his side. She would die long before the King and Ahrkyn would live the rest of his life without her.

How terribly sad. How long would he be alone? How long would he wait before seeking another to stay by his side while he ruled?

And why did the thought of him taking another mate after her death send jealousy coursing through her like fog across the grass?

She had no right to be jealous of anything that would happen once she was buried in the ground. She should only desire his happiness. Yet she couldn't kick the feeling of wanting to be his only love.

Selfishness was a new trait for Freyda and not one of which she was proud.

Turning her back on the mirror, she steadied herself to walk into a room where everyone would stare. She was the newcomer, after all. The daughter of their enemy. The stepdaughter of Emperor Ehmile, the ruler of the southern region of Mhahzin.

How many times had she said those very words in her own mind? How many times had she been referred to in that exact same manner? Yet now the title and relationship felt like a lie, like more a curse than a birthright.

This was her home now. Ahrkyn was her family. She would grieve her mother, she would miss her regardless of the strained and unemotional relationship or attachment. But Freyda knew she was exactly where she was meant to be. The Mother wouldn't allow otherwise.

The hallway outside the room she would one day share with Ahrkyn was empty, but she heard soft, feminine voices floating in the air. Following the sound, she found only the Queen and the woman introduced as Valdis in the living area filled with couches, winged-back chairs, and settees.

"Was your time alone enjoyable, daughter-in-law?" Queen Ahlmeda asked.

"Yes, Your Majesty. Thank you," Freyda said with a slight curtsy and bow of her head.

The Queen waved a hand in the air. "Please. Call me Ahlma when we are alone. You are my daughter now. I assume you do not refer to your biological mother with such formal titles."

Yes. She did. At least when there was anyone in the room, and Freyda couldn't remember the last time she was alone with her mother.

"Thank you," Freyda said, unsure of what she was thanking the Queen for, whether it was the permission to address her informally or because she would finally have a woman who could possibly care for her the way a mother should.

"You must be famished. Would you care to join us for lunch? Or, if you prefer, we could dine together on the patio, just the three of us."

Freyda frowned. "The King and Prince do not dine with you?"

The Emperor rarely dined with Freyda and her mother. She assumed it must have been that way in Ahdlai, as well. They were, after all, merely women.

"If you would like, we could join them in the dining hall," the Queen offered.

"I'm sure Ihsander is already complaining," Valdis said with a shake of her head. She turned her attention to Freyda. "Ihsander is always hungry. I swear he is like a cow and possesses four stomachs."

Freyda had no idea what that meant or why a cow would have four stomachs. While she was taught to read by Rhamzin, she wasn't taught much else. Because…she was a woman. In the Emperor's eyes, females of every species only had one role and that was to please a man and to bless them with heirs, to continue their bloodlines.

"I don't want you to change your life for me. I will follow your lead. If you normally join your King and the Prince in the dining hall, I will join you there."

Queen Ahlmeda tilted her head and studied Freyda long enough that Freyda fought the urge to squirm under her scrutiny. For what was she looking? A sign of discomfort from the Princess?

She would find none. Freyda had become quite adept at hiding her emotions.

Freyda waited as the Queen and Valdis rose. The Queen held out a hand and Freyda frowned at it for a heartbeat, unsure of what was expected of her.

"Please. This way," the Queen said, patiently waiting with her hand outheld.

Looking to Valdis, she slid her hand into the Queen's at Valdis's nod and allowed her to guide Freyda through the house.

"Seek your mate and my son. Let them know it's time for lunch," the Queen said.

Valdis nodded at Queen Ahlmeda, winked at Freyda, then disappeared around a corner.

A door opened and closed as Freyda was led into a room similar to the dining hall in the Palace of Mhahzin. There were over a dozen chairs situated around the table, much like the one at home, the King waiting at the head.

"They chose wisely for you," King Nhaeem said. "That dress is very becoming. I can see why my son chose you."

Freyda tensed and waited for the leering and inappropriate comments to begin. She had witnessed her stepfather coming on to many women who entered the Palace, had seen him lead them to his private sleeping chambers on just as many occasions.

"Thank you, Your Majesty," Freyda said with a curtsy.

She kept her eyes averted out of both fear and respect.

"Have I said something to make you uncomfortable?" the King asked.

"No, Your Majesty," Freyda replied, eyes still glued to the table in front of her.

"You may call me Nhaeem. My mate has told you, there is no reason for such formalities from our new daughter, not when there are no others around."

"Do you fear my mate?" the Queen asked.

Freyda raised her eyes to Ahlmeda's face and searched her eyes. There was no malice, no humor, nothing but genuine curiosity.

"I apologize. He…men make me nervous," she admitted.

Might as well get it out there now.

"You have no reason to fear me or any other man within this town. If you choose to wander the woods the way Valdis used to enjoy, I do ask that you bring a larger number of guards to keep you safe from any…well, from the *Ihllr* should they be hiding in wait for you or others whom they might enslave."

"Yes, Your Maj…I…I'm unsure of what to say."

Ahlmeda squeezed her hand lightly. "You are not required to say or do anything except be happy. And, maybe, give me a grandchild if you decide to one day give Ahrkyn an heir."

Freyda felt the knots in her shoulders relax minutely. Until a door opened and the sounds of many men filtered through the house. The carriers of those voices spilled into the dining room, pulling chairs from the table and watching the Queen closely, waiting for permission to sit, or perhaps waiting for the Royal family to be seated first.

Ahrkyn entered toward the back of the group of men, his eyes finding her immediately. Her heart did a funny little flip in her chest, and she fought the urge to run to him and throw her arms around his waist and hold him close.

Already, he felt familiar to her. He felt like home.

Hurrying to her side, he took her face in his hands and tilted her head back. "Did my mother tell you any embarrassing stories about me?"

That was not what Freyda expected. Part of her expected the Prince to lower his lips to hers. The other half expected some form of inquisition of her extended absence.

"No, Your Highness," she said.

His lips twitched as he held back a smile. "I am your mate. At no point are you required to address me as anything more than my name, *khaere*."

Khaere. She knew that word. Had heard it spoken many times, although never by the Emperor. And Ahrkyn had called her that once before. He had used a term of endearment in front of his subjects, in front of his guard.

The same guard members who were surrounding the table and appeared as though they would be dining with the Royal family. No one batted an eye, no one reacted to his treatment of her, no one stared or leered at her.

Instead, they all looked as though they were becoming impatient to eat and nothing more.

Ahrkyn pulled out a chair two down from the head and waited as Freyda smoothed the back of her skirt and lowered. He then took the chair beside her and at his father's left elbow while Queen Ahlmeda took the chair at the King's right elbow.

Then everyone sat and turned to watch the staff carry in bowls and trays of food.

No one remained silent, no one sat ramrod straight the way Freyda did. They all conversed and laughed and teased each other, told stories of their recent patrols. They attempted to include Freyda in their conversations, but she had nothing to add.

Plates were sat first in front of the Royal family, including Freyda, then the guard around the table.

"Is there anything you don't enjoy, Your Highness?" Elabeth, the same servant woman who'd helped with Freyda's hair, asked.

Freyda stared into the woman's vibrant green eyes. She had a choice of what she would eat?

Looking around the table, she realized the others were given bowls and platters to pass around and take what they wanted.

"I…I'm unsure," she admitted.

Being voluptuous and full figured was preferred by the *Ihllr* Elves of Mhahzin. She had been, more or less, forced to consume more food than was required to survive, but she couldn't quite remember despising anything she was fed.

"If there's something you don't enjoy, either pass it by or leave it on your plate and the staff will feed it to the livestock," Ahrkyn said, leaning close to be heard over the chatter of the group.

She nodded.

The food was delicious. The desserts were even better.

Every single person at the table constantly tried to pull her into conversation, asked her opinion on various topics, or asked questions about herself. Yet, she found herself at a loss for words.

When was the last time anyone had truly cared what she thought or felt? When was the last time anyone other than Rhamzin talked to her or treated her as a human being, as a living, thinking creature rather than a vessel for a stranger's child?

"Where is Rhamzin?" she asked Ahrkyn.

"He declined to dine with us. He is with the guards in training, eating his meal," he answered.

She might have felt more at ease had there been another familiar face at the table.

It would take time. She would have to remind herself every day that the *Vhtir* were nothing like the *Ihllr* of her home region. She would have to remind herself every day that the King was not romantically interested in her, that Ahrkyn would not allow anyone to harm her.

And she had to remind herself every day that she had made the right decision by following her heart. She had made the right decision to choose her own path and to follow that path to Ahrkyn.

Chapter Eleven

Freyda remained reserved throughout lunch. Ahrkyn knew she must feel overwhelmed by a new home and all the new faces. Not to mention the dress she wore now covered more of her body than the others he'd seen her wear.

Not that he minded seeing more of her flesh. And hoped he would see even more sooner rather than later.

For now, he must do whatever he could to aid her in growing more comfortable with her new home.

The guard, Valdis, and his parents had left the table, leaving the newly mated couple alone. And now, they sat in awkward silence, the table long since cleared.

"Was the clothing my staff left for you to your liking?" Ahrkyn asked.

She turned her face up toward him and he found himself dumbstruck once more by her beauty. How had he been blessed by such a remarkable creature, such a stunning woman?

"They were beautiful. But that's not what you want to ask me."

He frowned down at her, unsure of her meaning.

"You want to know whether I will lay with you tonight. And as far as I see it, I don't have a choice."

Ahrkyn stood and offered his hand. She sighed heavily, lifted her chin, and slid her petite hand in his.

Instead of leading her toward the bedroom she now occupied, he veered off and led her outside to the shaded patio.

It was her turn to frown at him as he gestured toward one of the empty chairs.

Once she was seated, he took the chair beside her, moved it until it sat directly across from her, and lowered himself onto it.

Without asking or waiting, he took both her hands in his and held them. "I expect nothing from you, *khaere*. Is that not why you chose to flee Mhahzin, why you chose to come live here with me?"

She blinked rapidly as tears welled in her eyes. "I'm so…confused. I don't know how to feel or what I'm supposed to say. And your parents are so…they're so loving and kind. And your friends were being so nice to me. And I sat there not knowing how I'm expected to behave. And I know you all keep saying nothing is expected of me, but you have to give me time. Twenty-three years of being trained to be a specific person isn't going to be changed within a few hours."

She inhaled deeply and blew it out.

"And I like when you call me *khaere*," she admitted.

A smile stretched on his face. "Then I shall call you *khaere* every day of your life."

Not *our* life. *Her* life. There was that terrifying, heart shattering fact being shoved right in their faces. She would not live the long life he would. There would come a time when he would have to learn to live without her, how to survive without her, how to allow his heart to mend without seeking an end to his life.

But not today. Today, he had her in his life and in his arms. Or at least within arm's reach.

"Did everyone overwhelm you?" he asked.

Her head bobbed side to side. "It was unfamiliar. The guard of Mhahzin don't dine with the Royal family. And it's rare for my stepfather to sit at the same table with me and my mother. His presence at any meal has become almost a warning. It signifies he has something to discuss and it's rarely something I enjoy."

Ahrkyn nodded, maintaining eye contact as he listened.

"The last time he sat to dinner with Mother and me was when he declared his intention of gifting me to a stranger."

"I can see why you say it's usually uncomfortable when he joins you," he said.

"The time before that, he threatened to execute Rhamzin."

Ahrkyn frowned. "Why?"

Her narrow shoulders lifted and fell. "I assume he felt I was becoming too spirited. Or perhaps I had done something to displease him. He never gave me a reason and didn't make it a habit to explain his actions or decisions to me."

"I've never met the Emperor but have heard many stories of Ehmile. And I've had more than my share of interactions with the men he hires to do his bidding."

Freyda nodded. "Rhamzin isn't like that, you know. He has never…he would never do anything untoward to a woman."

"He has never Claimed a woman against her will?"

"I can't really speak for him. But I have not seen him with a mate in the time I've lived within the Palace walls."

"Are you sure he can be trusted?"

Her head nodded emphatically. "I trust him with my life. He is the only one who truly looked out for my best interest and protected me from the attentions of the other less scrupulous guards."

Ahrkyn glanced toward the glass doors leading inside. There was no one standing there, but he pictured his mother straining to hear their conversation outside, cheering him on, and hoping Freyda would soon allow Ahrkyn to fill her belly with his child.

"Would you like him to remain your personal guard? I can't see him being amenable to working alongside my people to protect the borders of Ahdlai. He might be loyal to you, but that doesn't mean he would be loyal to those he had been raised to hate."

"Why do you hate Mhahzin?" she asked, tilting her head to the side and narrowing her eyes.

"I hate no one. I only hate those who prey on innocents and the most vulnerable like humans or females wandering the woods alone."

"Have you been to Mhahzin?"

Ahrkyn shook his head. "Not since I was a child. I remember the beauty of the land. I remember the ruler before your stepfather took over."

She watched him a few more moments and he could practically see a question forming in her mind.

"Were you alive during the time of the human war?"

"I was merely a toddler at the time. I barely remember much before the non-humans took over."

"But humans ruled the planet before then?"

He nodded.

Her eyes moved to the side, and he could once again see the thoughts form in her mind and could feel her rush of conflicting emotions. Without asking, he knew she was trying to imagine a time when her kind wasn't so low on the food chain, when humans were feared instead of hunted. When they were allowed to live their lives without fear of various supernatural and paranormal creatures taking them as slaves or forcing connections or children on them.

Most of what he knew about that time was merely from stories passed down from older generations. A child's memory was more like a dream that faded upon waking – the images came in foggy flashes with very few emotions tied to them.

The sun was high in the sky, the shade moving across the patio as they enjoyed each other's company and Freyda struggled to come to terms with her new life.

He hoped it would be easier since this was her choice and not something forced on her. He hoped she would one day come to love Ahdlai as much as he did, love the people as much as he did.

Come to love him as much as he was already growing to love her. Or perhaps it was the Bond convincing him of feelings that were far stronger than anything he had ever experienced.

While lunch had been a lot to mentally digest, the time alone with Ahrkyn had finally eased her nerves. She was with the man her heart had screamed for since the moment she had laid eyes on him.

Yet he barely touched her, hadn't kissed her, hadn't demanded anything from her. He had even given up his personal sleeping quarters and offered to sleep elsewhere if it would put her at ease.

As nervous as she was about being in the same bed with another man, the thought of sleeping alone in a strange room, in a strange house, surrounded by strangers caused her more anxiety than being beside Ahrkyn ever could. She wanted to stay near him, wanted him to wrap his strong arms around her so she could pull from his strength and assure herself that she was safe and would never again be treated like livestock to be auctioned off to the highest bidder.

"Would you like to see the rest of the Palace and the grounds? You should familiarize yourself with the area so you can find your way around without a guide," he said.

Freyda frowned at him. "Won't I have a guard escorting me?"

He blinked at her a couple times and shrugged up his broad shoulders. "If you prefer a guard with you, I can assign one of my men. But I assure you that you are safe within these walls. None of my people would let any harm come to you and none would dare lay a finger on you or do anything to make you uncomfortable."

She could hear the words he didn't speak through their link. They wouldn't dare touch her or they would answer to him.

How? How could she *hear* the words? Was it more of a simple emotion, an understanding of what was in his heart?

There were so many things about this union she didn't understand, and might possibly never learn the answers. Although, she had noticed Bond brands on the King and Queen, as well as Valdis and her mate. Perhaps they would have some answers for her.

It would take time for her to grow to trust them, unfortunately. Trust was not something that came easily for her. It had shocked her how at ease she was around Ahrkyn in such a short period of time. She felt as though she could put her very life in his hands and he would treat it as a precious gift.

"What of Rhamzin?" she asked.

"You prefer he escort you?"

"I only want to know he will not be mistreated. I swear to you, he is not like the others."

"He doesn't appear to trust nor like us," Ahrkyn said.

A muscle jumped in his cheek, but he kept his face neutral.

"All *Ihllr*, as well as the human and non-Elf residents, were raised to believe those in your region were…well, devils. Evil. Demons who would slaughter us if given the chance."

"Do you still believe that?" he asked, his voice soft, his expression pensive.

He still hadn't moved closer to her, had barely touched her since they'd stepped onto the patio after lunch. He kept his distance, left a space for her to move should she wish to flee his side.

"I want to say no. I don't believe you're like that. But…twenty years of being taught something is hard to forget," she admitted.

Everyone she had seen appeared no different than those in Mhahzin. The *Vhtir* were calm and treated her kindly. Although, her stepfather treated newcomers and guests with kindness to get what he wanted from them.

Could they be attempting to ply her with food, drink, and pretty clothes? She had not been given any wine, and she was not so full that she couldn't struggle or run if the need arose.

So, maybe, just maybe, these people, the *Vhtir* and the Royal family were as they appeared. Maybe they were simply good people who wanted the best for the residents of Ahdlai.

"How about we start with a tour? Invite Rhamzin so he, too, can familiarize himself with the grounds and Palace. That way, if you feel more comfortable having him at your side, he'll know exactly where to go."

"You won't remain by my side if I choose to stay here?"

Confusion and something akin to pain flashed through his brilliant icy eyes. "You have not decided to stay? You're still considering moving on?"

Had she decided? More importantly, did she truly have a say in that decision? She didn't fear Ahrkyn would force her into chains to keep her in Ahdlai, or to keep her within the walls of the Palace. But would the Mother allow her to walk away from the man chosen for Freyda? Would Mother Universe allow her heart to beat the same rhythm if it was missing a piece?

"We don't need to discuss that now. You've had a trying day. And I'm sure you're overwhelmed by so many changes."

"Yes. I am," she admitted then huffed a laugh. "But I would enjoy a tour. And I would appreciate if you would truly allow Rhamzin to accompany us."

"Of course."

He unfolded to his full height and lowered a hand to her. Allowing him to help her to her feet, she didn't immediately pull from his grasp, enjoying his touch far too much to relinquish her hold just yet.

"Where is Princess Freyda's guard?" Ahrkyn asked one of his own guard members as they entered the Palace.

"I'll retrieve him," the guard member said, hurrying from the room after a quick dip of the head.

Ahrkyn turned his hand so his fingers twined through hers. There were callouses along his palms, but his grip was gentle yet firm. His thumb made soft circles on the back of her hand as he led her through the Palace, through the front door, and onto the landing looking over the expanse of property along the front of the building.

"How many people reside in Ahdlai?" she asked as he helped her down the stairs.

The gown wasn't so long that she feared tripping, but she did have to hitch the front up a little to avoid stepping on the vibrantly colored fabric.

"There are somewhere near three hundred in Ahdlai proper. I'm unsure of how many actually reside within the borders of Ahdlai as not all choose to live within the many towns spread throughout our territory," Ahrkyn explained.

"I was told you have many wild beings in the woods surrounding the Palace."

He nodded as they strolled. "There are humans who have chosen to live in the forests and caves throughout all of Ahdlai, as well as other beings. And not all are civilized. There are many creatures out there who would feast on flesh of any, whether human or Elf."

Mhahzin had such creatures within their territory as well such as the vampires and Strigoi. Among others. She'd believed they were all stories told to keep the younger generations from wandering too far from the wall, but Rhamzin had assured her of the terrifying monsters who wandered free at night. And, apparently, they wandered this part of the world, too.

As they ambled toward a large expanse of garden, Rhamzin appeared around the corner of the building, his brows pinched together, his eyes narrowed as he sought Freyda through the bright sunlight.

When his gaze fell on her, he walked briskly in her direction, ignoring the man who walked beside him until he was at Freyda's side.

"Are you well?" he asked, barely glancing at Ahrkyn before turning his attention back to the Princess.

"I'm fine. Thank you. Ahrkyn is going to show me the Palace and the grounds. We both thought it would be wise for you to join."

"You will allow me to stay by her side?" Rhamzin asked Ahrkyn.

"You are more than welcome to remain within Ahdlai as long as it pleases Freyda."

The large *Ihllr* guard shocked both Freyda and Ahrkyn when he dipped his head and bowed slightly at the waist.

"You have my gratitude, Your Highness."

Ahrkyn waved him off. "You don't have to address me with such formalities. I, too, am a member of Ahdlai's guard. I only ask that you use my title when among the residents when I am attending my Royal duties."

Rhamzin frowned a few more moments before nodding and following a few steps behind the Prince and Princess to learn the layout of the land within the walls of the Palace. It took several hours, but only because they kept a leisurely pace. They took the time to get to know each other better, to speak without such a large audience.

Even Rhamzin stayed so silent Freyda, at times, forgot he followed them, never interjecting an opinion nor making a noise of displeasure when Freyda told Ahrkyn of Emperor Ehmile's treatment of those who lived within Mhahzin.

"Why have none of your people risen up against him? If there are as many as you say in the territory, it should be easy to overthrow the Emperor."

"Because those who support him are given power over the women they capture as well as being paid heavily in food and supplies," Rhamzin said.

Ahrkyn slowed to a stop, turning to look at the guard.

"You're saying there are those in Mhahzin who would rather live under a dictator with the promise of a steady influx of women and food?"

Rhamzin nodded his head once.

Ahrkyn turned to look at Freyda. "Even at the expense of his own daughter." Fury lit a fire behind the Prince's eyes, bright silvery light flashing from them. "Sick bastard."

Rhamzin huffed a deep laugh but didn't crack a smile. He merely stood and waited for the two Royals to continue their exploration.

As they passed a large vegetable garden, several people working in the sun stopped and bowed their heads.

"This is Princess Freyda. Hopefully," he said with a wink down at her, "you will see her around a lot. Please treat her as you would the Queen."

Her eyes growing wide, Freyda shook her head emphatically. "No. I want to be treated as you all treat each other," she corrected, and hoped she hadn't overstepped. Such would cause a severe punishment in Mhahzin.

"Yes, Your Highness," a few said in unison.

Well, damn. That was the exact opposite of what she wanted.

She had grown tired of the deference from the women in her home territory and the leers from the men. The men here didn't make her feel as though they were mentally undressing her or waiting for the moment they would catch her alone in a hallway. They would nod their heads and avert their eyes. Those who'd dined had attempted to include her in their conversations, but their gazes never lingered, their attention never dropped to her chest.

Respected. That was the only word she could find to describe how she felt in Ahdlai.

For once, she wanted to walk around without the extra attention. More than once, she had thanked the Mother for not making her a beauty like her mother or Queen Ahlmeda.

Although not being a great beauty hadn't stopped the Emperor from finding those who would be willing to fight to the death to earn the rights to make her their mate and breed with her.

How long had the guard of Mhahzin lingered near the border of Ahdlai? Were they still out there? Was her stepfather foolish enough to send someone into the northern territory to attempt to steal her back? She was, after all, the prize he had offered for the stupid games. He would look like a liar if he no longer had the Princess to offer as a gift to the winner of whatever competitions he had planned.

A new wave of fear touched her heart. She was given freedom to roam within the walls, but she knew her stepfather had found allies who were capable of breaching their security and entering the town. Luckily, none of the civilians had been slaughtered during that raid.

"What if my stepfather attacks?" she blurted while Ahrkyn was in the middle of discussing the types of crops they grew and livestock they raised.

"Then we will hold them off," Ahrkyn said after a beat.

"Your guard members could be hurt. Or killed. Simply because of my presence."

"And they would be willing to go through the same for any resident of this region. You are now a member of Ahdlai and a member of the Royal family. As such, you will be protected."

Freyda turned to look back at Rhamzin, who was doing his best to pretend not to eavesdrop.

"You should have taught me to fight," she said to her only friend.

His eyes flitted to her face and he frowned.

"And when would I have done that? With all the guard watching? While your father kept close tabs on you? I will keep you safe. Should any member of the guard fall, you will still have me to stand between you and those who wish you harm."

His statement did nothing to quell her fear. It was yet another living person willing to sacrifice his life for her. She wasn't worth so much trouble. She wasn't worth so much pain.

Yet…she would be more than willing to put herself between Ahrkyn and a sword aimed for his heart. She might not know how to fight, but she knew what she felt for the Prince was deep. Surely, his feelings for her were as strong. And Rhamzin was her friend. He had been her friend and protector for two decades. She would do what she could to keep him safe if she had any idea how to swing a sword or pull the string of a bow.

"It's not too late."

Her attention bounced between the only two men in her life she trusted. The only two people in her life she trusted.

"Do you wish to learn to fight?" Prince Ahrkyn asked.

"I wish to learn to defend myself and help protect the people of Ahdlai."

Ahrkyn shook his head. "It's not your job to protect the people. That is the job of myself and the rest of the guard. Jhelan is the head of the guard. I would have to speak to him first, but I know he will not allow you to join the guard. The only reason I'm permitted as the Prince is because my mother fought for me to–"

"I don't wish to join the royal guard. I only wish to not be a hindrance."

"How would you be a hindrance?" he asked.

Ahrkyn moved closer, their hands still entwined, and brushed loose hair from her face.

"I have lived in a cage my whole life. I have had men standing guard outside my sleeping quarters every day of my life. I only wish to be able to protect myself should the need arise. I wish to be able to wield a sword instead of running, hiding, and praying one of you find me in time."

Freyda hid her shock when Ahrkyn visually consulted with Rhamzin. The big guard shrugged slightly.

"It's her decision."

Ahrkyn nodded slowly, his head bobbing up and down as his eyes moved back to Freyda. "Very well. I'll ask Valdis to begin your training when you have settled in."

Elation filled her. Was she truly free? Was she truly being given the right to choose for herself, to choose the life she wanted to live, to choose how she wanted to live?

Grinning up at Ahrkyn, she couldn't stop herself from throwing her arms around his neck and squeezing tightly. For the first time in her young life, she felt she could finally follow dreams she thought would remain nothing more than that – simply dreams.

For the first time in her twenty-three years of life, she felt free.

132

Chapter Twelve

There were so many families in the town of Ahdlai proper. So many little ones. And everyone behaved as a family, helping each other with their chores, with the running of the town, and watching over each other.

And they were all super friendly toward Freyda.

But they also insisted on referring to her as *Your Highness* rather than using her first name. She supposed she would simply have to accept the title as a show of respect. Maybe in time they would come to see her as more of an equal.

Although they referred to Ahrkyn in the same manner.

Ahdlai was nothing like what she had conjured in her mind. It was beautiful, albeit lacking some of the exotic fruits to which she was accustomed. But the soil was rich, the crops bountiful, and the people kind and welcoming.

The sun was crossing the sky as evening approached.

"What about the town outside the wall?" she asked.

They had passed through two gates to get to the Palace. She had only caught glimpses of the people and their homes. It would be nice to form friendships with the people she would live among if she chose to remain there.

Who was she kidding? The choice had already been made for her, and she couldn't find any anger over that fact.

Ahrkyn had remained sweet and gentlemanly the entire time he had shown her around the property and inside the Palace. He had even attempted to engage Rhamzin in conversation a few times, though she knew it was because he knew the guard should be familiar with the most secure rooms and locations within the Palace walls and inside the building itself.

"Would you like to see the houses?" he asked.

"I would."

He frowned the slightest bit, a crease barely appearing between his brows. "You know you will remain within the Palace, though. You can have a room to yourself for as long as you need it, but it's not safe for you to be out there."

It was her turn to frown. "There's a wall around the town, just as big as the one here," she said, motioning toward the tall, impenetrable wall. "Why would I be any safer in the Palace than I would be out there?"

"For one, the Palace has safe rooms. And a basement. And for two…I will be nearby. As will Rhamzin."

"I'm sleeping in the Palace?" the big guard asked.

Freyda's eyes widened. "You allow the guard to sleep in the same quarters as the Royal family?"

"We won't be sharing a bed, if that's what you're asking," he said to Rhamzin, then turned back to Freyda. "And the guard all have their own homes in Ahdlai proper. But I know having him near will make you more comfortable and lend you a greater sense of safety. I only want your happiness, Princess," he said.

Warmth unfurled in her chest. Stepping closer, she sighed when he opened his arms and wrapped them around her. Everything felt so right when she was close to Ahrkyn. It felt as though she was exactly where she was meant to be when he held her like this.

"Thank you," she whispered.

Ahrkyn pressed a kiss to the top of her hair, then pulled away enough to look into her face. "Dinner will be soon. I know eating with the entire group was a lot this afternoon. Would you prefer the three of us dine alone? Or…the two of us?"

Rhamzin made a sound in the back of his throat but said nothing.

"You always dine the same way? Every meal is with your parents and the guard?"

"Only the higher-ranking guard members. Those in training eat elsewhere. It's…it's a promotion of sorts when they are permitted and trusted enough to dine at the same table with the King and Queen," Ahrkyn explained. "Do you not often dine with staff?"

"Meals were usually only my mother and me. And they definitely weren't considered staff in Mhahzin."

Ahrkyn nodded, pressing his lips into a thin line. "Servants?"

"More like slaves," Rhamzin said under his breath.

"The staff here have volunteered for their positions. Each uses their strengths or gifts for the role. Everyone contributes to make the town run smoothly," Ahrkyn answered. "They have what humans used to call a break room to dine during the hours they work in the Palace. Otherwise, they return to their own homes to eat."

The place sounded like a home and a family. Nothing like where she'd grown up or how she'd lived.

"I want to eat with the family. With the group," she said.

No doubt it would still be overwhelming, but it would be something to which she needed to grow accustomed. And maybe, one day, enjoy.

Ahrkyn released his hold on her and reached for her hand. They continued their slow stroll through toward the first gate leading toward the town encased by the second wall. She still couldn't believe the Royal family had taken so much care to keep its residents safe and to ensure they were as heavily guarded as themselves. Emperor Ehmile would rather use the residents as shields against a threat than protect them.

There were a lot of people milling around outside, working on various things throughout the town. Some worked on smaller gardens of fresh foods, some tended to smaller livestock like chickens, turkeys, and ducks. And there were quite a few children running and playing.

"I thought your children were sent away to be raised by someone else after birth," Freyda said.

She couldn't hide the smile as a little girl ran directly up to her and extended a hand, a bright yellow dandelion clutched in her dirty little fingers.

Freyda took it and thanked the girl with as much fervor as if she had been gifted the most beautiful of flowers.

Ahrkyn ruffled the child's hair and nodded for her to join the rest of her friends. "If the mother chooses to remain in the town, she has a part in her child's upbringing. But, if she chooses to return to her

Clan in the woods, the caves, or another town, the child stays here and is risen by the Elves and remaining human women."

She nodded as she listened. She had believed the children were ripped from their mothers' arms and shipped off to be raised by strangers. She wasn't aware of a single woman in Mhahzin who had been given the opportunity to stay in their child's life, let alone be a part of raising him or her.

That information was one of the main reasons she'd had no interest in carrying someone's child – she would give birth to a beautiful baby, and, if she survived, wouldn't be a mother. She would simply be a vessel to grow another man's bloodline.

But here? Here she could raise her child. She could watch her son or daughter grow into an adult.

Unfortunately, her child would live a life long after she was gone. Since the child would be an Elf halfling, they would live centuries to her mere decades. If she was lucky, she would make it to her eighties, nineties if she took great care of herself, didn't get ill, or wasn't murdered by some monster.

That was a major *if*, though. She would more than likely only have another forty or so years left on this planet.

Pushing thoughts of pregnancy and motherhood to the back of her mind, Freyda listened as Ahrkyn gave her a bit of history about the town, about the homes there being the first built in the entire northern region after the fall of human civilization.

Ahrkyn damned near shuffled his feet as he stood outside his own bedroom door. Freyda stood just inside, her hands fisted in the billowy fabric of the gown loaned to her by members of the town. Or, more than likely, by his mother. Very few women in Ahdlai wore such extravagant clothing; it wasn't realistic to wear something that could get in the way when tending to crops or livestock.

"Would you prefer if Valdis stayed with you?"

"Valdis has her own bed," Jhelan called from the living room.

Why Ahrkyn thought either of the mated duo would be willing to sleep separately was ludicrous, and there was no way in hell Ahrkyn would allow another man to sleep in the same room with the Princess.

"I'll be fine."

"Where's my room?" Rhamzin asked.

"Give me a moment to get the Princess settled in and I'll show you where you'll sleep."

"I'm sleeping here," the large guard said. "I want to bathe before settling in."

Anger and a wave of possessiveness rushed through Ahrkyn.

"You will not sleep in the same room with my mate."

Rhamzin's head snapped back in surprise. "I know damned well I won't be sleeping in the same room with the Princess. I'll post a chair outside her room as I've done nearly every day of her life."

"It's fine, Rhamzin. I'm safe here."

Affection filled Ahrkyn, pushing away the anger. She felt safe. After less than twenty-four hours in Ahdlai, after less than twenty-four hours of being at Ahrkyn's side, she trusted his word when he told her she was safe in the Palace.

Rhamzin didn't move from his spot as sentry in the hallway, though.

"You don't have any changes of clothes, either," Freyda said after a few moments.

Neither had carried anything in satchels or knapsacks on the backs of their horses. They had literally escaped with the clothing on their backs.

"I'll speak with members of the guard and find something that fits you," Ahrkyn said.

"I won't wear the emblem of Ahdlai," Rhamzin said with a lift of his chin.

"I don't expect you to. But you will need clean clothing and we don't expect you to wash what you're wearing in the bathroom sink each day."

He'd meant it to come out as a joke, a tease, but was having a hard time forcing his anger over the guard refusing to leave Freyda's side. She was Ahrkyn's mate, damn it. She was *his* to guard, *his* to protect.

He needed to remember Rhamzin was simply one more barrier between Freyda and any danger…like her stepfather.

The three stood there for a few moments in awkward silence. Ahrkyn knew he needed to leave Freyda to change into one of the sleeping gowns the women from town had loaned her until she was able to get her own clothing. She needed to wind down and let her thoughts settle after such a full and interesting day.

One day. She'd only been in his territory one day, yet it felt like she'd been in his life for years. He felt as though he'd known her for years, as though they had always been fated to meet and form a bond.

And now, he didn't want to leave her side, didn't want to close his eyes and fall asleep for fear he would wake to find this was all a dream.

"Either get me a chair or show me where I'm supposed to sleep," Rhamzin finally said, breaking the silence.

Freyda's body shook softly with a quiet laugh. "He wasn't lying when he said he was posted outside my sleeping quarters nearly every night since I was merely a toddler."

Ahrkyn reached forward and cupped the Princess's cheek. "Would you feel better if he were outside your room?"

She held her hand against his, keeping his touch on her face. "No. It's fine. I'm sure he would much rather sleep in a bed than sit up staring at the wall all night. Besides, he's already been awake for almost twenty-four hours. He needs rest, too."

"I'm fine," Rhamzin said.

But the weariness was there in the dark circles under his eyes and the lines bracketing his mouth. The man definitely needed sleep. He had been tense since the moment the two had ridden over the border and into Ahdlai. He hadn't taken a single moment to relax. Ahrkyn was told that until Rhamzin was beckoned to familiarize himself with the Palace and grounds, he had paced like a caged animal, uneasy and ready for battle in a blink of an eye.

He must have been exhausted, tired to the bone, yet he stood there, shoulders squared, chin lifted, gaze missing nothing as he constantly surveyed their surroundings even inside the house.

"Goodnight, Freyda. I'll instruct the staff to give you privacy until you're ready to join the rest of the household in the morning. Should you wake after breakfast has been served, the staff will make you something to hold you over until lunch."

"They don't need to go out of their way for me," she said.

He waved a dismissive hand. "The staff who work in the Palace and in the kitchen are caregivers to their core. No way would they allow you to go so many hours without something in your belly."

Freyda smiled at that, amusement and affection twinkling in her brown eyes.

Leaning closer, he pressed his lips to Freyda's cheek and left a kiss. She wrapped a hand around the back of his neck and held him there a moment longer, stepping until their bodies were lined and she could wrap her arms around his waist.

"Thank you, Ahrkyn."

"For what?" he whispered, snaking his own arms around her back.

"For giving me freedom."

Shaking his head, he had to reach up to dislodge her hair that got stuck in his stubble. "You earned your own freedom. Rhamzin helped you to escape. All I did was wait for you with open arms."

Chapter Thirteen

Freyda rolled onto her side and stared at the sliver of light peeking through the gap in the curtains. She'd been in Ahdlai for exactly one week as of this morning. And in that time, no one had burst through the door at sunrise demanding she rise to get dressed and have her hair braided and twisted into intricate styles.

The Queen wore her hair in elegant styles, but they were soft, not as severe as those worn in Mhahzin. The staff of the Palace and residents of Ahdlai also wore their hair in braided styles but theirs appeared out of comfort, a way to keep their hair out of their faces and off their necks while still appearing feminine and fashionable.

The Queen was the only woman in town who regularly painted her face with the various creams and powders. Valdis had only used the same colors twice, and it was far more subdued than the vibrant colors Queen Ahlmeda wore.

Freyda had chosen to forego the powders and creams. It was nice to wear her face naturally and not be expected to dress or behave in a certain manner. She still hadn't broken the people of town from referring to her formally, but those closest to Ahrkyn had finally began to refer to her by her first name. They might not have been friends, but they were, hopefully, on their way.

Rhamzin…

She sighed. He kept his distance from the other guard, always keeping an eye on anyone who moved close to her, always watching the Palace grounds. And he was always at her door when she stepped from her sleeping quarters in the morning. He had slept in his own room since that first night, but rose before the sun to ensure no one bothered her before she was ready.

It was obvious he was uneasy in Ahdlai and felt like an outcast. He was no more an outcast than Freyda.

Not completely true. He was born and raised as an *Ihllr* Elf, living among the *Vhtir*. They were of different bloodlines, and had been at war for centuries, long before the humans destroyed the planet and their way of life.

It had only grown worse since the non-humans took control, since the fallout of the war rendered so many of the non-humans unable to breed children with their own kind. They depended on human women to carry their offspring. And very few humans were willing to carry *Ihllr* Elf children because of the way they were treated.

But there were many humans living in the town near the Palace. And, according to Valdis during one of their many conversations over the past week, there were many humans living in the towns throughout the region of Ahdlai. Those she'd met all seemed content. Happy. Comfortable with their lives among the *Vhtir*.

Freyda, too, was quickly growing comfortable there. It was easy when no one treated her as though she were up for sale. They treated her with respect. The men put her on a pedestal, although she had a feeling it was partly because she was their Prince's mate and she, herself, was a Princess from her own region.

Whatever the reason, she enjoyed being treated like a person rather than an object to be obtained or a challenge to be conquered.

Enough lounging in bed. She could hear others moving around within the Palace and assumed Rhamzin would be in his usual place outside her door. He wouldn't even have breakfast before she stepped from the room as though he were afraid someone would hurt her in the minutes it took him to finish a meal.

Tossing back the blankets, she threw her legs over the side and stretched. She was still wearing clothing lent to her by residents of Ahdlai, but the Queen had loaned Freyda a few of her personal gowns. While they were far more conservative than what she was accustomed to, the manner of dress was more familiar than the casual tunics, tights, or breeches worn by the other women.

It had only been a week, but Freyda was growing restless. Everyone else in the town had a role. All she did was sit on the patio when Ahrkyn went on patrol and read one of the hundreds of books from the royal library. When he was home, they would wander the Palace lawn and talk and talk and talk.

She didn't think she had ever felt as though she'd known someone as well as she knew the Prince. He was genuine and kind and very funny, albeit reserved.

And he had barely kissed her since she had joined him in his territory.

While she wasn't sure she was ready to carry his child in her belly, the urge to feel his hands on her, to feel his bare skin against hers grew stronger every day until she wasn't sure how much longer she could go before she asked him to sleep beside her in his bed.

Hurrying through her morning routine of bathing, then twisting and braiding her hair back away from her face, she pulled on one of Queen Ahlmeda's gowns.

No matter how many times the Queen insisted, Freyda couldn't quite make herself refer to her as anything other than her formal title, and especially not mother, even though Freyda saw the hurt in the Queen's eyes at her refusal.

After a quick once over in the mirror to ensure she looked the part of her place in society, Freyda slid her feet into the only shoes she owned, squared her shoulders, and prepared to step from the room.

As she reached for the knob, a tap on the door startled her.

Pulling the door open, she couldn't stop the smile that stretched across her face at the appearance of Ahrkyn standing in front of her door. Well, *his* door. He had given her the space she needed.

Now, she wanted him to join her in his bed and for longer than a single night. Each night they went without completing the bond, the brands on her arms grew that much more uncomfortable. Not quite painful, but the ache and burn was nagging, like a light sunburn in the beginning of summer.

How long before that nagging would grow unbearable?

"Good morning," Ahrkyn said, his smile matching hers.

Even after spending every minute possible together over the past week, her heart hadn't ceased from racing each time she saw his face or heard his voice. Her stomach would flip and butterflies would flap their wings like crazy deep inside her belly.

The brands on her arm throbbed with the need to be closer to Ahrkyn. Stepping out of the room, she sighed when he placed a finger under her chin and tilted her head up to brush the lightest kiss across her lips.

"I thought we could have breakfast in the garden this morning," he said.

Opening her mouth to ask about Rhamzin, she frowned at the empty spot he'd occupied every morning.

"Where's Rhamzin?"

"Believe it or not, he actually volunteered for a perimeter patrol today. He's out with a group of other guards."

Freyda's head snapped back and she blinked at Ahrkyn's statement. It appeared she wasn't the only one growing used to her new home. It might take Rhamzin a lot longer to feel as though these people were his friends or family, but at least he was interested in keeping the area and the residents safe.

Or perhaps he was merely thinking of Freyda's safety.

But it said a lot that he felt she was safe enough to leave in the care of Ahrkyn while he went on the mission with the others. That had to mean he was growing to trust and respect he Prince. Or at least trust her judgement of the Prince and his people.

Stepping back, he stretched his hand out and waited with a smile as she slid her hand into his and let him guide her from the room.

"Did I miss breakfast?" she asked, tilting her head back to look up into his face.

She wasn't a small woman, but Ahrkyn and the rest of his men all had at least six inches and so many pounds of muscle on her.

"No."

"Then why are we eating in the garden?" she asked.

He pulled her hand from his and wrapped it around the crook of his elbow, causing her to have to step closer to his side as they walked.

She loved moments like this, when it felt like they were old friends, or as if they'd known each other their whole lives. She was comfortable with him, felt safe and cared for, felt cherished and adored.

Especially on days like this.

He had only gone on patrol twice in the week she'd been in the territory and had been back within hours while the others stayed in the woods for days. According to Valdis, it was odd for the Prince to hurry back without the others. He preferred to patrol, to check the perimeter and hunt for *Ihllr* Elves who trespassed or attacked the humans who lived within the territory.

And he returned so quickly each time just for her. To spend time with her. To strengthen their bond…

Only, it wasn't the bond they needed to complete.

Nerves tickled her belly as she thought about addressing the specific aspects that went into the Bond. There was no blood exchange the way they did in Mhahzin. All that was left was for the two of them to make love.

And, honestly, at this point, she was pretty sure she would willingly lie with him whether they carried matching brands or not. She wanted him. She wanted him in a way she had never wanted a man. She wanted him in a way that burned her soul, the way the heroines craved the heroes in her favorite fairy tales.

"It's a nice day. And I wanted to have you all to myself for once."

She ducked her eyes to the ground as her cheeks heated. They wouldn't technically be alone since there would be residents milling around doing their daily chores, but it was the closest to privacy they'd had since she'd arrived. Rhamzin had shadowed her every movement, and every meal was shared with the King and Queen and the higher ranking guards.

He led her to a table where plates, platters, and bowls were waiting. There were no staff members lingering around as though they had disappeared when they spotted the couple arriving.

After Ahrkyn helped Freyda situate her gown and take a seat, he sat across from her and winked.

Since there was no one there to plate their food, it took Freyda a moment to realize she would be doing it herself. She rarely did anything for herself. The small gesture made her feel almost normal, like a regular person, an average human.

She had earned her freedom. She had found her Fated Mate and carried his brands. And now, she was enjoying the peace of the morning with the man her heart warmed for more each day she knew him.

"Do you have to patrol today?" she asked after taking a sip of tea.

Ahrkyn shook his head. "No. My father granted me the next few weeks off."

She frowned. That didn't mesh with the person Valdis had described, the person who demanded he join the guard, the person who wanted to be on the frontline to keep his people safe even though he was next in line for the throne.

Had he requested that time off, or had the King ordered it? And why?

"We, uh…"

It was Ahrkyn's turn to duck his eyes as his cheeks turned bright pink.

"What's wrong? What has happened?" she asked.

His behavior didn't indicate he'd changed his mind about her presence in his life. Quite the opposite.

"I was wondering if, uh…" He rubbed the back of his neck. Pushed hair that had come loose from his braid away from his face. "I'm the damn Prince. Why can't I find the words?"

The longer it took him to speak his mind, the more her anxiety grew.

"What is it? Has something happened?"

His brows shot up to his hairline. "No. Nothing has happened. You're still completely safe and absolutely welcome here. The residents love you."

"I don't know how. They barely speak to me."

"It's not you. It's your station. They're not trying to be rude but showing you respect."

"They speak to you," she pointed out.

"Because I have fought alongside many of them through the years."

That made sense. He would feel more like one of them rather than one of the Royal family if he wielded his sword in battle beside them.

She, on the other hand, drifted around in gowns loaned to her by the Queen, continued to behave in the manner she was trained as a child, and waited for her orders from those who were above her.

This wasn't Mhahzin. They didn't expect the same things from her, didn't expect her to behave any in manner, didn't expect her to avert her eyes when the Royal family entered the room.

Perhaps she could begin to dress like the women in Ahdlai. She could wear the tunics, could ask to be assigned a job in the gardens or something similar. If Ahrkyn could hold a job as the Prince, why couldn't she?

First, though, she needed to find out exactly what it was that her mate was having such a hard time saying.

"Just say it. Whatever it is, we'll get past it."

She *hoped*. As long as it wasn't something along the lines of him wanting her to live elsewhere, they could get past anything.

Why the hell couldn't he simply spit it out? It wasn't a secret that the two of them were mates. And not simply mates, but Fated Mates, Blessed by Mother Universe, and carried matching brands that told the story of their lives lived and the lives they would build. It would take them years to decipher the markings.

But there was more that needed to be done before the Bond was completed. He was terrified of broaching the subject and making her feel the way her stepfather or all those other men had.

If he were honest with himself, he wanted her for more reasons than simply completing the Bond. He'd wanted her from the moment he'd seen her. When he had laid eyes on her curves and the cleavage that spilled over the top of her gown, his body had stayed perpetually hard.

Even now, as she watched him closely with an open and curious expression, his trousers were snug as his body hardened simply from being near her.

"Ahrkyn?"

"Would you feel comfortable if I slept in my room with you tonight?" he blurted out before he lost the nerve.

She stared at him as her lips popped open, her lashes fluttering as she blinked rapidly.

"If I tell you something, you have to promise not to laugh," she whispered.

He tilted his head and waited.

"I was going to ask if you'd sleep with me tonight."

The breath left his lungs in a rush as the muscles in his neck and shoulders relaxed.

"Ahrkyn?" she whispered.

"Yes, *khaere*?"

Her cheeks went pink at his term of endearment. "Are you okay?"

He frowned at her as his heart raced madly in his chest.

"Yes. I'm perfectly fine," he said. He was more than fine. He was elated. She finally felt comfortable enough and safe enough around him to have him sleep in the same room. Hopefully, she'd meant in the same bed.

"You look…scared. Or shocked."

Struggling to get his heartrate and libido under control, he smiled. "I'm pleased. You trust me. That makes me happier than I can put into words."

"I know it was inappropriate for me to ask, but I also know you were waiting for permission."

Her cheeks grew darker as she ducked her gaze to her mostly empty plate.

"You know we expect nothing from you. We don't expect you to behave in any manner. If there is something you wish to say to me or ask me, please do so. At no point should you fear being yourself."

Cheeks still bright pink, she raised her eyes to his face and smiled. "Then let me be honest – I wondered if it was all an act. As if you were all trying to get me to lower my guard so you could…I don't know…pounce on me."

Ahrkyn sucked his lips into his mouth to hold back the smile at her choice of words.

"All of you, everyone in Ahdlai, are nothing like what we were warned of in Mhahzin. You all seem so happy. Content. Like you all truly care about each other."

"Of course we do. And everyone cares about you, as well. And I promise it's not solely because you're mated to the Prince."

He winked at her.

"Do you think it would be alright if I wore clothes like Valdis?"

"You don't like the gowns?" he asked, his eyes dropping to what he could see of her torso.

"It's not that. I just…I've never been able to choose my own clothing. Each gown was chosen for me each morning before I woke. The servants would dress me, braid my hair, and use creams and powders on my face every day. I might not want to continue wearing the tunics, but it would be nice to…"

Her cheeks once again acquired the pink hue.

"*Khaere*," he said, reaching across the table to take her hand. "You have choice here. If you would rather wear the tunics the women of town wear, be my guest. You would be beautiful naked."

It was his turn to blush as her eyes widened, her lips popped open to form a perfect circle, and she sat up straighter.

"I didn't mean it like that," he blurted out.

A couple seconds went by before the surprised look fell from her face, a wry grin stretched across her lips, and she laughed. Her laugh was growing less reserved, like she was no longer doing as she was trained and remaining the picture-perfect member of royalty.

No. Now her laugh sounded full of humor and joy. Every day, she grew more at ease and Ahrkyn was slowly learning who the real Freyda was rather than the Princess molded by a dictator.

And he couldn't wait until her full personality shone through. He had a feeling she would be a firecracker, a perfect member of Ahdlai, and exactly who the Mother had created her to be before the Emperor of Mhahzin had sank his claws into her.

Chapter Fourteen

Freyda's stomach was in knots. The nerves prevented her from finishing her dinner, but she ate enough to curb the hunger pangs and avoid anyone noticing her odd behavior. The last thing she needed was for someone to point out her countenance and guessing at the reason why.

She had officially asked Ahrkyn to join her in his bedroom for the night, which still seemed peculiar to her that he had waited for permission to sleep in his own quarters and in his own bed.

But she appreciated it. She appreciated him giving her time to get her mind and heart situated, to grow comfortable around this huge group of strangers.

But they didn't quite feel like strangers, not anymore. In the short time she'd been in Ahdlai, she had seen more love and compassion than she had in her entire life in Mhahzin, or at least the life she could remember. She had no memories of her time before her mother had become the Empress.

And in the time she'd been in Ahdlai, in the short week, she'd begun to feel how trapped and invisible she'd been for twenty years. She'd begun to forget the person she'd been forced to be when she'd been the Princess of Mhahzin.

Perhaps not forget entirely, but that person, the person she'd pretended to be, was like a stranger, like a character in a dream that was quickly fading from her memory.

She wasn't completely who she wanted to be, hadn't completely let loose and tried to discover who she was without the title, but she was trying. And Ahrkyn was making that even more possible with every ounce of freedom he awarded her, every time he encouraged her to do as she pleased rather than what was expected of her.

Ahrkyn hadn't batted an eye when she'd requested tunics like the women of the town. He'd been curious but hadn't judged her in the least. She was tempted to leave her hair loose instead of braiding it back each morning like the rest of the Elven population. After all, she wasn't an Elf. She was human. Why not make her own rules, create her own personal fashion around her tastes and desires?

The moment the word desire floated through her head, her body grew warm. Which meant her cheeks would carry a flush and give away her inner thoughts. If anyone noticed, she would have to come up with a quick excuse, maybe pretend she was feeling warm or feverish.

Could the Elves smell her arousal? She knew there were other species who could scent such things, whose senses were so acute they could detect the difference between human and non-human, detect whether a woman was Claimed or already carrying a child.

But she'd never had the opportunity to ask anyone in Mhahzin. That would have been seen as highly inappropriate.

Not here. So far, she'd yet to be reprimanded, yet to receive a look of disapproval.

How tempted she was to push the boundaries, to see how truly genuine each person she'd encountered was when they declared they only wanted her happy.

She had earlier mentioned wanting to learn to defend herself. What would Ahrkyn say if she requested she be permitted to train alongside Valdis and the lower ranking guard members? She would never be a guard, had no intention of being responsible for the safety of so many, but it would be so much better if she wasn't a hindrance, someone whom others felt they needed to protect with their own lives.

As each member of the guard finished their meals and looked to the King or Queen for permission to be excused, the table slowly emptied until it was only the Royal family and Freyda.

Technically, she was part of the Royal family since she was Ahrkyn's mate.

Family. She had her mother. The Empress was her biological family. But she had felt like a stranger to Freyda for so many years. The Emperor had affectively beaten any semblance of the woman who had given birth to Freyda out of her over a decade earlier.

Freyda hadn't known the feeling of a family, of the love and care one receives through those who had her best interest in heart...ever. If she'd experienced it when her father was alive, the memory had long since faded into nothing.

"Ahrkyn tells me you've requested a change in clothing," the Queen said as she lifted her goblet to her lips.

There was a beat of silence where Freyda's heart jumped. But that beat faded as quickly. This was not Mhahzin. The people sitting before her were not her stepfather.

"I've never been given the opportunity to choose my own clothing. I simply wanted to try something new," Freyda answered with a shrug.

Ahlmeda studied Freyda for a few more moments before nodding. "I'll find some women in the town who are close to your height and size. We'll get you a variety to choose from. And if you decide you prefer the gowns, we shall find some of your own so you can choose those, as well, instead of feeling as though I'm dressing you in my own image."

There was a twinkle of mirth and affection in the Queen's eyes.

"I was also wondering if I could possibly..." Freyda waved a hand toward her hair. "Do my hair differently than yours. I know Elves have a particular style–"

"But you're not Elven and wish to find your own way," the Queen cut her off and finished for her.

"Exactly."

There was no judgement in the Royal family's eyes. And she was relieved that they understood her desire for some form of autonomy without going into further explanation.

Her nerves about what might or might not happen tonight faded as elation over finally taking full control of her life took over and filled her with joy and excitement. Now, she was almost impatient to go to bed.

Because she couldn't wait to wake and start her whole new life.

Ahrkyn leaned back in his seat, resting his forearm on the table, and watched as Freyda spoke up for herself, as she addressed his mother about her desire for full freedom to choose her own life, as she looked the Queen directly in the eye without dropping her gaze.

One week. If she had grown so much in one week, she would be unstoppable within a month. She would become the perfect woman to rule at his side one day.

But that was something that might never happen. She would leave him one day; she would die long before Ahrkyn and he would be left to sit on the throne alone.

Once again, he forced himself to push the dread and fear of the future to the back of his mind where he locked it in a box to be shoved deep in the darkest corners of his mind. He would dedicate his life to enjoying every moment the Mother gave him with Freyda.

The fact his parents didn't bat an eye when she'd confirmed her request to choose her clothing didn't surprise Ahrkyn. His parents were kind, they were understanding, and they were ecstatic about the possibility of their first grandchild coming soon.

He was rather excited to see Freyda in something other than the flowy gowns his mother had loaned her. He'd felt on the dirty side when he would lust after her when she floated around in the same frocks as the woman who'd raised him.

What would she choose? Would she request the tunic and leggings worn by the women who worked the gardens? Would she request something less restrictive such as the clothing Valdis wore?

Or would she return to something more revealing like the dresses she'd worn in Mhahzin?

As much as he wanted to see more of her flesh, he wasn't sure he could control his possessive nature if one of the other men in the guard were to ogle her full breasts. He wanted to be the only one to see her soft skin, to run his hands over her curves, to use his tongue to—

"I do have another request," Freyda said, breaking into his thoughts.

Ahrkyn's mother dipped her head once.

"I mentioned it before, but I would like to learn to fight. I'm not asking to do as Valdis. I could never win in a battle against another. But it would be nice to at least know how to wield a sword. Or, in the least, defend myself should my stepfather choose to attack because I chose to escape to your territory."

Ahrkyn's heart hammered in his chest at both the thought of Freyda having to fight for her life and the fact there was a very real possibility of the Emperor of Mhazin attacking Ahdlai in an attempt to drag her back.

He would cut the fucker's throat if Emperor Ehmile came anywhere near his mate.

"I don't see where that would be a problem," his father said, looking to the Queen.

"I think it's a good idea. Every woman should know how to handle a weapon and should be able to defend herself."

Ahrkyn's mother was damned handy with a sword and had helped hold off the *Ihllr* when they'd attacked months ago. She had endured a few wounds before Valdis had shown up to even the numbers, but she had held her own against the enemy.

The head of the guard had a mother who was the first female guard member in *Vhtir* history. She was large for a woman and formidable with a sword or bow. Hell, she could take on multiple enemies at a time bare handed if the need arose.

But Freyda was not a large woman – although she was a few inches taller than Valdis – nor had she been trained since birth to fight. Being trained by Valdis or any member of the guard would be the first time she would have been face to face with any form of battle. And it scared the shit out of Ahrkyn.

He knew no one in Ahdlai would ever intentionally hurt his mate, but that didn't mean she wouldn't incur injuries while training. Valdis had. Freyda wasn't of Fae or Elven blood, though. She wouldn't heal quickly like those of his kind.

Heart still racing, he forced himself to keep his lips clamped shut instead of voicing every reason for her to avoid handling weapons. He knew she was right; every woman should be able to defend herself.

He also knew himself well enough to know he might have to keep his ass as far away as possible during that training. Otherwise, he might end up killing anyone who left so much as a scratch on her beautiful body.

Freyda's smile stretched on her face, and he could practically feel the joy radiating from her. Within a week, her entire life had changed. And she was the one advocating for those choices. Ahrkyn knew enough about her stepfather and the *Ihllr* Elves to know women weren't given choices. They didn't choose their mates, they didn't choose whether or not they would carry children, they didn't get to choose something as simple and mundane as the clothing they wore to cover their bodies.

She was free. His mate was truly free. And she was finally grasping that truth. He would never stand in her way of anything she chose to do, even if that meant hiding away while she endured cuts, bruises, or, Mother forbid, broken bones while learning to protect herself from any and all enemies.

Her shoulders were squared, her chin raised as she smiled at his parents, then turned that look of pure joy to Ahrkyn. And he found himself wanting to do everything in his power to see that smile every single day for the rest of her life.

"Would you like one of my staff to seek some new clothing for you tonight? Or would you prefer to wait until tomorrow?" the Queen asked.

"If it's okay, I would love something tonight. Any chance there is something more comfortable to sleep in?"

The moment the words left her mouth, that pretty pink returned to her cheeks as her eyes darted to Ahrkyn before dropping to her hands folded in her lap.

"Do you prefer nightgowns or would you like some shorts and camisoles?"

Freyda's pretty doe eyes widened as she looked to the Queen. "I...actually don't know. I've never worn shorts. Or pants."

"I'll find several pairs of each so you can discover which you favor," Ahrkyn's mother said.

"Thank you so much."

"Now that we have that out of the way, I'm afraid we have something a little more uncomfortable to discuss," his father said.

Frowning at the King, he tilted his head and waited. What could they have to discuss that could be considered uncomfortable?

"Have you decided whether you would desire to carry an heir for my son?"

That was definitely in the category of uncomfortable. And, in Ahrkyn's opinion, a little inappropriate. What business was it of either of his parents whether he and his mate chose to have a family or not? He already knew there was no way he would ever allow his child to be raised by anyone but Freyda and himself. Ahrkyn had never known his biological mother. And while he loved the Queen, it would have been nice to have had at least some memories of the woman who had birthed him.

Ahrkyn's anger rose as Freyda shifted in her seat, fidgeting with the fabric of her gown.

"I have not decided."

The King narrowed his eyes for a moment but nodded his head. "You have plenty of time. And it will not be held against you should you choose not to carry his heir. Are you opposed to your mate fathering a child with another—"

"Father!" Ahrkyn said, cutting off the King.

His father might have been the ruler of the northern region, but he was way out of line with his questioning.

"Do you believe I would have been content with your fathering children with another woman after we completed our Bond?" his mother asked, a frown matching Ahrkyn's on her ethereally beautiful face.

The King's lips twitched, but he held back his smile. "I believe you threatened my…manhood, should I ever contemplate such."

"Freyda, the choice is yours. Should you decide you have no interest in motherhood, you will remain a member of this family and will always be welcome in Ahdlai. Please ignore my mate. He has been dreaming of a grandchild for decades. Don't let his eagerness ruin your evening."

"And, of course, if you should choose to carry my grandchild," the King said, smirking at his mate before turning his attention back to Freyda, "you will remain by his or her side and watch as I spoil my first grandchild mercilessly."

Ahrkyn groaned and dropped his face into his hand. Any dreams he'd had of finally making love to his mate tonight was quickly dissipating with each word spoken by his parents. It felt as though they were taking turns dousing both Freyda and Ahrkyn in ice water.

Peeking at his mate through a small gap in his fingers, he found her struggling to hide her smile, but the small shake of her body told him she found this conversation oddly amusing.

Perhaps there was still hope yet.

"I think we should excuse ourselves before my darling parents say anything else," Ahrkyn said, pushing his chair from the table.

He lowered his hand toward Freyda and helped her to her feet, shooting both parents a forced glare. They merely chuckled, the sound following Ahrkyn out of the dining area.

"I've never seen a family like yours," Freyda said.

She let Ahrkyn guide her through the house and onto the lawn.

The sun had moved across the sky, but the days were longer now, the air warm and filled with the sounds of the evening insects starting their song as the night grew closer.

He'd always loved those sounds. Since he was a child, he'd loved the warmer months, loved to sit outside and listen to the sounds of the wild around him.

Glancing down at Freyda, he sighed inwardly at the soft uptick of her lips. She appeared happy.

"I'm not sure there are any families like mine. I'm pretty sure both parents have made it their mission in life to embarrass me as often as possible."

"The Queen isn't human, so she's not your biological mother. Do you remember her?"

He shook his head. "I don't know that I ever met her after she gave birth to me. That was a different time. I'm closing in on eighty years old. If she's still alive, she's beyond elderly at this point. She was one of the first humans to volunteer to mate with the Elves. My mother

– the Queen – came along when I was still a baby. She's raised me as though I were her own from day one."

Freyda's soft smile grew then faded a little.

"Thinking about your mother?" he guessed.

Her narrow shoulders rose and fell. "I feel like I should miss her, but I don't. We weren't close. But then I start feeling guilty because I don't miss her." She tilted her head back to look into Ahrkyn's eyes as they continued to walk. "I love her. I just…we weren't like you are with your parents."

"Your father?"

"I was a baby when he died. I don't remember him. Mother used to tell me stories, but those stopped a long time ago."

Ahrkyn assumed they stopped around the time she became mated to Emperor Ehmile.

He turned his hand and twined his fingers through hers, giving her hand a supportive squeeze. It was the best he could offer for now. He couldn't change her past. Couldn't force her mother to have a closer relationship with her only daughter.

All he could do was be there for his mate, to show her she had a family who loved her now, who cared for her for who she was rather than what she had to offer them.

Chapter Fifteen

Ahrkyn's warm hand lent her a touch of comfort, but it wasn't quite enough. As much as she loved being in Ahdlai, as much as she loved being with Ahrkyn and watching the interaction between he and his parents, it made her grieve for something she'd never had. She wasn't sure whether her mother even loved her anymore. Or ever had.

For the past twenty years, Freyda had felt as though she was nothing more than a burden to her only living parent, to the only person who should have had her best interests at heart.

Instead, Freyda had watched as her mother sat silently while the Emperor had made plans for Freyda's future, one that included being given away as a gift to some stranger to breed like livestock.

Forcing her focus on the positive, she wondered what kind of frocks would be left for her by the end of the night. She would have choices. It wasn't that she disliked the Queen's gowns, but they weren't hers, nor were they chosen by her. She wanted to decide what she preferred to wear. She wanted to discover who she was beneath all the training she'd received through the years to behave like the perfectly subservient Princess of Mhahzin.

She knew she would never be as fierce and strong as Valdis. From what Freyda had learned, Valdis had lived among the humans, fighting off the *Ihllr* Elves when they would attack her Clan. Long before she'd come to live within the town of Ahdlai proper, long before she'd been mated to the head of the guard, Jhelan, she had fought and won on many occasions.

Freyda didn't have the long life with which Valdis was granted. She didn't have the accelerated healing of the Elves and Fae. But she could at least learn how to hold someone off long enough for the cavalry to arrive. Or, if she trained hard enough, maybe she could even learn to fight in earnest, learn to take down one or two opponents and prevent being taken by the *Ihllr* or any other enemies of Ahdlai.

There were so many what-ifs in her strategy, though, and not nearly enough absolutes.

"Do you remember anything about the world before?" Freyda asked, doing anything she could to distract herself from the woes in her mind, as well as the possibilities of the night that was to come.

"Very little. I was young when the humans went to war."

He led her to a large tree and helped her lower to the ground, then took a seat beside her, both leaning their backs against the trunk of the old oak.

The air around them was warm, but in the shade and with the breeze blowing, she was quite comfortable.

Situating her skirt around her the way she'd done thousands of times throughout her life to ensure nothing beneath the skirt was visible, she turned her upper body to look into Ahrkyn's face.

"Can you tell me anything? All I know is what I've read in novels through the years. The Elves in my territory didn't care to speak with me, other than Rhamzin, and he had it in his mind that speaking of the past would only confuse me or cause me fear."

Ahrkyn huffed a soft laugh. "He cares about you."

"Does that anger you?"

He turned his head and looked down into her eyes. "In the beginning, yes. I feared he wanted you in a romantic capacity. But he appears to see you as a younger sibling or even a daughter figure. So, no. It doesn't anger me."

Freyda could hear a silent *but* in his sentence, but didn't push him any further.

"What has Rhamzin told you?" he asked.

"Only that humans once ruled the planet. And that there was a war that decimated our numbers greatly."

Ahrkyn nodded as she spoke.

"I was barely a toddler when the war erupted, so a majority of what I know is what I've been told by the elder *Vhtir*."

Drawing her knees up and securing her skirt, she wrapped her arms around her shins and rested her cheek upon knees so she could see Ahrkyn's face.

His eyes looked as though he were seeing into the past instead of seeing the present.

"We lived in the woods. Like the humans who choose to live outside of the towns now. That's how we lived, in the trees, the caves. Some were able to live among the humans, those who didn't appear abnormal, those without pointed ears or glowing eyes. But the rest…we lived in the wild. We survived. We hunted. We grew our own crops. Our population was much smaller then."

Cheek still resting on her knees, Freyda closed her eyes and tried to picture the world as he described it.

"There were tall buildings. Thriving metropolises throughout the world. Vehicles. People rarely travelled by horse. They drove things called cars."

She read about those and only had the images from the children's books to go upon.

"The air…it wasn't so clean then. It smelled of smoke, oil, pollution. People were poisoned by chemicals used in their food. Those same chemicals seeped into water supplies. The humans were plagued with so many diseases, something called cancer, so many disorders of their immune systems."

While she grew drowsy listening, she hung on every word until it felt as though she were in the time of which he spoke.

She imagined a world where humans wandered, tried to imagine a place with modern buildings, only without chunks missing like those that were still standing after the war. She imagined families living inside houses, going about their lives unaware of the non-humans living among them or hiding from them.

"There was a government. Many governments. Each region had their own. I believe they called the regions countries," Ahrkyn continued. "The governments made their rules and laws for the humans to follow. But they're also the ones who caused the problems."

It didn't sound much different than the rulers they had in each region now. The rulers, the Emperors and Kings, made and enforced the rules and laws. And they were the ones who declared war on each other. She had already lived through three wars started by her stepfather during her short life.

"When the wars started, it was only in small areas. They fought much the way they had before with guns and bombs. But then the entire world seemed to…implode. The entire world began pointing their weapons at each other. Nuclear weapons and biological weapons were deployed. Millions of humans were lost. The non-human women were left unable to reproduce, with the exception of the Shifters. Their biology didn't change. But we – the Elves, Fae, and such – were left with two options: go into extinction or find another way to increase our numbers."

"Human women. How many were left? You said millions were lost."

His hand landed on her back and slowly and softly made strokes up and down her spine.

"There were some, those who were more adept at surviving. They had created bunkers underground. Members of the government hid their higher-ranking members in the same manor. From over six billion humans, only a few thousand were left."

Freyda opened her eyes to look up at Ahrkyn. "Six billion?"

She couldn't wrap her mind around that number. Billions. There had been billions of humans on the planet.

He nodded, his slow caresses continuing.

"In the beginning, human women weren't given choices. Since the humans were so outnumbered, non-humans would simply choose someone whom they thought could carry their offspring without both the child and the mother dying and force her into mating. But, eventually, when those like my father came into power and took over regions, they declared it should be the human's choice whether she mothered a child she wouldn't raise."

"Why weren't the women allowed to raise their own children?"

It was still that way in Mhahzin. Yet she had never been given a reason that made any sense. Or any reason, for that matter. Those like Emperor Ehmile didn't find it necessary to explain their actions to those they deemed lesser.

His hand raised until his fingers toyed with her braids. "Originally, it was thought a human wouldn't be able to raise an Elven child. That those who were born with strong gifts would be too much for the mother, or that the child could injure the mother unintentionally. There were some mothers who had no desire to raise the child, but enjoyed the luxuries provided by the Palace such as plenty of food and extra protection for their Clans. But now…I think the tradition is antiquated. Those who live within town have plenty of backup to raise children with gifts. There is no legitimate reason the mother can't be involved in their child's upbringing."

"I can't stand the thought of having a child and never seeing her."

"Her?" Ahrkyn said, an obvious tease in his voice.

She shrugged. "I would love to have a daughter. Then treat her the way I wasn't. I would let her make up her own mind about her life. If she wanted to train to be a guard, I would support her. And she definitely wouldn't have to hide the fact a member of the guard was teaching her to read in secret."

"You learned to read in secret?"

She turned her eyes to his face. "Rhamzin taught me. I'm still not sure whether my stepfather is aware I can read and write just as well as the men in our territory."

"*Their* territory," Ahrkyn said.

"What?"

"Ahdlai is your home. This is your territory now."

A smile pulled up her lips. Her home. This was now her home. Ahrkyn was her family. The King and Queen were her family. The people of this region were her family.

And she honestly wasn't sure how she felt about all that. She didn't know how to treat family, or how to allow herself to be truly loved.

But she would learn. She wanted to learn.

"You and your family lived in the woods?"

He nodded. "Yes. We actually had log cabins we built with our own hands deep within the woods, far enough away no humans would wander out and find us. Well, I didn't help build anything. I was too young," he said with a wink.

"I wish I could have seen the world before. I read a lot of books, but they don't often describe the world, only the world around them in the moment. It's hard to picture the reality through only the words."

"Other than the way humans have been treated since then, the world is actually much cleaner, quieter, and, believe it or not, safer. Humans killed each other at alarming rates long before the war that ended everything."

"They killed each other? Why?"

How ridiculous. What reason would humans have to kill each other? Now, they tended to band together to protect their race. Or so she'd been told. Her world experience ended at the gates of Mhahzin until a week ago.

Ahrkyn stretched his legs out in front of him, crossing them at the ankles. But he never ceased touching her whether running his fingers along the line of her spine or toying with her braided hair.

"You would have to ask them. They killed each other out of hate. Jealousy. I was told stories of humans who killed each other while stealing from them. And many humans suffered from mental issues. It was a much different time."

She tried to hold back her laughter, but it came out as a snort.

Ahrkyn's brows shot to his hairline as a grin stretched across his face. "That was a becoming sound."

With a roll of her eyes, she sat up and shook her head. "Mental issues still seem to be a problem among all humanoids. How else would you explain people like my stepfather?"

He looked thoughtful for a moment then bobbed his head side to side. "Good point."

How long had they sat in the grass under the tree? The sky had grown to dark gray and deep lavender. The evening insects made their presence known, their song growing louder with each passing minute.

She was getting tired. Which meant it would soon be time to retire.

And now her nerves were taut. She would sleep beside her mate for the first time. It was actually the first time she would sleep beside a man at all.

What if he wanted her to…

What if *she* wanted to?

Jhelan and Valdis passed, their hands intertwined.

"Hey, Princess. I hear you're training with me tomorrow," Valdis called out.

The thought of holding a sword in her hand pushed the fear of the night's unknowns to the back of her mind.

"I'm surprised you didn't demand to train her yourself," Jhelan said to Ahrkyn.

"Yeah. Right. If he's anything like you, someone will end up with a black eye after sparring with her," Valdis said.

Freyda's brows shot high. "You gave someone a black eye for sparring with Valdis?"

"Only because my sparring partner actually knocked me down. But he's gotten better about not treating me like glass," Valdis said, raising her free hand to pat Jhelan on the cheek.

"I won't be watching her train," Ahrkyn said.

Freyda frowned at him. Did he not approve? He'd appeared as though he supported her decision. "Why not?"

His look turned sheepish as he shrugged. "Because I don't want to lash out at anyone, especially Valdis, if you get hurt while training."

After a few slow blinks, Freyda caught on to his meaning. She could get injured while training. She knew Valdis or any of the younger guard trainees would never intentionally inflict pain on her, but she would have to learn to fight. Which meant taking a hit every once in a while.

Erasing the shock and mild fear from her face so Ahrkyn wouldn't decide it was all too much for her, she smiled at her mate.

"You really don't mind that I want to learn to fight?"

His hand raised and cupped her cheek in his palm. "I want you safe. If that involves you learning to swing a sword or fist, I support it fully. But that doesn't mean I want to watch anyone taking a swing at you," he admitted.

Lowering his head, he pressed his lips gingerly to hers, letting the kiss linger a moment more before pulling away.

"Were we that disgusting?" Freyda heard Valdis ask.

"You still are," Ahrkyn said, but his eyes were locked onto hers.

She was fully aware they were no longer alone. She was fully aware the sun hadn't fully set.

Yet all she could think about was Ahrkyn lifting her into his arms and carrying her to the bedroom so they could complete the Blessed bond.

She wanted to feel his hands on her body, to feel his muscular body atop hers, his weight pressing down on her.

Every inch of her body felt hypersensitive. She needed her mate in a way she had never needed another person in her life.

Were his eyes glowing? They had to be. Because every cell in his body felt as if they were being licked by fire.

There was something about the way Freyda now looked at him that turned his insides to magma. He wanted her. Needed her. Now.

When he opened his mouth to ask if she was ready for bed, he was startled when she practically lunged to her feet, reached for his hand, and tugged until he, too, stood.

And then she was nearly dragging him across the lawn toward the Palace.

Ahrkyn mentally warned Jhelan and Valdis to keep their mouths shut. One inappropriate comment might very well stop Freyda in her tracks, therein stopping the trajectory of the evening's events.

And please, Mother Universe, let him be right about what was to come the moment they were behind the closed door of his bedroom.

Their bedroom. After tonight, after he officially made her his life mate, they would share the room. And if she decided she wished for more privacy, he would personally build her the home of her dreams with his bare hands if he had to.

They were practically running toward the castle. If she noticed the curious looks being thrown their way by those still out and about, she ignored them.

Ahrkyn fought the urge to lift her into his arms so they could close the space between the lawn and the Palace. His long legs and preternatural speed would get them to the bedroom much quicker, but he wanted this to be her choice, wanted the timing and pace to be set by her.

He wanted her in control, wanted her to choose what she would do with every single aspect of her life, including making love with him for their first time.

Her first time.

The fact he could cause her discomfort while changing her status of Untouched didn't bode well with him, but it was unavoidable. He would ensure her body was ready for him and would take it as slowly as she needed. He would ensure she experienced as much pleasure as possible before seeking his own release.

There were no staff wandering the halls as they entered through the front door; his parents were nowhere to be seen. They would have a modicum of privacy as they rushed to his bedroom, lust burning through their veins. At least it was burning through his. The scent of arousal permeated from her, as well.

He was nearly out of his mind with need by the time she pushed through the door, pulling him after her. He kicked the door shut and opened his arms to embrace her as she threw herself at him, her arms immediately going around his neck, her lips finding his as she rose onto her toes and he bent to meet her.

There was no slow exploration of lips, no gentle caresses. They crashed together, the moment no less powerful than a lightning strike as electricity slithered across his flesh and caused his brands to throb along with his heartbeat. Or perhaps he was feeling hers.

Even now, before they had completed the Blessed bond, he could feel her emotions, could feel the need deep inside of her, feel her confusion, fear, and excitement. He'd felt her before, felt when she was rushing toward him, rushing toward his territory. Rushing to join him and into his arms.

Before the Bond was completed, the connection between them was stronger than anything he had felt in his life. And he partially feared how deeply he would feel her once the Bond was completed. Would he be able to do his job of guard? Would he be able to walk away from her for days on end while he patrolled the border of Ahdlai?

He would have no choice. He would do as Jhelan had and learn to focus on the task at hand, checking on her periodically to ensure his mate was safe.

Freyda's hands were frantic as they ran from the back of his neck, across his shoulders, then down his chest. The damn leather of his battle armor kept him from feeling her caress. He needed to feel her. He needed to feel all of her, every touch of her flesh, every dip, swell, and curve of her body.

Pulling away only long enough to pull his battle armor over his head, he once more closed the space between them and worked at the leather straps of his shirt while exploring the satiny sweetness of her mouth, his tongue dancing and dueling with hers.

For someone who came to him Untouched, she kissed with such skill and passion.

Her hands continued to roam his shoulders and chest as he struggled to undo his shirt. Again, he pulled away so he could pull the fabric over his head, tossing it to the floor without any thought. He wanted to shuck his pants, as well, but knew the moment she was naked before him he would plunge deep into her warmth. He would wait. He would keep himself covered and restrained until he knew she was ready for him, for his length and girth, for him to make the Princess his forever.

The cutest and most frustrated groan escaped her lips when he pulled his mouth from hers yet again, this time putting space between them. The gown she wore would take work to remove. And he wasn't sure how much longer he could wait. He would not simply lift the hem and take her. He wanted to see her, see every inch of her, to see the flesh he had fantasized about since the moment he had found her just over their border.

The buttons and strings were so small, his hands shaky. Ahrkyn began to wonder if it wouldn't be faster to rip the dress from her body or slit the front open with a dagger.

But the gown belonged to his mother, and he didn't want to scare his mate by drawing a knife so near her heart.

Releasing a curse under his breath, he smiled sheepishly when she giggled.

"Here," she said, pushing his hands away and making quick work of releasing all the bindings that kept the gown closed.

The moment the last button and closure was free, it separated, revealing the full swell of her breasts, and Ahrkyn's knees damned near buckled. His cock thumped against his breeches, begging to be set free.

Not yet. He had to repeat the words over and over in his mind, both to remind himself her body wasn't quite ready, that he wanted her to set the pace…and to distract himself enough to avoid spilling his seed in his breeches rather than inside his mate's warmth.

Freyda gasped through parted lips as Ahrkyn slid his hands beneath the fabric to lift the weight of her breasts in each hand. Her eyes rolled shut when he rolled her hardened nipples between his thumb and forefinger.

He needed to taste her. All of her.

Pushing the fabric apart, he lowered until his face was level with her chest and kissed a path across the mound of one breast, still fondling the other, until his lips closed around the hardened pink tip.

Her fingers tangled in his hair, catching in the braids he had carefully twisted back this morning. He wished his hair was free. He wanted to feel her nails rake against his scalp unhindered by the traditional style of the *Vhtir* Elves.

"Ahrkyn," she moaned softly.

His name on her lips sounded like music to his ears.

Leaving her breast, he switched to the other, giving it as much attention as he had the first. It wasn't enough. He needed more. Needed to taste more of her flesh. Wanted to run his lips and tongue across her soft, rounded stomach to the apex of her thighs.

But the damn dress was still in the way.

Rising, he pushed the dress off her shoulders and helped her stay steady on her feet as she stepped free of the chiffon and lace. There was yet another border between him and what he wanted more than his next breath.

Ahrkyn dropped to his knees, hooking his fingers into the sides of the undergarments worn beneath her gown. As he pulled it free, moving it over her hips and down her legs, he followed the movement with his lips, kissing a path, nipping at her ribs until she twitched with a surprised giggle, then finally buried his face in the dark thatch of curls between her legs.

And was instantly drunk on the sweetness of her sex.

Chapter Sixteen

Freyda knew she must have died at some point and moved on to another plane. Because she was sure there was no such pleasure on this planet.

Ahrkyn's lips were soft, his breath warm as he kissed a path down her belly until his mouth found her core. His tongue made a slow stroke through her folds before he kissed her there as fervently as he had devoured her mouth.

Pressure was building low in her belly, a pressure she'd never felt. A pressure she would have begged him to help her find a release for if she knew what exactly he could to do help.

Yet, something deep inside of her told her Ahrkyn was the source of the pressure *and* the solution.

"Ahrkyn," she half moaned, half begged.

The pressure continued to build, as did the pleasure until she felt as though she would burst or implode. Either would suffice as long as she could find a release.

And then, stars began to erupt behind her closed eyes, explosions started low in her belly where that blasted pressure had begun. Throwing her head back, she cried out. Wave after wave of ecstasy stole her breath until her legs shook and felt like jelly.

His arms wrapped around her, helping her as she lowered to the ground to kneel before him.

Her lips opened then closed. She couldn't find the right words, couldn't articulate a single coherent thought. Other than she wanted to experience more of what he had just done.

Ahrkyn's chest rose and fell, his breathing matching hers as they both panted. His face was flushed, his lips parted as a beautiful silver glow shone from his irises.

The brands on her arms throbbed and tingled. It wasn't painful, but she swore she could feel Ahrkyn's need, his emotions, everything he didn't say through those marks.

Reaching for him, she wrapped her fingers around his neck and pulled his mouth down to hers. The motion pushed Freyda backward, bringing Ahrkyn with her until they were lying on the thick rug covering the cool hardwood floor.

She was fully naked, yet his bottom half was still covered by his breeches and big, heavy boots.

"Ahrkyn," she whispered against his lips between kisses.

His lips left her mouth and nipped and kissed her throat and the sensitive spot below her ear.

"I need…"

She didn't know what she needed other than him. She knew what sex entailed, knew after tonight she would no longer carry the status of Unclaimed. And was overjoyed that she had been able to wait for the person the Mother and her heart had chosen for her.

"Tell me, *khaere*. Tell me what you need. I will give you anything."

His breath was warm against her flesh, his hands roving her body, stroking her shoulders, her breasts, before sliding down her stomach where his fingers found that sensitive place where he'd just made love with his mouth.

"I need you. I want to feel you, Ahrkyn. I want to feel all of you."

When he pulled from her, cool air rushed between them as he hastily doffed his breeches, shoving them down his hips and over his legs while simultaneously toeing his boots off. In the end, he had to stop long enough to undo the laces that held his boots on.

And then finally, *finally*, he was naked, kneeling before her, his erection jutting toward her and sending fear and excitement skittering through her system.

Her brands throbbed more, the tingling now a slight burn. Yet the sensation still wasn't exactly unpleasant, only foreign. Different. And she knew in a few moments she would be bound to Ahrkyn in a way no force on the planet could sever. Only death would tear them apart, and even then, the person left behind would never be the same.

Ahrkyn leaned forward, slid one arm beneath Freyda's knees, one behind her back, and lifted her against his chest. He carried her the short space across the room and lowered her onto the bed. She would have been content making love with him right there on the floor, but this was even better.

The mattress dipped beneath his weight as he knelt before her. His hands were gentle as they pushed at her shoulders, urging her onto her back. Moving forward, he positioned his body between her knees, urging her thighs apart further as he stared down at her bared sex.

"So beautiful," he murmured with a tone full of reverence and awe.

Slowly, he crawled up her body. A muscle jumped in his jaw as though he were barely restraining himself from plunging into her in one hard thrust.

The moment the tip of his erection brushed her core, she shuddered.

His hand slid between them as he guided himself to her opening. "If it's too much, tell me. We'll go as slowly as you need."

Reaching down, she brushed her fingers over the velvety skin of his cock as Ahrkyn pushed forward, one agonizingly slow inch at a time.

There was a slight pinch, but her mate had taken so much time preparing her body the discomfort waned and was quickly replaced with more pleasure.

And then he stopped moving.

Locking eyes with the man who'd stolen her heart from the moment they'd met, she watched as he clenched his teeth and waited for her body to adjust to the new invasion.

"Ahrkyn," she begged. "Please. I need you to move. I need more."

Slowly, he withdrew, then, just as slowly, pushed back in again.

Freyda's eyes rolled shut as his pace picked up, his pumps growing faster, harder, until the mattress moved below her. Her fingers fisted in the sheets, then she raised her hands and gripped at the arms holding his torso up. The muscles in his biceps tensed and relaxed, rolling under her hands.

She wished she could spend the time getting to know his body the way he had hers. She wanted to do as Ahrkyn had and lick and kiss every inch of his body, taste the saltiness of his flesh, take his length into her mouth, run her fingers over every single part of his body.

That would have to wait for another day. For now, she was enjoying the sensations tingling through her body, the pressure building low in her body once more. The pressure no longer took her by surprise. She knew he would push her over the edge of the precipice, and nearly begged him to take her harder, faster, to help her find another release.

And another. One night with Ahrkyn and she was addicted to what he could do to her body, what he could do with his fingers and mouth, with the way he moved his hips, his length hitting places she was unaware existed.

She had feared being with a man, feared what would happen to her body, feared the pain so many women had warned her of.

There was no pain. Only bliss.

Ahrkyn and Freyda were the only two people in the universe at that moment. When she opened her eyes, she smiled softly up at him as he watched her closely.

Lowering onto his forearms, he framed her face with his hands and lowered his mouth to hers, his movements slowing as he kissed her tenderly, deeply.

Then something happened. Something…clicked between them.

They gasped in unison the moment her brands burned white hot, the throbbing growing intense. Ahrkyn raised up to sit on his knees between her thighs, cupping her behind to lift her so he could get a better angle. His thrusts became frantic, hurried, desperate.

The brands on his arms appeared to glow as his hips moved in the perfect rhythm, pushing her further and further toward the edge.

Unable to hold back any longer, she threw her head back, opened her mouth, and released a cry as ripples of power and pleasure flowed across her flesh like a wave of fire and water. It should have been painful. It should have brought tears to her eyes.

But instead, she felt nearly invincible. She felt as though a piece of Ahrkyn's soul had melded with her own, lending her some of his magic, feeding her with his magic.

Ahrkyn followed her over that edge within moments as his hips slammed into her once more and he filled her with his seed, her name escaping his lips on a long, deep moan.

He dropped forward, resting his head on the pillow beside hers, his breath fanning the hair that had come loose from her braids.

It was done. She was fully Bound to Ahrkyn. She was fully and truly mated. No one could ever take her from him. No one could ever tear them apart.

The fact he had finished inside her was there in the back of her mind, reminding her there was a chance they could very well have produced his heir during their first time together.

But she couldn't find it in her heart to care. In fact, now that the Blessed Bond was completed, the thought of becoming a mother to Ahrkyn's child filled her with joy.

And hope that her belly would one day grow round with their first offspring.

His heart was slamming against his ribs and would surely burst through at any moment.

He'd had sex with many women through the decades. But he had never felt so lost in a woman before. A bomb could have gone off outside the bedroom door and he wouldn't have noticed. There had been nothing in the world that would have stopped him from fully Claiming his mate, Claiming the most beautiful woman he had ever laid his eyes upon.

"Are you okay?" he muttered.

She shoved at his chest a little.

Lifting onto his forearms, he frowned down at her. Had he hurt her? She'd appeared to have enjoyed herself. He'd felt her inner muscles clamp down on him as he'd pushed her to a second orgasm.

Freyda smiled up at him. "Sorry. You were squishing me," she said with a girly giggle.

"Did I hurt you?"

She shook her head on the pillow. Her braids had come loose in places, some tendrils stuck to her damp face.

"That was…incredible," she breathed then grinned wide. "Am I supposed to say that? I mean, the other women…" She blinked up at him, that grin still in place. "They always behaved as though they hated laying with their mate. They said being with a man hurt. That definitely did not hurt."

He wouldn't tell her exactly why those women didn't enjoy themselves. At least not while he was still buried inside of her.

"It is enjoyable when you're with someone you care for," he said.

He pressed his lips to her forehead, then eased from her and rolled onto his side, taking the weight off her delectable body. Already, another wave of need was rising, as was his cock. Would he ever grow tired of seeing her like this, disheveled, lips swollen from his kisses, her skin dewy with the glow of orgasm and the perspiration of their exertions?

As their breathing slowed and his heartrate returned to normal, Ahrkyn trailed his fingertips over the swell of one breast, down the valley between them, and over the swell of the other. He let his touch roam down her ribcage, causing her to jerk with a giggle, then trailed over the soft swell of her round belly.

He had always loved a woman with curves, a woman with full breasts, hips, and a plump ass with a nicely rounded stomach. There was something about it that screamed femininity and fertility. Perhaps it was his primal side that was attracted to those things.

But his cock sure didn't mind them, either, because the more he touched her the harder he grew.

It was getting late, but it wasn't that late. Perhaps they could make love once more before climbing under the blankets together for their first night as a fully Bound couple.

Shifting to pull her on top of him, a tentative tap on the door stilled his movements.

Freyda raised her brows at him in question. No way would he allow her to answer the door. Even if she were to pull a gown over her nude body, they would still see the flushed cheeks and how delicious she looked with the after-sex glow. And then he would have to kill a member of his family or guard.

Pushing to his feet with a groan, he grabbed the blanket from the end of his bed and wrapped it around his torso, just enough to cover his once again hard cock.

Rhamzin stood outside the door, a glower on his face, his eyes averted, and a large stack of fabric in both hands.

"I wasn't sure whether I should leave these outside the door," he said, still refusing to make eye contact with Ahrkyn.

No doubt the Mhahzin guard had heard every noise made inside the bedroom. They weren't exactly quiet, and Freyda cried out when she came. While Ahrkyn relished the sound, he prayed to the Mother that Rhamzin hadn't heard their sounds of love making.

He prayed even harder Freyda didn't think about the fact anyone within the house might have heard them. She might very well refuse to make love to him again until they had a home of their own or were far away from anyone who could hear them.

Rhamzin's eyes flitted toward the mostly closed door then darted away again. "Is she alright?"

"You know I would never do anything to harm her. She's well."

Rhamzin finally made eye contact with Ahrkyn. He studied him for a brief moment, nodded once, then handed over the large stack of clothing. The Prince knew nothing of women's clothing, but he recognized the various fabric textures and colors. There would be a decent variety from which Freyda could choose.

Rhamzin turned on his heel and disappeared around the corner of the hallway without another backward glance. Ahrkyn knew there was no chance he would find the large guard standing sentry outside the bedroom door in the morning. The Princess was officially mated and was now Ahrkyn's to keep safe. She would sleep beside him, and he would keep her safely nestled against his side every night.

Except the nights when he would spend patrolling the perimeter. His father had already granted him a couple weeks off his guard duties to spend with his mate. They would have some time before he had to return to his work.

Closing the door, he carried the clothing to the bed and set it at the end. "Looks like a lot of people were more than happy to donate a few choices for you."

Freyda's face lit up as she rolled onto her knees and crawled to the clothing. And Ahrkyn almost lost his damn mind. Seeing her like that, naked, still glowing, braids coming loose, and on her hands and knees, sent so many images rushing through his head of him taking her from behind.

He wanted to see her hair loose. He wanted to see the length trail down her back.

More than that, he wanted to see her in the shower, the water sluicing down her curves. He wanted to soap up his hands and run them across her flesh until she was begging for him to take her again.

Slow down. She'd only just lost her status of Untouched. He didn't know whether she was sore, or whether she would want to make love again so soon. But he sure as fuck hoped he would have the opportunity to take her at least once more before they fell asleep.

"Oh my gosh," she said.

She sat back on her haunches and pulled the large stack closer to her. And the move made her full breasts sway.

"*Khaere*," he groaned.

She raised her eyes to his face and waited.

He nodded at her breasts. "Either you need to cover that delicious body or I'm going to lose myself in it again."

Her cheeks flushed a bright pink. And for a second, it looked like she was trying to decide whether she wanted to cover her body or not.

In the end, she lifted the sheet they'd managed to push to the foot of the bed and covered herself as much as possible so she could peruse her new selection of clothing.

Ahrkyn released a dramatic sigh and picked up his breeches from where he'd left them discarded on the floor. Pulling them up his legs and over his hips, he left the straps open, but kept himself tucked away. There was a damned good possibility he would still be hard when they finally drifted to sleep. And when he woke in the morning with her in his bed.

Freyda was torn. There were so many options of clothing lying before her.

Yet…her mate was currently wearing only his breeches. Since he hadn't bothered to redo the leather ties, they hung low on his hips and his erection was perfectly outlined by the material.

She would love to feel him inside her again. She would love to feel his hands and mouth on her again.

But she had never in her life been given a choice about her own life. She could literally choose any piece of clothing from this pile and wear it and no one would have a single complaint. They wouldn't give her a hard time, tell her she needed to reveal more flesh if she wanted to be appealing to the opposite sex. She was even given permission to do as she pleased with her hair. She could find her own style. She could discover who she was beyond the title of Princess, beyond the status of stepdaughter to the Emperor of Mhahzin, beyond the role of mate to the Prince of Ahdlai.

Hugging the clothes to her chest, she smiled up at Ahrkyn. "I have no idea which to wear."

"Try them all. See which appeals to you. If you find a favorite, we'll ask the seamstress to duplicate it in varying colors so you'll have more variety."

He made their life in Ahdlai sound so easy, so carefree. If she wanted something, she simply needed to ask and it would be done. It was like she was a Princess in one of her favorite fairy tales. Her Prince had swept her away from the tower and was showing her how beautiful and joyful life could be.

Perhaps it truly was. Perhaps it wasn't merely appearance but a life they had built for themselves and the laws set by fair and compassionate rulers.

With a squeal, Freyda lunged to her feet, allowing the sheet to drop from her body, and hurried to the bathroom. She swore she could feel his eyes on her behind and felt a wave of lust burn through their brands before she closed the door.

Setting the load on the top of the vanity, she quickly undid all the braids, then hurried into the shower to wash away the day. She had always loved to linger in warm baths, but wanted more to discover who she was beneath the façade she had worn for so many years.

Hastily dragging a towel across her skin, she ripped a brush through her long locks, then began to hold each frock up, inspecting them.

The gowns she set aside. She had worn such for years. She knew how she would look and feel in those. She wanted to know the feeling of more casual and comfortable clothing.

The first item she chose was a tunic similar to what she'd seen the women who worked the gardens wear. It hung below her knees, the sleeves reaching just past her shoulders. The fabric was soft, but not quite as smooth against her bare flesh as the gowns she'd worn since birth.

Not bothering with undergarments, breeches, or tights, she pulled open the door and stepped out to show her mate.

He lounged on the bed, resting on his side, propped up on one elbow. And looked positively edible. His breeches were still undone, that rock hard erection still evident, his eyes still holding a slight glow.

The iridescence blazed brighter at the sight of Freyda.

"I wondered if I would find you more or less desirable. I have come to the conclusion you could smear yourself in mud from the garden and I would still want you," he admitted, his eyes doing a slow perusal of her body. "Your hair is long."

It hung to her hips, and, when allowed to dry before being braided, would wave. Not curl, but wave and become somewhat unruly at times. But it was her hair. She was not Elven and could choose how to wear her hair, and that included letting her hair be wild.

"Do you like this one?" she asked, doing a slow twirl for him.

"Do you? I told you. It doesn't matter to me what you choose to wear. You will still appeal to me like no other."

She ran her hands down the fabric. "I want to try the others."

Turning on her heel, she hurried from the room and stepped into the bathroom, swinging the door closed behind her. There was no reason for her modesty, not after he had seen her at her most vulnerable, not after he had tasted her body and had been buried deep inside of her. But it was habit. She was to never undress in front of a man lest he get the wrong idea. It was one of the few lessons her mother had taught her before shutting down and no longer acknowledging the existence of her daughter.

Pulling on another tunic, one similar to what Valdis wore, she tied up the leather straps along the front and viewed herself in the mirror. This one dipped lower in the front. Not quite as much as the gowns she wore in Mhahzin, but not quite as conservative as those worn by the residents of town.

The fabric was also much softer and gave way when she moved. It had a stretch to it, as though to prevent restricting her movement. It was dyed the shade of the needles of the evergreen trees in the forest and made her eyes appear more hazel than brown.

This one she liked. Far more comfortable than the gown, less restrictive, and she wouldn't have to lift the hem when climbing stairs or stepping over items on the ground.

Pulling the door open, she stepped out and nearly barked out a laugh. Ahrkyn was in the same position he had been when she'd entered the bathroom to change. His eyes held the same glow, his erection still straining against his pants, only this time, there was a look of anticipation in his beautiful eyes.

"Why do you look so excited?" she asked with a laugh.

"Because you're excited. You finally seem…happy."

Her smile slipped a touch and her brows drew together. "Have I not appeared happy? Because I am. I've been happy."

"You've been reserved. I feel like I'm watching the real Freyda step out of the bathroom each time. Like…I don't know. As if with each change your personality shines more."

Her smile was tentative at first. He said it as though it were a good thing. And perhaps it was. Had she not told herself she could finally discover who she was now that she was out from under her stepfather's rule?

"I don't really know who I am. But I want to learn. That's why I wanted some physical changes. I don't know what I like. I don't know what foods are my favorite. I don't know…I like to read. I love the fairy tales written by the humans, the ones where the Princesses escape with the love of the life."

"I believe you're living your very own fairy tale…Princess Freyda," he said with a bow of his head.

She chuckled softly. Gripping the short hem of her tunic, she curtsied. "Indeed, you're correct, Prince Ahrkyn."

And she was. She was truly living her very own fairy tale. Only in this story, no evil witch would arrive with a poisonous apple. There was no cruel stepmother to lock her away from her love.

She was in a place where she could be accepted for the person she was instead of the womb she possessed and the power she could award someone by Claiming her.

Chapter Seventeen

Freyda rolled onto her back and froze. For a brief moment, she'd forgotten Ahrkyn had slept beside her last night.

And then, the entirety of the night and the events that had unfolded for hours returned to her memory.

They'd finally made love. Actually, they'd made love quite a few times after she had tried on that last tunic. It was obvious the Prince cared for her for more than her status. Otherwise, he would have preferred to see her in the low cut, revealing gowns of her territory or the fancy gowns his mother had loaned her.

But he just wanted…her. As she was. In the gowns, the tunics, and especially nude. As they both were now.

Neither had bothered donning clothing when they had finally collapsed, exhausted, onto the pillows. He had pulled the blankets up over her shoulder, then spooned his big body behind hers. The fronts of his legs were still molded to the backs of hers, his groin was pushed against her behind, his chest against her back.

She could feel his slow, steady breaths ruffling her hair as his head rested on her pillow. They had barely separated an inch throughout the night, as though even in sleep they needed to be as near the other as possible.

As much as she would love to linger in bed, to enjoy the warmth of his big, strong body cradling hers, her bladder demanded she leave the bed.

Slowly and carefully extricating herself from the arm Ahrkyn had draped across her middle, she tiptoed to the bathroom to relieve herself.

After washing her hands, she reached for her toothbrush and froze as she stared at the reflection staring back at her. That person was a stranger.

The hair that was always so carefully braided away from her face was tangled and a tad frizzy from drying during their many rounds of vigorous love making. Her eyes, while still the same color, seemed brighter somehow. There was a flush to her cheeks and her lips were kiss swollen.

And she looked happy. As Ahrkyn had said last night, she was becoming a different person. A happier person. But she still had a lot of work to do to truly discover who the woman was inside.

Tempted to shower, she decided she liked being covered in Ahrkyn's scent. She might not have been able to smell it as strongly as the Elves, but anyone who came near would know exactly what they had done last night. While the brands wouldn't be as dark to any who saw them, they would be darker, more detailed, the future of their lives laid out in designs and curves they would one day learn to decipher.

She was Claimed. And he had finished inside of her each time they had been together. Even now, she could be carrying the Prince's child.

As foolish as it was, she couldn't help but turn to the side and run a hand over her belly.

The thought of carrying an Elf's heir had been terrifying to her. It had sickened her.

But Ahrkyn was no mere Elf. He had been chosen by the Mother, had been sent to her, had been chosen by her very own soul.

Shaking her head at her silliness – there would be no chance of a child showing so early – she brushed her teeth, did her best to tame her hair, and left it hanging freely down her back. Ahrkyn would wake soon. She wanted to be fresh when he laid his eyes on her this morning.

As quietly as possible, she pulled the bathroom door open a crack and peeked out. Ahrkyn laid in the same position, his eyes still closed, his breathing still slow and deep.

And for some reason, seeing him so peaceful and vulnerable warmed her body. Why? Why after being so reluctant to a Claim for so long did she feel insatiable when it came to her mate?

Because he wasn't merely a stranger, wasn't merely a man who wanted what being with her would award him.

Ahrkyn loved her. He hadn't said those words. *She* hadn't said those words. Yet, she'd felt it through the brands each time he'd stroked his fingers along her cheek, each time he'd pressed his lips gingerly to hers, each time he'd slid his hardness into her core.

Freyda tiptoed across the room. The mattress dipped below her as she knelt on the edge and slowly peeled the blanket away from his body. Still, he didn't move.

He behaved as though her body was the most glorious thing he had ever seen, yet she was currently staring down at utter masculine perfection. His muscles were defined, honed from years of battle with his enemy. She had pulled his braids free last night after one of their bouts of love making and it now fanned on the pillow, the length reaching nearly to the middle of his back when hanging loose.

His thighs were toned, his stomach flat, and, as she'd learned after running her fingers across it several times last night, rippled with muscles. He was a living weapon, tuned to perfection.

She hadn't had the opportunity to taste him last night, but this morning, she wanted nothing more.

Gingerly, she urged him onto his back. He made a sound as though rousing, but didn't speak.

Freyda positioned herself between his knees, lowering her face until she could press her lips to either side of his long, thick erection. It twitched as her breath fanned across the delicate, velvety soft skin.

As she opened her mouth and lapped her tongue across the flared head, he raised one of his knees as though finally waking.

"*Khaere*," he muttered, his voice hoarse with sleep.

"Shhh," she said.

Flicking tentatively across the head again, she then licked a slow line from the base to the tip. She had never tasted a man before, had never seen a man's cock before last night. She didn't exactly know what to do, wasn't exactly taught anything much about sex, but instinct guided her as it did last night.

Opening her mouth, she slowly lowered it over the head, then took him slowly and deeply, wrapping her lips around him. His fingers threaded in her hair, tightening into a fist. And then he began to push and pull, urging her to bob her mouth on him.

He wasn't touching anything other than her hair, yet she felt that pressure building low in her belly, the pressure she knew he would help ease.

But not yet. Not until after she gave him the same pleasure he had given her over and over last night.

After a few strokes of her mouth, his hips began to rise from the bed and his other hand gripped her hair.

"*Khaere*, you have to stop."

She didn't want to stop. She liked the way he behaved when she made love to him with her mouth. She liked the way he appeared as though he would lose control. She liked the primal feeling, the powerful feeling she had deep inside with her mouth on him.

Only a few strokes later, he hastily pulled her mouth from him and flipped her until she was on her hands and knees. There was no slow teasing, no talking. He gripped himself and entered her in one hard thrust, pushing her forward with the motion.

Freyda's mouth opened and a cry escaped her. He stopped, his hand landing on her back.

"Please don't stop," she begged, surprised by the wanton stranger speaking.

She was begging a man to take her from behind? She was begging a man to make love to her in such an animalistic manner?

Yes. She was. And loved every second of it.

Ahrkyn lied on his back, an arm thrown over his eyes, panting as sweat dried on his skin. Waking up to his mate's mouth on him…he'd thought he was dreaming at first. But as he'd grown more conscious, there was a moment he wondered if he'd died and moved on to another plane. It was…

There were no words. He had no words for how he'd felt waking and no words for how he felt now. Other than absolutely sated and content. He could have never dreamed being mated would make his heart thump so wildly, or that something as simple as lying beside her could bring him such joy.

A rumble came from Freyda's stomach and he chuckled.

Pulling his arm from his eyes, he turned his head on the pillow and looked at his mate. "Hungry, are we?"

She still glowed, sweat made her skin dewy, her lips were pink and swollen. Smiling, she nodded. "Famished."

"We burned quite a few calories over the past few hours."

"*Few* hours?"

The mattress shook beneath him as she chuckled.

Pushing onto his elbows, he turned his head and let his gaze roam her body. "I can't believe I'm going to say this, but I need you to get dressed. I need to feed my mate, and I'm not sure I can leave this room if you stay naked a moment longer."

Oh, how she tempted him. He would much rather stay in bed for the rest of his life, starving to death while he feasted on her body.

But her belly continued to grumble from hunger. He would allow himself discomfort, but never her. Never his Freyda.

Rolling off the side of the bed, he pulled his breeches up his legs, then pulled a shirt over his head.

"I'm close to begging you to dress, *khaere*," he said, his tone bordering on a whine.

The giggle that escaped her mouth was so feminine and full of humor as she tossed the blanket off and stood. Her ass and breasts jiggled and swayed with each moment.

"I'm going to wait outside," he said as his cock once more stood at attention.

How long would it be before he could see his mate without walking around in a state of constant arousal? And how much teasing would he earn from his friends when he walked out of the room with a raging erection?

Hopefully, the sounds of their activities hadn't been too loud. He would never quiet her when she cried out with pleasure, but neither did he want anyone to make her self-conscious by bringing up those same sounds.

Her laughter followed him into the hallway.

Rhamzin wasn't present. Ahrkyn assumed he knew what had happened in the bedroom last night when he'd delivered the clothing and had rightly assumed he wouldn't want to be witness to any further acts of romance.

The sounds of conversation filtered through the house. He could hear his mother and father, as well as Jhelan, Ahdeben, and Ihsander. Valdis spoke up periodically, but it was mostly the men who spoke.

And none sounded happy.

Leaving his mate to dress in privacy, he followed the voices and found the small party congregated in the living area.

Jhelan leaned forward, his elbows resting on his knees. His brows were knitted tightly together. Valdis sat beside him, her sword atop the coffee table. Why was she armed inside the Palace? There was no threat, no reason to have her weapon close at hand.

A quick survey showed all three of Ahrkyn's friends and fellow guards were also armed and their looks were as angry as Jhelan's.

"What's happened?" Ahrkyn asked.

The world could have exploded around him through the night and he wouldn't have noticed. He'd been too distracted by Claiming his mate and completing their Bond. Moreso, he was distracted by getting lost in her soft body.

"We have received word from Mhahzin," his father said.

Ahrkyn's brows instantly slammed together as fury burned a path through his veins. It had only taken a week. Although, Ahrkyn was mildly surprised it had taken that long.

One week. They'd had one week together before the fucking Emperor reared his evil head. Ahrkyn had assumed it was only a matter of time, but it would have been so much better if he'd been able to spend months, perhaps years with his mate before having to fight her stepfather and the members of her former territory.

"What is it? What threat is being made?" Ahrkyn asked, moving further into the room.

Freyda would join them any moment. He wanted to get as much information as possible before breaking the news to her after such a wonderful night. And morning.

"A member of the Mhahzin guard is currently at the border. He brought news that Princess Freyda's mother is ill. She's dying."

That wasn't the news Ahrkyn had expected.

"It's bullshit. We all know this is absolute bullshit," Jhelan said. "It's a ploy to get the Princess to return. Once she's in his claws again, it will take the whole of our army – and some friends – to break her free once more."

"If her mother is ill, she should be made aware," the Queen said.

"She's not leaving Ahdlai," Ahrkyn said. He knew he had no right to hold her captive, but he also knew Jhelan was right – this was nothing more than a ruse to get her out of Ahdlai and back to Mhahzin where she could be sold or used as a tool to gain more wealth and power.

"I agree she is safer here, but it must be her choice, Ahrkyn," his mother said.

"I will not allow her to be taken to that bastard," Ahrkyn said.

"Son," his father said, raising his voice. "It will be her choice. We do not hold anyone captive here. You know that."

"Then I'll accompany her."

"We'll talk to your mate, see whether she cares to return to say goodbye to her mother. If she desires to return temporarily, we'll present the Emperor with our terms of her return back here," his father said.

Soft footsteps sounded down the hall as Freyda left their bedroom in search of Ahrkyn. She rounded the corner, her long hair hanging loose down her back, the last tunic she'd worn before he'd pulled it over her head last night covering her body, a pair of cotton breeches covering her legs.

"I knew you would like that one," Valdis said. "My clothing is far more comfortable. Easier to fight in, too."

Soft pink colored Freyda's cheeks. All the men, including the King, rose as she entered the room, then waited for her to lower onto one of the cushions before retaking their seats.

She looked around and instantly picked up on the tension permeating the room. "What is it?"

While she was dressed like Valdis, she sat ramrod straight like the Queen, her hands folded in her lap, her ankles crossed delicately. She had been far more at ease in the privacy of the bedroom. Now that she was surrounded by others, now that she detected a problem, she reverted back to the training she'd received to behave as a respectable member of a Royal family.

"There's been contact from your stepfather. A messenger arrived at our border. He said your mother is ill and might not make it. He thought you might wish to say goodbye," the King said.

His words were emotionless and matter of fact, but sorrow, fear, and anger were there in his glowing eyes.

"Your mate and the head of my guard, Jhelan, both believe this is a ruse to get you to return. They feel it is dangerous. But the choice whether you return or stay here will always be yours, daughter-in-law."

Her eyes widened slightly at the King's words, mostly at his use of the word *daughter*.

She turned her attention to Ahrkyn, her gaze bouncing between his eyes before looking to each person sitting around the room. She had met Ahdeben and Ihsander, but didn't know them as well. Valdis was truly the only person other than the Prince and Royal couple Freyda had had time to get to know in the short time she'd been in Ahdlai.

With the exception of the King and Queen, each person wore the same expression: anger and doubt. They highly doubted the Emperor gave a shit whether or not his mate was dying and whether or not her daughter might want to say goodbye. And anger over the fact he would do nearly anything to get his prize back.

"I don't think it wise, *khaere*."

"What if you come with me?" she asked. She turned to look at Valdis, then Jhelan. "What if you all come with me? I can say goodbye to my mother, then we can all return. Surely, my stepfather isn't so daft as to try to attack while I have my own guard."

The King raised one brow. "He sent his guards and enlisted others to attack my territory knowing his people could be slaughtered. He cares for nothing but himself."

Tears welled in Freyda's eyes. She blinked them back quickly, and inhaled a shaky breath. "I can't simply let my mother die without at least telling her goodbye. We weren't close, but she is the last of my flesh and blood left on this planet."

Not the last of her family. The last of her flesh and blood. Hopefully, that meant she already saw Ahrkyn and his family as her own.

"I doubt the Emperor will allow so many *Vhtir* to enter his territory. He'll consider it an act of war. We could all be slain, including your mate," Jhelan said.

The tears welled again in her eyes. Her bottom lip quivered.

"Rhamzin. I'll take Rhamzin with me. He would never allow anyone to harm me. And he'll ensure I leave after. Even if we have to escape the way we did the last time," she said.

So much emotion moved through their Bond and straight through Ahrkyn's brands he fought tears of his own.

Jhelan looked to the King, who remained silent. He'd said the decision was Freyda's and would say nothing to persuade her in one direction or the other. Ahrkyn had always respected his father's refusal to command one's loyalty or obedience, but this was one of those times he begrudged his father for it.

"Where is Rhamzin?" Freyda asked. "He should be here for this."

"I'll find him." Ahdeben pushed to his feet and left the room, the front door opening and closing with more force than necessary.

He didn't know Freyda well. Had barely spoken to her. But Ahdeben would protect her with his life. She was the mate of his Prince, of his friend. And she was officially a member of Ahdlai.

She was also very human and very fragile. She could never withstand the injuries the Elves had incurred through their many battles.

"If he accompanies me, I can go, tell my mother goodbye, then return. The Emperor might be cruel, but he isn't stupid. He knows holding me against my will, especially after Bonding with the Prince, would bring Ahdlai's wrath down upon him and all of Mhahzin. I was told there were many lost in the last battle with you."

"We had others who helped with that battle," Ahrkyn said. There was no reason to hide the risks from her. This was her home and her people now. "Had we not had that help, we might not have come out the victors. Ahdlai could have fallen. The women here…" He let the words trail into the air. She didn't need him to detail exactly what would happen to the women of Ahdlai were the *Ihllr* Elves to be in control. Their laws didn't prohibit the forced Claiming of women.

"Who helped? What if we asked them to escort me along with Rhamzin?"

That didn't set well with Ahrkyn. She would prefer strangers to be at her side rather than her own mate? He knew it was to protect him from being slain at her stepfather's hand, but didn't make him feel much better about her choice.

"Those who helped were unexpected visitors," the Queen said. "They were descendants of Valdis, arriving in hopes of coercing her to join them. They only stayed to help because they didn't wish to see another Fairy fall."

Freyda's eyes widened as she turned them on Valdis. "You're Fae?"

"I am," she said.

Valdis and Jhelan would never have a family, she would never carry a child in her belly, but they were happy. The fact didn't diminish the love they had for each other.

"Will they help again? I mean, if my stepfather attacks, will your family help again?"

"They're not my family. They're…more like great-great-great aunts. Or something along those lines." Valdis's tone said she had no intention of discussing her Fae lineage any further.

Tears shone anew in Freyda's eyes. "I have to go back, Ahrkyn," she said, turning and grabbing one of his hands in both of hers. "I have to say goodbye. Surely you understand. What if it was your mother? Or father? What if you were far away and received news they were close to death? Wouldn't you at least want to try to get there before it was too late? There is so much I want to say to her before it's too late."

A tear escaped over her lashes and trailed down her pale cheek. Ahrkyn used his free hand to wipe it away.

He couldn't deny her this. Yet, standing by while she crossed over the border and into the land of their enemy made him sick to his stomach.

The front door slammed open, hitting the far wall, heavy stomps following after. Rhamzin rounded the corner, his face a mask of rage.

"Absolutely not," he nearly bellowed.

Ahrkyn's hackles rose. No one raised their voice at his mate.

Unfolding to his full height, Ahrkyn positioned himself to stand directly in front of Freyda.

"Stand down. You know I would never hurt the Princess," Rhamzin said. His eyes were bright silver, lines bracketed his mouth and eyes, his nostrils flared with each breath. "And I won't allow anyone else to hurt her, either." Turning his eyes down to where Freyda still sat, he shook his head. "He is trying to lure you back with the only thing he knows will work. If you step foot over that border, he will have you back in his possession. Do you truly believe he'll let you walk away freely once your mother is dead?"

Freyda's small hand landed on Ahrkyn's arm and pushed him aside. She stood, lifting her chin defiantly. "I escaped on my own without you. I escaped with you at my side. I can escape again if this is nothing more than a trap."

"Bull shit," Rhamzin growled.

He began to pace the space, his steps jerky and full of agitation. He cared about Freyda. Cared for her the way a father would, cared enough about her that he was willing to receive the wrath of the Royal family of Ahdlai for cursing at the Princess.

"What about the ogre Brizio?" Valdis spoke up. "Is there a way to get word to him? He is neither friend nor foe to any region. He could accompany them. Act as another guard."

"He is a wanderer. There is no way to reach him. At least not in time. Even if we were to somehow get word flowing through the woods, there is no guarantee he would arrive in time. Not if the Empress is in as bad of shape as the *Ihllr* say," the King said.

"I'm going back to Mhahzin. I will tell my mother goodbye. I will tell her I forgive her. And then I'll return home."

Ahrkyn's heart raced, only he wasn't sure whether it was his own beat or Freyda's. He could feel all the things she didn't say, could feel the guilt over leaving her mother there with the cruel Emperor, could feel the fear of not seeing her mother again before it was too late.

He could also feel the fear of returning to her former territory, the agony of leaving Ahrkyn's side, the fear of not being able to return as she promised.

If she truly set her mind to returning long enough to say goodbye to her mother, Ahrkyn would stand right there at the border and wait for her return. He would pack as much as he needed in a knapsack and await her return. And if she didn't return within a few days' time, he would rally every single member of Ahdlai's guard and invade Mhahzin. He would kill anyone and everyone who stood in his way of getting to his mate.

For now, he would pray to the Mother someone would find a way to change her mind before that time came.

 Chapter Eighteen

Freyda trembled as she threw her leg over the mare she'd ridden when she'd arrived in Ahdlai. She had wanted to learn to fight, learn to wield a sword and protect herself. There hadn't been time.

Within a few days, her mother would be lowered into the ground. If Freyda didn't make it to her side in time to at least let her know she was forgiven, Freyda would carry that in her heart forever.

Her mother wasn't a bad person, nor a bad mother. She was merely another victim of the Emperor. He had changed her, beaten her into submission, something he had tried with all his might to do to Freyda. But she'd been able to escape before it was too late and she, too, became a shell of a person.

Rhamzin waited until she was situated atop her animal before climbing onto the saddle of his.

"Please, *khaere*," Ahrkyn said. "Please be careful. Please return to me."

His hand was on her leg, his grip tight. She curled her fingers around it and brought it to her lips, bending at the waist to reach, and left kisses along his knuckles, then turned his hand to press her lips to his palm.

"I will return. I promise."

She would return to him. She had to. If somehow the Emperor was able to keep her a captive permanently, she would find a way to end her own life. She would rather be dead and allow Ahrkyn the chance to grieve her than to carry the child of another and risk Ahrkyn rushing into a war and getting himself killed.

The world would continue to turn once she was gone, but she couldn't imagine a universe where Ahrkyn didn't exist in some manner. She was human, after all. Her life would end long before his.

"I still say this is a stupid idea," Jhelan said.

"Jhelan," the King barked out in warning.

Jhelan clamped his lips shut, but didn't stop glowering.

"Keep her safe," Ahrkyn told Rhamzin. "Please. I will give you anything you want if you'll bring her back to me."

"I need nothing," Rhamzin said. "It is my job to protect the Princess."

The two would never be friends, but it was obvious they held a mutual respect toward each other because of her.

"Bring her back to me. Please."

Freyda could feel Ahrkyn through her veins, through their brands, and in her heart. Their fear was nearly identical. The same fear that she very well might not return. The fear that one or both of them would have to say goodbye forever.

Rhamzin reached over and grabbed the lead of Freyda's horse and started them on their journey. It was for the best. Because the longer she stood there holding her mate's hand, the harder it was becoming to leave.

Members of the Ahdlai guard escorted the duo through the woods and to the border where members of Mhahzin's guard waited. She recognized a few of them, despised a few of them, as well. They weren't much different than her stepfather or a majority of the *Ihllr*.

Not all the *Ihllr* were sick, twisted bastards. But so many had gotten away with so much for so long it had become engrained in their minds that they were superior to all females of every species.

Freyda fought the urge to look back once more, but failed. There, in the distance, she caught a silhouette of her mate watching over her. He hadn't followed closely, didn't alert any others to his presence. But he was there for her, waiting in case she needed him.

Tears burned the backs of her eyes but she kept them at bay, kept her stepfather's men from seeing them. Head held high, she bid goodbye to those who'd escorted her and rode beside Rhamzin as they were engulfed by the Mhahzin guard. They created a barrier around them, flanking them on all sides.

Should she change her mind and wish to turn the horse, they would stop her. She knew in her heart they would stop her.

Jhelan had been right. Ahrkyn had been right. This was a ruse. A trap.

She had to keep her emotions at bay to prevent Ahrkyn from feeling them through their Bond brands. He would rush forward and start a fight with the guard. Someone would get hurt. They could die. And she couldn't live with that. They would die because of her, protecting her.

She had put herself in this position. Once she discovered what the Emperor had planned, she would make her own plans. She would escape as she had before and she would never look back.

"Is she truly sick?" Freyda asked when the group was far enough from Ahdlai's border to avoid being overheard.

"She is," a guard said. "That is why we were sent for you. She has been unwell since you left."

Guilt slammed into Freyda's heart. Could the loss of her daughter be what caused her mother's illness? From what she'd read in books, there were diseases and infections that made humans sick. But could heartache cause someone to be close to death?

She hadn't properly told Ahrkyn goodbye, just as she hadn't told her mother goodbye. What if that moment, the moment she'd spied him watching her in the trees, was the last she would ever glimpse of him?

Why hadn't she told him how deeply her feelings for him ran? It was beyond the Blessed Bond. Beyond being drawn together by Mother Universe's force.

She loved him. In such a short time, she had grown to love him more than she loved anything else in the world. She hadn't told him.

And she might never again get the chance.

If she was correct, if Jhelan and the others were correct and this was some form of trap to coerce her back to Mhahzin, she would need to find a way to send word to Ahrkyn. She would ask Rhamzin to bring word to Ahrkyn, to tell him of the joy he had brought into her life, of the freedom he'd given her no matter how fleeting in duration.

She would ensure Rhamzin reminded him Freyda's life would have been short in comparison to the long years he would live and that he would one day have had to find a way to live without her. She wanted him to be happy. If that meant grieving her loss and finding another who brought him a sliver of peace and contentment, she wanted him to know he had her blessing.

First, she needed to discover whether her mother was sick at all and what exactly her stepfather had planned for her stay in her former territory.

Rhamzin rode so closely to her she occasionally felt his horse brush her leg. The others barely spared her a glance, speaking only between themselves while affectively ignoring her entirely.

That wasn't exactly uncommon. She was a woman, the stepdaughter of the Emperor, the human Princess of Mhahzin. They were ordered to keep their distance lest they suffer the consequences of defiling the purity of the Emperor's prized possession.

Since they weren't racing toward anything, the trek to Mhahzin took the entire day and most of the night. By the time the gates leading toward the Palace came into view, Freyda's stomach grumbled, her behind was sore, and her heart ached.

Focusing on the brands she shared with Ahrkyn, she could feel his own ache deep in his heart. He grieved her absence as she did his, felt the same discomfort in his chest, felt the same emptiness in his soul as she.

She must close the link, block him from feeling her, because the moment he felt an ounce of her fear, he would charge forward. He would rally the guard and rush toward her, toward Mhahzin, rush to the gates where the Emperor would surely have his men ready to slaughter every single *Vhtir* who dared show their face.

Ahrkyn wasn't sure how long he waited. He sat atop his horse watching as the other piece of his soul rode away from him surrounded by the enemy. And there wasn't a damn thing he could do to stop her.

He had told Freyda she was free, free to make her own decisions and to come and go as she pleased. He hadn't intended her to use that freedom to walk right back into the lion's den. But he trusted Rhamzin. He had to trust the large guard to keep his Princess safe.

He'd watched as her shape grew smaller, until she'd disappeared over the hills. The sun had set hours ago, yet he still sat in the saddle watching the place where she'd disappeared.

He had packed several days' rations in a knapsack and intended to stay right there until she returned to him. She had promised she would return. He hung on to that promise as though it were a lifeline.

Over and over, he focused on their connection through their brands, tracking her emotions.

Until she had somehow figured out a way to close him out. He could no longer feel her. He knew she was alive, could still feel her heart beating in his own chest, but he could no longer feel her anxiety or the pain leaving his side had caused her.

That didn't bode well with him. He'd wanted to track her travels through their link, to ensure himself she was safe by tracking her emotions. The moment he'd felt an inkling of true terror, he had planned to bury his heel in his horse's side and rush to her.

Perhaps that was why she had shut him out, to prevent him from going headfirst into an ambush. A slaughter at the hands of the Emperor's men.

Was that his plan all along? To use Princess Freyda as bait so Ahrkyn would end up with his head on the chopping block? That would surely start a war between the two territories. And his people were unaware whether or not Mhahzin had been successful at growing their numbers after the last battle with Ahdlai.

As he thought about his mate being surrounded by *Ihllr* Elves, his own anxiety and fear spiked. It might very well be a good thing she had closed down the connection between them, at least temporarily. She needed to focus on what was coming rather than Ahrkyn's emotions.

The night insects and nocturnal creatures scurried and sang and chirped. He couldn't sit in the saddle for the next few hours. Or days. Or however long it took for her to return.

Throwing his leg over the side, he set his feet on the ground, spread a pelt on the grass, and prepared to get comfortable. He was sure he would get little sleep, but he needed to be as rested as possible. Just in case. In case she needed him. In case she came rushing toward the border as she had a week ago.

Ahrkyn laid on his back and threw an arm over his eyes. He had to focus on staying calm. He had to trust in Rhamzin to keep Freyda safe. Had to trust she would once more be in his arms. Sooner rather than later.

Memories of lying with her, of feeling her lush body beneath his hands, of her warmth wrapped around him, sent peace through him. His body didn't harden as it had every time he thought of her, but rather his heart reached for her. He needed to feel her in his arms again. Needed to have her in his bed, sleeping soundly beside him again.

Needed her in his life for as long as he could have her.

She was no more than a few years over twenty. If she stayed in good health, he might have another sixty years with her. Unless he could find a way to prolong her life. The only solution he could conjure was finding a vampire and asking the vile creature to turn her. But that would mean no more walks in the sunlight, it would mean sustaining on the blood of humans and animals.

It was a curse he refused to accept for his selfish need to keep her with him longer.

He could always follow her into the afterlife. That would be a far better outcome than suffering for decades, maybe even centuries after she left this world. He knew of others through the years who'd lost their mates who had been sent by the Mother. They slowly went mad until they either ended their lives at their own hand or begged another to do the task for them.

Yes, death would be far better than living another day without Freyda by his side. Even after such a short time, his life, his heart, mind, and soul had been irrevocably altered by her mere presence.

For so long, Ahrkyn had been resistant to mating, to Claiming a woman. He knew now it was for fear of being so deeply connected to another person, to being so connected that their absence created a crater in his heart.

His thoughts were consumed by Freyda. He feared every moment they were apart, feared for her safety, feared he wouldn't be there for her when she needed him.

He couldn't fail her.

But he couldn't ride into Mhahzin alone. That would be a suicide mission and would be of no use to his mate.

The humans married. He might not remember much from before the nuclear war, but he remembered hearing of weddings where the women would wear beautiful white gowns. They would have lavish parties, celebrate with wine and cake.

When she returned to him – and he refused to believe otherwise – he would ask his mother to help him plan a wedding in the manner of the humans before. He would ask the seamstress to make her a gown that rivaled any worn by the Royal women around the world. He would ensure there was music and dancing and a great feast.

Then he would carry her cradled against his chest to their own home where they were awarded privacy. He would lavish her body in kisses, relish every inch of her body, then make love to her until neither could stay awake another moment.

With a sigh, Ahrkyn crossed his arms over his chest and stared up at the stars, waiting for sleep to finally find him. He counted each twinkling light overhead and wondered if his beautiful mate was looking at the same starts, if she, too, was dwelling on their future. If she, too, was counting the moments before they were once more united.

Chapter Nineteen

Freyda's heart slammed against her ribs as she was escorted across the Palace lawn and toward her former cage. She had hoped to never see this place again, had hoped to never again set foot on the grass surrounding the Palace.

It was different now. The place she had called home for so long seemed so strange to her. She no longer saw the beauty in the opulent building, the stained-glass windows, or the statues carved from stones that decorated the gardens.

The men she had seen day in and day out were the enemy. She saw them as they were, not that she had ever seen them as anything more than people of which she should be leery.

But she no longer feared them. She had seen how good men behaved, seen true loyalty. These men were not loyal to the Emperor. They simply enjoyed the spoils they were awarded for doing his bidding. They enjoyed the endless supply of women to produce their heirs, the endless supply of food and wine those outside the walls rarely experienced.

While the residents of Mhahzin suffered and went to bed hungry on most nights, those within the Emperor's employ had rounded bellies. They never experienced the pain one experienced after days without sustenance.

While Freyda had always wanted to escape, now she hated herself for not doing more to help the people who were forced to live within this territory. The land was beautiful. The people who lived outside the tall, thick walls were good people. They simply wanted to survive, to have families and provide for them. It was the Emperor's fault that hard times always befell them.

Taxes. He'd called the theft of the food they grew and the livestock they raised taxes. He took what he wanted instead of doing as they did in Ahdlai and working as a community. The only thing the

Emperor did was take. He took and took until those around him had nothing.

Why couldn't this have happened a few weeks later? Had she been able to receive at least a little training, she might have been able to fight for her freedom if the situation turned sour. She might even be able to slash her stepfather's throat and free the people of Mhahzin.

She could always try. If she was given a moment alone with her stepfather, she could always reach for the sharpest thing she could find and end the misery of all *Ihllr* Elves.

A smile pulled up the corners of her lips unbidden. It was a terrible plan, but at least it was a plan. Until that moment, she'd had no idea what she would do or what would happen the moment she was through the Palace doors once more.

It was late. There was very little light coming from any of the windows. But someone was definitely up, whether her stepfather or the guard, awaiting her arrival.

Rhamzin climbed from his horse and reached up to help the Princess down from hers. He stayed beside her, his arm brushing her shoulder with each step.

Until he was stopped at the doors.

"I stay with the Princess. It is my job to guard her," he demanded.

He had been the head of her stepfather's guard for years. He towered over most of the men under the Emperor's employ by several inches and had quite a few pounds of muscle on them.

But he was far outnumbered.

"You are no longer tasked with her employ. You couldn't keep a single woman from leaving the territory. You have officially been demoted," one of the men said, a smug look on his stupid face.

She might not have been able to physically fight, but already she could feel the strength inside of her welling.

"He is my personal guard. I demand he stay by my side."

That same smug guard rolled his eyes. "You are in no position to demand anything, *Princess*." The title was said in a mocking tone and angered Freyda.

"Where is my mother? I was told she was ill. I demand to see her now."

Several men chuckled. Others looked uncomfortable.

"Your father wishes to speak with you first."

"You would wake the Emperor over something as petty as his stepdaughter's arrival?"

The smug jerks snickered.

"We're under strict orders to wake him the moment you grace the Palace with your presence."

He gripped her upper arm a little too tightly. Rhamzin lunged forward, ready to tear the guard's arm from his body, but was stopped by a wall of black leather encasing muscle.

"Release the Princess," Rhamzin demanded.

But the smug jerk ignored his demands and continued dragging her up the stairs and into the Palace. Anything else said was silenced with the slamming door.

The guard's grip never lessened as he led her through the halls toward the Emperor's sleeping quarters. She had never set foot in her stepfather's private quarters. The fact she was being taken directly to him while he slept sent a new wave of fear coursing through her veins.

"Why can't I see my mother first? Let the Emperor get his sleep. I'm sure he wouldn't mind speaking with me in the morning," Freyda said, attempting to negotiate with the jerk manhandling her.

"My orders stand. Unlike your friend, I do as I'm told. You are to be brought directly to Emperor Ehmile the second you arrive."

She attempted to jerk her arm from him. She could very well walk on her own two feet, damn it. She didn't need this brute to drag her through the house. She knew the halls like the back of her hand. Since she was rarely allowed outside the walls without an escort, she often paced the Palace while reading one of her favorite books.

He only tightened his hold, jerking her toward him until she nearly lost her balance.

She wasn't a small woman, neither in height nor stature. But every man in her stepfather's employ was huge. Much like the *Vhtir* Elves, they all towered over her. And while she wasn't a waif of a woman, they were packed with muscles honed from work and battle while she was soft in a womanly way.

Why had she come back here? She should have heeded the warning from Jhelan, from Ahrkyn, from the others. But how could she forgive herself without being with her mother when she took her last breath?

She was pulled to a stop outside her stepfather's sleeping quarters. The guard raised his free hand and knocked several times before the door was ripped open.

And the man she had hoped to never see again stood backlit by candlelight, a scowl etched in his face.

That scowl never eased, even when he discovered why he was disturbed.

"Good. Take her to her room. Position two guards outside her door until morning. Make sure there are others outside her bedroom window should she decide to grow brave and jump the two stories to once more escape."

"So, I'm a prisoner?" she asked, jutting her chin forward.

"Were you not told of your mother's condition?"

"I was. If I'm not a prisoner, why do you fear I'll leave? I came, did I not? I'm here to see my mother before she leaves this plane."

A muscle jumped in the Emperor's cheek. He raised his eyes to the guard. "Do as I say. She may visit with my mate in the morning. For now, make sure no others disturb me without cause."

"Yes, Your Highness," the guard said, yanking Freyda away from the door.

He dragged her down the hall, much as he had to her stepfather's room, and to the sleeping quarters she'd occupied the past twenty years.

The door slammed closed after she'd been nearly tossed inside.

Stumbling, she grabbed the side of a chest of drawers to keep from falling on her face and had a look around. Nothing had changed. Her bed had been made since last she slept in it, but it was often made by the servants immediately after she left it. But everything else was exactly where she'd left them.

With one exception – all her books were missing from the shelves lining one side of her bedroom wall. Someone had stolen all her books, the only items she cherished, the words she had used to escape mentally from the cage she'd been held within for so long.

And she was once more thrust in the gilded cage.

There wasn't a single doubt in her mind that her stepfather would find one excuse after another to keep Freyda within Mhahzin. Even after her mother passed – *if* she was truly sick – he would find a reason to keep her there.

With two guards outside her door and more below her window, she had no idea how the hell she would escape this time. There were no secret tunnels or passages hidden in her walls like in some of her books. There was no magic potion she could use to drug the guards into doing her bidding.

She would have to bide her time, possibly do what she must to earn the trust of one or more of the guards, until the time to escape presented itself.

Where was Rhamzin? Why would they not let him join her? Would he be punished for aiding in her escape?

Oh no. He would. He had been demoted, but she had no idea what that entailed. Would he be sent away? Sent far away from the border of Mhahzin, far away from Freyda?

She had no one on her side, no one to keep those who would risk the Emperor's wrath for a chance to lie with the Princess.

She was mated. She shared the Blessed Bond of the Mother. She carried the brands of her true mate. Surely, that had to mean something, even to those with the darkest of hearts.

Freyda still wore the tunic loaned to her by Valdis. The chest of drawers and closet were full of clothing, but she refused to don any of them. She refused to return to the person she was before Ahrkyn. Refused to wear the clothing that revealed so much of her breasts and hugged her body. Such clothing was used to snare men. She had no desire to do such.

She had a man. A real man. A man of honor and loyalty and love. A man who would slaughter the guard who'd manhandled her when he found out. *If* he found out.

Sitting on the edge of her bed, she opened herself to the link formed between their brands and sought Ahrkyn. As she closed her eyes, she swore she could see what he saw, could feel the hard ground beneath him.

He'd remained in the forest after she'd left. She knew of the creatures that lurked about after dark, knew of the dangers of being alone in the woods, knew of the monsters that feasted on the flesh and blood of any humanoid.

Why hadn't he returned to the Palace? Why had he not asked one of his friends to accompany him to the woods, to stay with him while he waited for her?

And she knew that was exactly what he was doing, waiting for her return.

Lying back on the mattress, she closed her eyes and focused on Ahrkyn, on her mate. She opened herself as much as she could and hoped he could feel her. She wanted him to feel the love she felt for him, the gratitude she held in her heart for him and his family. They had given her a real life, albeit the time was short.

She stayed linked to Ahrkyn as long as she could, but, slowly, her eyes grew heavy. The physical toll of the travel and the emotional strain of being separated from her mate along with the unknowns of what was to come caught up with her.

As sleep swept her under, she clung to Ahrkyn, clung to the hope she would wake in his arms once more.

Heavy knocking on her door woke Freyda. She had moved at some point and was lying on her side, facing the window of her room. Sunlight filtered through the thin curtains. Unaware of how much sleep she'd actually gotten, she knew it was officially morning.

And time to face her stepfather.

Blinking heavily to get the dreams and sleep to fade away, she pushed to her feet and shuffled to the door. A different guard from last night stood before her, two others on either side of the door.

"The Emperor requests your presence," the guard said. Unlike the man from last night, he was cordial and to the point. He was merely doing as he was ordered.

"I want to see my mother. If she's as sick as I was told, time is running out."

His eyes over her head, the guard repeated himself. "The Emperor has requested your presence, Your Highness."

He stepped out of the way so she could leave her room and waited until she was beside him before he moved forward. He didn't touch her, didn't grab her arm, didn't speak another word as they traversed the halls, stopping in the dining hall where her stepfather currently ate his morning meal.

"Thank you, Heune," the Emperor said.

The guard, Heune, left with a bow, pulling the tall doors shut behind him.

"Where's my mother?" she asked, getting to the point. There was only one reason she had returned, and it had nothing to do with conversing with the man who had made the lives of so many an absolute nightmare.

"You will see her soon enough. Sit. Have some breakfast. We have much to discuss."

"We have nothing to discuss."

Unlike before, she didn't avert her eyes, didn't defer to him in any way. He was nothing to her. He was no longer in control of her. She was an adult woman with a new family. She had a mate who was waiting for her to return. And she very well could be carrying a child in her womb at that very moment, though they wouldn't know for weeks.

"Sit," he ordered, locking eyes with her, the glow entering his irises and reminding her he carried something in his veins she did not – magic.

She had not seen the full extent of his power, but even the slightest measure of magic could overcome a human with ease.

Chin held high and shoulders squared, she rounded the table and took a seat at the foot of the table, as far from him as she could get while being in the same room.

A servant scurried into the room, setting plates and bowls and cups in front of her. Eying the knife beside the fork, she quickly pulled her attention away from it. She could use it as a weapon if needed and didn't want him to see her plan in her eyes.

"Do you believe those marks on your arms will protect you from defying my orders?" he asked, his tone as conversational as though he'd asked about the weather.

"They are the Bond brands. I have a mate and our union has been blessed by the Mother."

The Emperor glanced up briefly, a smirk on his, before refocusing his attention on his meal.

"You might want to eat. You'll need the energy."

Freyda frowned. "I'm not hungry."

She would need the energy? For what? Could it possibly be he intended to let her leave after all?

"Where is my mother?"

Her stepfather pushed his plate forward and waved away the servant who hurried forward to clear his place.

"Leave," he told those who waited for his commands.

The room emptied, servants scampering from the room in a frenzy. Doors *snicked* quietly behind them; the only sound left was the crackling of a fire in the tall hearth.

As her stepfather leaned back in his seat, folding his hands over his stomach, she had a hard time seeing him as a leader. He was a dictator. True leaders led by example. They would never ask the men they employed to do something they themselves would not. They didn't send their men out to imprison innocent women, to kill entire Clans for simply trying to survive.

Ehmile was a coward. He hid behind his guard, stayed within the security of the walls of Mhahzin proper. He would never lift a sword to defend his people as King Nhaeem and Queen Ahlmeda had.

Meeting his gaze, her own unwavering, she refused to speak first. If he had something to say, he could say it. Then she would seek out her mother, tell her everything in her heart, then demand Rhamzin be allowed to escort her back to her home.

Because this place was not her home. It had *never* been her home.

"Do you understand the repercussions of your actions?" he asked after several moments of silence.

Still, she refused to answer.

"Had we cancelled the games, others might have seen it as a weakness. After all, what kind of Emperor can't control his own daughter?"

"*Step*daughter," she corrected on impulse.

"Rulers around the world would have attacked, they could have attempted to take my crown. All because I raised a spoiled brat."

As his words began to sink in, her heart began to race painfully and her breath came in short pants.

*Had he cancelled the games…*he still planned to give her away as a prize. He hadn't changed his plans, still didn't plan to change what he'd planned for her life regardless of the brands on her arm.

"I am mated. I am mated to the Prince of Ahdlai. I am no one's property. You can't gift me to someone else when I am already Claimed."

He waved his hand in the air as though shooing away a fly. And she was just as significant to the Emperor as any other pest.

Spoiled brat. He truly believed he had raised her or spoiled her in any manner? She'd learned to read in secret, had been watched over like a criminal her whole life, and now was being held against her will.

"If you attempt to hold me here, my mate and the entirety of Ahdlai will see it as an act of war. They will attack."

"Oh, I'm planning on it."

Her heart stuttered. *Planning on it*. He'd planned for this. Planned for her mate to come for her. Planned for Ahdlai to come to her rescue.

He was hoping they would, was planning some form of ambush. Perhaps he would wait until the games to send word she would not be returned. He could use her as a way to win against his enemy by awarding her to any who bested the Royal family and stole the crown.

The man sat on a throne of ash and dust. Of lies. Of betrayal and evil.

"No," she said. She sat against the back of her chair and crossed her arms over her chest. "I am Claimed. I have a mate. Mother Universe will never stand for it."

He threw his head back and laughed. "Who taught you such stupid superstitions? Had to be Rhamzin."

"Where is he?"

"Around."

Tears burned the backs of her eyes as her heart clenched. "Is he still alive?"

A smirk appeared again on his face. "For now."

Ensuring the connection between herself and Ahrkyn was fully blocked, she prepared to square off with her stepfather. She wouldn't allow him to sell her off like cattle. She wouldn't allow him to punish Rhamzin for something he was against. He hadn't wanted her to leave the Palace walls, but felt it safer for her to have a companion.

"You will not use me as a reward for your sick games. And you will let Rhamzin leave. He had nothing to do with my escape. He tried to stop me. He tried to talk me out of it, but felt I wasn't safe traveling alone."

"Do you really believe he doesn't have the strength to throw you over his shoulder and carry you back to your chambers? He made a choice. As did you."

"Is my mother sick? Or was it a ruse?"

"Oh, she's sick. But it might have something to do with something she was fed."

Anger quickly replaced any fear that had caused her heart to race. "You poisoned my mother?"

He shrugged it off. "She was beyond child bearing years and no longer of any use to me."

"You sick son of a bitch."

Grabbing the knife, she lunged to her feet so quickly the chair upon which she had sat hit the ground. She rushed around the table, the knife held high, intent on slamming the blade deep into his heart.

Unfortunately, he was not only much stronger and faster, but he was an Elf. His magic stopped her in her tracks and stole the air from her lungs.

Like a statue, she stood there, her arm raised over her head, the knife clenched in her fist, as she struggled to suck in a single breath of oxygen.

Freyda watched in horror as the Emperor casually stood, pushing his chair back into place, then closed the space between them. He plucked the knife from her hand, tossed it onto the table, then drew back his arm.

When he let it fly forward, his knuckles made contact with her right cheek, knocking her to the ground and breaking the spell he'd put her under.

Breathing deep, she tried to force the stars from her vision. Her face throbbed, her head ached, her knees burned where they'd been abraded by the thick rug running alongside the table.

Fire erupted in her scalp when her stepfather wrapped his fist in her long hair and yanked her to her feet.

"I see you're as stubborn as your mother. Don't worry; I beat the fire out of her. And I'll have no problem beating the fire out of you. By the time we're done, you'll be more than ready to move on to a new man and will be the perfect submissive Princess."

Chapter Twenty

Ahrkyn jerked awake. His sword was in his hand before he was fully awake or on his feet.

Crunching leaves alerted him to someone's approach, but it only took a second to recognize the scent of fellow *Vhtir*. His friends had come to join him in the woods while he waited.

"Why do you keep coming out here by yourself?" Jhelan asked. "It's my fucking job to protect you."

"You knew where I was," Ahrkyn said, sheathing his sword now that there was no imminent danger.

"He's been out here with you for hours," Ihsander said, shrugging with a grin while Jhelan glared at him. "He stayed downwind so you wouldn't detect him."

"It's my job," Jhelan said.

"Any word?" Ahdeben asked.

Ahrkyn picked up his pelt and shoved it deep inside the knapsack with a shake of his head.

"Nothing."

"It's been less than twenty-four hours. It's a long trek to the Palace of Mhahzin. Be patient. Rhamzin will watch over her."

If he was still alive.

While any in Ahdlai were free to come and go as they pleased, if any member of the guard openly defied King Nhaeem, there would be harsh penalties. Rhamzin could have been executed before they arrived to the gates. Or perhaps Emperor Ehmile would make a show of it, proving that death was the penalty for going against their ruler.

"Have you felt anything from her?"

"She closed off the link. I haven't felt anything from her since last night."

"Any reason we should be concerned?" Ahdeben asked.

Of the four, his powers were the most powerful. A simple thought from him could fry a man's brains, scramble them as easily as an egg over fire.

"I felt her fear and anxiety. But I expected that. It's the first time she's gone home since escaping. And she was told her mother was dying. That alone could have caused those emotions."

Ahdeben didn't look convinced. His hand rested on the hilt of his short sword hanging from his belt and his eyes were fixed on the horizon.

"We could always wander a little closer, stay under the radar. Make sure your mate isn't in need of our services," he offered.

The plan sounded perfect to Ahrkyn, but if they were unable to stay under the radar, as Ahdeben put it, they could be found by members of the Mhahzin guard. If they were killed, they couldn't get to Freyda. While Ahrkyn knew his father would ensure his new daughter-in-law would always be protected, there was no reason to poke the hornet's nest. Not yet.

However, the moment he felt true fear from his mate, he would be on his horse, racing toward the Palace, consequences be damned.

"Do you plan on waiting out here until she returns?" Ihsander asked.

Ahrkyn nodded.

His stomach grumbled. Pulling an apple from his knapsack, he couldn't fight the smile as he looked down at it in his hand. They had shared an apple on the first morning together, when she'd attempted to flee her region the first time.

Ihsander eyed the apple.

"I'm not sharing. If you're hungry, you should have either brought your own or ate before you left."

"He already ate," Jhelan said.

"And I'm hungry again."

The man was always hungry. He trained, patrolled, and fought as fiercely as the rest, yet his body was leanly muscled instead of bulky like the rest. The sinewy nature of his body didn't slow him down. He didn't appear ill. It was simply the way he had been born.

"I'm not sharing," Ahrkyn repeated.

He'd only brought a few days' rations. If he shared his food, he would have to return to town to restock. And then might not be there waiting when Freyda returned.

His brands throbbed, but he couldn't feel his mate's emotions. Couldn't pinpoint her location. So why were they reacting?

Jhelan's eyes lowered as Ahrkyn rubbed his free hand along the brands lining his left arm from fingertips to over his shoulder.

"What is it?"

With a shake of his head, he looked in the direction of Mhahzin. "I don't know."

"Can you feel her?"

"No. She's still blocking me. But my brands…they're throbbing to my heartbeat."

No. Not his heartbeat. The pattern was far quicker than the cadence of his own heart. His marks were throbbing to the beat of her heart. And it was racing.

That could be good news, though. She could be on her horse, galloping toward him as they stood there waiting.

After a while, Ihsander tired of standing and lowered to the forest floor, leaning his back against a tree. Ahdeben and Jhelan followed suit.

Ahrkyn continued to stare in the direction from where Freyda would arrive.

"You're going to make yourself crazy standing there like a statue, waiting for her to come home," Jhelan said.

With a heavy sigh – and an equally heavy heart – he abandoned his position and joined his friends under the trees.

"Well?" Ihsander asked.

Ahrkyn frowned. "Well, what?"

"Will she carry your heir? Have you discussed growing a family with her?"

They had only had one night together. Granted, they'd made love several times, but had only spent one night together in bed. And whether or not they would bear children hadn't been a topic they'd addressed.

"I don't know," he admitted.

He had finished inside her each time, filling her with his seed and she hadn't protested. So, perhaps that meant she was amenable to carrying his first child. First of many, he hoped.

And they would raise them together. Of course he would accept the help of the town, especially when he was tasked with patrolling for days at a time, but he imagined his mother would dote on her first grandchild enough to make up for his absence.

"She has the body for a mother," Ahdeben said. While that comment should have angered Ahrkyn, he detected a hint of jealousy in Ahdeben's words. He'd been wanting an heir for a while. Both he and Ihsander had been interested in Claiming a woman, but none in town were interested.

And since the *Vhtir* were determined to allow the women, human and otherwise, to choose their life's paths, both men would have to wait until an opportunity arose.

Both Jhelan and Ahrkyn had found their mates, the mates chosen by the Mother, by happenstance. The duo would have to wait until either the Mother sent them her choice for their mate or until they found someone willing to carry their heirs.

Hours passed while the men chatted and munched on the meager snacks they'd packed in their knapsacks. Jhelan, Ihsander, and Ahdeben would eventually have to return to town. They hadn't brought enough supplies to stay the night with Ahrkyn. Not unless they wanted to spend the night hungry.

He hadn't been teasing when he'd refused to share his food. He needed enough so that he wouldn't have to leave this spot. Even if it took days and he ran out of food and fresh water, he would continue to camp under the stars until Freyda returned.

The sun was crossing the horizon and would set soon.

"You should head back," Ahrkyn told the group as a whole.

"I'm staying with you. The King will have my head if I let something happen to his son," Jhelan said.

"I'm going back. I'll grab more food and head back out to hang out with you guys a while longer," Ihsander said as he unfolded himself from the ground.

He pulled his hands over his head and stretched; the time spent on the ground had made him stiff as it had Ahrkyn.

"Do you plan on moving from here?" Ihsander asked.

He slid his foot into a stirrup and threw the other leg over the horse.

"No. We'll be here," Ahrkyn answered. At least he would. The others were under no obligation to wait with him.

Ihsander nodded once and nudged his horse forward. Ahdeben didn't move. He stayed right where he sat, watching their friend ride off.

"He has worms," Ahdeben said.

Ahrkyn and Jhelan exchanged a look of horror and confusion.

"What?" Jhelan asked.

Ahdeben looked to the other two men. "How else can the bastard eat so much without gaining a pound? He must have worms."

That simple suggestion broke the tension in the air. Ahrkyn's lips quirked. Then he chuckled. Then Jhelan and Ahrkyn both laughed heartily, the sound bouncing off the trees around them.

The tension was broken, but Ahrkyn still couldn't ignore the throbbing of his brands. He didn't know whether it meant something was wrong, whether she was on her way back, or was merely anxious about being back in Mhahzin.

All he could do was wait. And patience had never been his strongest virtue.

Freyda groaned as she rolled onto her back. Every inch of her body ached. When she tried to open her eyes, one of her lids wouldn't lift fully. Her eye was swollen nearly shut.

Raising a trembling hand, she touched her face in places, wincing at the pain the tender touch caused.

She rolled back onto her side and attempted to sit up. It took a few tries. Even her damn back hurt as though she'd been tossed around like a ragdoll. Perhaps she had. The memories of last night were hazy.

The last thing she remembered was being dragged through the house by her hair while guard members watched on. Some snickered. Others refused to maintain eye contact with her.

What had happened? Had she been beaten then delivered back to her sleeping quarters? Why put her through so much pain to deposit her on her bed? Why not put her in the cells in the basement?

It was best not to wish for such things. At least here, she was warm. She had a bathroom she could use without an audience.

Placing both feet on the ground, she grunted as more pain shot up her leg starting at her ankle. She could move it so it wasn't broken. But it was swollen and bruised and couldn't hold much of her weight.

The trip to the bathroom took far longer than it should, but she eventually made it and stood in front of the mirror, horror seizing her. The last time she'd truly examined her reflection she'd looked happy. There was a glow to her face, her cheeks were flushed, her eyes bright.

The woman looking back at her now was…broken. Both literally and figuratively. There was so much bruising to the left side of her face she was nearly unrecognizable. Her bottom lip had been split, her left eye was turning an angry shade of purple and was swollen to the size of a lemon.

Her hair had been loose when she'd left Ahdlai. It was now tangled and matted in places with her blood.

Was this what her stepfather had done to her mother? Was this what he'd meant by beating her into submission? By breaking her?

He could beat Freyda all he wanted. She would never submit to his rule. She would never go with another man willingly. She would fight until her last breath.

What would happen today? She could almost picture her stepfather calmly sitting across from her at the dining table, pretending as though nothing happened, testing to see how pliant she was to his wishes.

Why would he think presenting his prize to hundreds of men all battered and bruised was a good idea?

Because the type of man who would kill others to then Claim a woman against her will didn't care about such things. The kind of man who would go along with this kind of foolishness would have no problem raising a hand to Freyda.

He had poisoned her mother. Did that mean she could still survive? What a sick, twisted bastard. She had given him sons in her younger years. Freyda knew none of her half-brothers as they had been raised by others, but they were out there. And cared for her as much as a majority of the *Ihllr* guard did.

Now that the Empress was older and of no use to him, the Emperor was prepared to discard her. Not simply release her to live as she pleased, but kill her.

Why hadn't Freyda tried harder last night? Why hadn't she been sneakier in her attempt to kill him?

It wouldn't have mattered. She could never best someone with magic, could never best an Elf. Hell, she couldn't best anyone. After being locked away and treated like a trinket or simple decoration for so long, she had zero survival skills.

Pushing from the vanity, she refused to allow her stepfather or anyone else to see her like this. She might not be able to do a thing about the bruising, but she could wash the blood from her skin and hair and redon the same tunic.

After a glance down at the frock she'd borrowed from Valdis, she grimaced.

Or not.

It was torn in so many places. It was completely ruined and stained with her blood. If she wore this among the guard and in front of her stepfather, it would both be a reminder of her abuse and would show more skin than she preferred. Her only other option was to wear one of the gowns that hung in her closet.

Unless…

After a quick shower and a lot of wincing as she pulled her brush through her long, wet hair, Freyda rummaged through her closet and drawers until she found something she could wear. A pair of thick tights and a long sleeping gown thick enough as to not be see through with a collar high enough to conceal her cleavage.

Her body was for her mate only. No other man on earth would ever see more than she was willing to show.

It wasn't quite the same as Valdis's tunics, but it would do.

Sliding her feet into a pair of shoes, she squared her shoulders and prepared to meet her stepfather head on.

If her mother died, would he still be considered her stepfather? They would have no familial ties after that, other than the half-brothers she'd never met. How could he maintain any control over Freyda if her mother was gone?

Right. Because he was the ruler of Mhahzin, the feared dictator who did as he pleased.

The door to her sleeping quarters was unlocked from the outside. That shocked her. Although there were still guards positioned outside of her room. What reason did they have to lock her in when she couldn't make it past the threshold?

"Princess," one of the guards addressed her.

"I want to see my mother," she demanded.

The one who'd addressed her looked over her head at the other. "Seek the Emperor. Ask whether she has permission."

"Why do I need permission to see my own damn mother?" she nearly yelled. "If she's dying, let me say goodbye before it's too late."

Since Freyda had no idea what her stepfather had used to poison his own mate, she had no idea how much time she had left before her last remaining flesh and blood relative left this plane.

The second guard left her sight. The first didn't look on her with disdain. He barely met her gaze at all. He might have been the only one she could reason with since Rhamzin wasn't allowed near her.

"Please. All I'm asking is to tell her goodbye. I won't try to escape. You can stay at my side. I'll even let you tie my hands together if it will make you feel better."

His eyes lowered to her face then rose to stare across the room again. "I'm sorry, Princess. After Rhamzin…" He shook his head. "I'm sorry. I must wait to hear from the Emperor."

"Where is he? Where is Rhamzin?"

The guard didn't answer, but she saw something flash through his eyes.

Tears burned the backs of her eyes and a lump grew in her throat. "Is he alive?" Had she gotten her first ever friend killed? Why hadn't she listened to his warnings?

Why hadn't she listened to her new family in Ahdlai when they warned her that this could be a trap? They were right. They knew so much more of life than Freyda ever would. She should have trusted their judgement.

Instead of dwelling on all that she should have done, she waited patiently, her hands folded in front of her, while the second guard sought permission from the Emperor.

She wouldn't put it past her stepfather to forbid it. He would wait until the only time Freyda could lay eyes on her mother was when they lowered her into the ground after her death.

Minutes passed, yet Freyda refused to show an ounce of frustration or any form of emotion. From here out, she vowed to hide anything she felt so her stepfather couldn't use it against her. Already, he was using her mother as a punishment. If she allowed him to see how much she missed her mate, how much she missed Ahdlai, he could attack the territory and slay as many as possible for no other reason than to break Freyda.

Little did he know that every action against her, every threat, every warning did nothing but fuel the fire burning deep inside of her.

As Freyda made plans in her mind, as she wondered what the future would hold, as she did her best to school her expressions to hide her inner thoughts, the second guard returned.

"The Emperor has granted her permission to visit with her mother."

While Freyda's heart leapt, she showed no emotion, didn't let her lips quirk, nothing.

Limping closely behind the second guard while the first who'd addressed her fell in step behind, she eyed the location of each guardsman positioned around the house. If she were to find a way to escape, she needed to know which areas to avoid, where she could duck into the shadows, where she could hide until the threat of discovery passed.

A few guards noticed her attention and raised a brow. The others kept their eyes straight ahead, ever the dutiful employees.

Her escorts led her to her mother's sleeping quarters. The Empress wasn't permitted to sleep in the same room as the Emperor. After all, when he brought a new female into his bed the three might very well not fit comfortably.

He had never been loyal to her mother, had never loved her, never cared for her. He protected the virtue of his stepdaughter, but only because her status of Untouched was of worth to him.

How could he continue with these stupid games? She was no longer Untouched, she was Claimed, and she held the brands of a Blessed Bond. She was worthless to a suitor looking for a mate to carry his heir.

Not true. Her status wouldn't prevent her body from accepting the seed of another. If she was already carrying the heir of her true mate, what would happen to that child? Would she be forced to abort her baby? Would they yank the child from her arms at birth and discard the Prince's heir?

None of those options were possible. Not to her, anyway. She would kill anyone who came near her body or any future child.

Her mother laid in her bed, the blankets pulled up to her chest, her arms resting atop. Her face was pale, as pale as one who'd already passed, but Freyda could see the slow rise and fall of her chest. Her mother still lived. Barely.

Freyda dropped the mask of indifference and rushed across the room, dropping onto the bed and taking one of her mother's hands in her own.

She was so cool to the touch, her skin clammy.

"I'm here, Mother. I'm here," she said, fighting the tears that welled in her eyes and blurred her vision.

Her mother's lashes fluttered as she struggled to open her eyes. When her lids finally lifted, her gaze was unfocused.

"Freyda?" she croaked out, her voice hoarse from lack of use and the grip of death.

"I'm here, Mother. I'm here."

Draping her upper body across her mother's, she let the tears fall, rolling from her cheek to soak into the blanket that covered the Empress.

"I'm so sorry. I shouldn't have left."

A shaky hand dropped onto Freyda's head. "Yes. You should have. You should have stayed away."

Freyda sat up to look into her mother's face. That was the most she had said to Freyda at one time in months. Perhaps years. She was always so closed off, indifferent, as though she was unaware Freyda occupied the same space as she.

"You should not have come."

Every word her mother spoke was forced. She gasped in air as though merely speaking exhausted her.

"I couldn't stay away. I had to tell you, Mother. I love you. I forgive you. I'm so sorry we weren't able to be closer."

Empress Medora's hand took one of Freyda's and squeezed gently. "It is I who is sorry. I thought by keeping my distance…" A deep gasp… "I was keeping you safe. I was wrong."

"I love you, Mother. Please know as you pass to the next plane that I love you."

Her mother gasped again, the intake shaky. "I have always loved you, my sweet girl. I should never have…" *gasp* "…brought you here. I thought it was best. Thought you would be safer."

"You didn't know. How could you know?"

Perhaps Freyda hadn't had her freedom, perhaps her stepfather had had cruel intentions for her all along, but she'd had food in her belly every night. She slept in a comfortable bed in a warm room, protected from the elements by a sturdy roof.

Had her mother not accepted the Emperor's request of a Claim, he might have taken her against her will. Or, they could have died of starvation or disease while trying to survive in the wild.

"He poisoned you, Mother. You're not ill. Ehmile poisoned you."

Her mother nodded. "I know. I was aware when he handed me the cup."

"Then why…" Freyda's voice broke as she tried to ask why her mother would accept the drink if she knew it would cause her death.

"I thought if I was gone, you would be free to live a life far from this place. There would be no ties to bind you to this place."

And the Emperor had used it, instead, to draw Freyda back.

"I will stay with you until the Mother comes for you," Freyda said. "I will be right here."

Her head wagged side to side on the pillow. "You must leave."

Another tear escaped Freyda's eye to roll down her cheek. Her stepfather wouldn't let her leave. It was obvious now the plans he had for her.

If her mother noticed the broken skin and bruising on her daughter's face, she didn't mention it. Perhaps she couldn't see Freyda clearly through the poison in her system.

That would be better. It would be better if her mother didn't die knowing her own mate had battered her daughter so badly.

"You must go, my sweet girl. Before it's too late."

There was no point in upsetting her mother any further. It was obvious she was close to the border of the two planes, her spirit already leaning toward the veil that separated this world from the next.

"I will. I'll sit with you a while longer, then I shall take my leave."

She leaned closer, as though to whisper conspiratorially.

"I'm mated, Mother. I have been Claimed and the Bond has been Blessed by Mother Universe. I carry his marks on my arm. He loves me. I love him. I found my soul's match."

A sweet, soft smile pulled up her lips. "That is all I ever hoped for you."

Her voice had grown weaker, her breaths slower. She was dying right before Freyda's eyes.

"Is there nothing you can take to help you live? Something to counteract the poison?"

Again, her mother's head wagged on the pillow. "I'm ready to go, sweet girl. I only wish I could have lived long enough to see you have your own children far from this place."

Her eyes fluttered closed then opened once more.

"My one regret is bringing you here. I have always loved you. Please know that. You were the only good thing in my life."

Regret, anger, sorrow. So many emotions rushed Freyda's heart at once. She could no longer control the flow of tears as they streamed down her face. If only they'd been able to form a closer bond before it was too late. If only her mother had been taken by another man. If only her father hadn't died when Freyda was so young.

Their lives would have been so different.

Things happened for a reason. The Mother of all things, the Mother of the Universe put them where they were meant to be at all times. Freyda might never know the reasoning behind her own mother's suffering while she walked the planet, but one day all the answers would be made clear to her.

For now, she would hold her remaining parent's hand and wait as her shuddering breaths grew further apart.

At any moment, the Emperor could demand she be pulled from the room. It would be more painful to leave her mother's side at that moment than any beating he could dole out.

Yet, no one came in the room, no one yanked her from the side of the bed, no one ordered her out of the room.

After a while, her mother's eyes never reopened. And Freyda sat silently staring down into her face as she took her last breath. A slow, shaky exhale, and then…nothing. The life fled from her as her spirit travelled to the next plane.

Freyda wasn't sure how long she sat there staring down into her mom's beautiful face, how long she held her cool hand.

But eventually, someone came to retrieve her, pulling her numbly from the room as she struggled to limp behind the guard.

She refused to let another tear escape as long as she was in the presence of a single Mhahzin guard member. She refused to let her stepfather see the pain in her eyes as she was brought to the dining hall to join him for their evening meal.

Evening meal. She'd sat with her mother for hours, toiling the hours away with her lifeless body.

As a plate was set before the empty space at the end of the table, Freyda kept her head high as she limped to her place. A chuckle followed her but she didn't acknowledge it.

She didn't trust that her stepfather hadn't poisoned her food, as well, but what good would she do him if she were dead? He'd demanded she stay behind so he could continue with his sick games with her as the prize.

Besides, she was hungry. She hadn't eaten more than a few bites last night and it had been many hours before that. She would need to keep her strength up if she were to find a way back to her mate.

Lifting her fork, she ate properly, her back straight, both feet on the ground, taking small bites as a Princess should.

One glance up at her stepfather made her stomach turn. He wasn't done with her yet. She could see it in the glow of his eyes, could see it in the cruel turn of his mouth. One wrong word, one wrong step, and she would be beaten again tonight.

So be it. She would never let him beat the spirit out of her. She would never let him beat the love she held for Ahrkyn and all of Ahdlai out of her.

He would have to kill her to accomplish such a feat.

Chapter Twenty-One

Two days. It had been two days since Freyda had ridden off on her horse and away from Ahrkyn. His heart was shattering sliver by sliver with every minute she was gone. And he was still struggling to feel her through their connection.

He'd felt a wave of dismay, of pure sorrow. He assumed that was the moment her mother had passed away.

But then there had been nothing else. She thought she was protecting him by closing herself off to him. Yet, all she was doing was driving him mad.

Did she not know that link would aid him in finding her should she be taken away? Did she not know the link would alert him should she need the guard of Ahdlai to rush over the border to help her?

Ihsander had returned last night as he'd said he would. Then returned to the Palace for more food before riding out to wait with Jhelan and Ahdeben.

"Your mate is going to kick your ass when you get home," Ihsander said.

Jhelan shook his head. "She's grown used to my being gone for days at a time during patrols. And she agrees the Prince shouldn't be out here alone."

"You sound as if I'm a child," Ahrkyn muttered.

"I sound as if I'm the head of the Royal guard and charged with the safety of the members of the Royal family," Jhelan retorted.

Ihsander grinned and opened his mouth, no doubt to throw an insult at one of them, but snapped it shut. All four heads whipped to the south. A scent rode on the wind.

It wasn't the Princess. Ahrkyn would know her scent anywhere, could track her with that alone.

But the scent wasn't unfamiliar, either.

Whoever was coming wasn't riding a horse and was travelling slowly.

"Should we cross?" Ahdeben asked.

Jhelan held up a hand and shook his head. "Could be an ambush. We wait."

Ahrkyn hated taking orders from anyone, especially his friend. He was the Prince, after all, the next in line to the throne of the northern region of Ahdlai.

But, as a fellow guard, he was to heed the head of the guard's orders, and that included standing down.

Ahrkyn's nerves grew taut as they waited. The scent grew stronger, and, eventually, the sounds of struggling steps met their ears. Whoever was coming was having a hard time staying on their feet.

When the top of Rhamzin's head came into view, Ahrkyn's heart nearly burst from his ribcage.

He was alone. He was barely able to walk. And he looked as though he'd been beaten nearly to death. Both eyes were nearly swollen shut, his face was battered until barely recognizable. He held one arm close to his body, his wrist at an odd angle. Each step involved dragging his left leg to catch up to his other as though he was forcing it to work. Blood trailed down the right side of his body and down the left side of his torso near his rib cage.

"Fuck this," Ahdeben growled.

He hastily crossed the border separating Ahdlai from Mhahzin and rushed to Rhamzin.

Ahrkyn threw a leg over his horse and kicked his side, forcing him to move forward at a fast clip. Rhamzin would not be able to walk much further. He would need the horse's back to return to Ahdlai.

"What has happened?" Ahrkyn asked when he reached Rhamzin.

He climbed from the horse and helped Ahdeben as they hoisted the massive guard onto the steed's back.

"They're holding her. She will not return on her own. They will not allow her to return," he said, his words garbled through split and swollen lips.

He looked as though he'd been trampled by a stampede of wild horses, but Ahrkyn knew it was fists, feet, and weapons that caused the damage.

"They left me for dead. They left me in the wild, thinking me gone. The Princess is in danger. Before I lost consciousness last night, I heard her scream out in pain. I couldn't get to her."

He reached down and gripped Ahrkyn by the front of the shirt. "I swear to you, Prince. I tried. I tried to get to her. I tried to get her away. But there were too many. They were ordered to execute me but thought to use me as an example. They thought to leave me for others to find my bones after wild animals or other creatures devoured my carcass."

"Fuck!" Ahrkyn bellowed, his voice bouncing from the trees and echoing in the air.

A flock of birds were startled from a tree overhead, taking flight with squawks and flaps of their wings.

"They'll be waiting for you," Rhamzin warned.

"Is that the reason for luring Freyda there? Did they hope to lure the Ahdlai army?"

"No. But they assume you will come for her. They are prepared. Many others will be entering Mhahzin soon. They will request their aid. Too many fuckers out there are hoping to win Freyda's hand."

"You mean her body," Ahdeben growled.

"How many do you have? There will be dozens against you. Perhaps more. They will be prepared and watching for your arrival."

"You said you heard her scream in pain," Ahrkyn said. His voice came out choked as he struggled against the urge to rush to the Palace and carry his mate away. "Who? Who hurt her?"

"I do not know. But my guess would be the Emperor. He will try to break her as he did her mother."

"Was the Empress truly sick?" Ihsander asked.

"She was. I heard mention of poison. I believe the Emperor poisoned his mate, though I don't know whether it was to lure Freyda or simply because her body was no longer of use to him."

"Sick fuck," Jhelan muttered.

He was pacing now, his movements agitated. It was his job to lead the entirety of the guard. It was his job to ensure all were trained for all forms of battle. But he knew as well as Ahrkyn they might not have the numbers to win a war against so many.

"There has to be a way to get word to Brizio and his witch friends. Perhaps your mate could persuade her descendants to help once more," Ihsander said to Jhelan.

Jhelan shook his head. "The Fae will not bother themselves with the affairs of others. They only came the once and warned Valdis that they would not again if she didn't return with them."

"What about the Shape Shifters? The King allowed the others to live and provided them with food. The *Vhtir* have allowed them to live in peace in our territory," Ahdeben said.

"*If* we can track them," Jhelan said.

The Shape Shifters were adept at keeping their location hidden from any they deemed the enemy. While the *Vhtir* Elves were of no threat to them, they also had no interest in following the rules set by King Nhaeem. They kept to themselves, governed themselves, punished those who stepped out of line. They were as close to wild animals as a humanoid could be.

"Find them. Find as many as you can gather," Ahrkyn barked out.

The sooner they could gather their forces, the sooner they could get to Freyda. And they had to get to her before it was too late. Should another man touch her, should another man attempt to lie with her…

His stomach turned. He couldn't allow such thoughts to enter his mind. He would go mad and burn down the whole of Mhahzin, and might not stop there. He would slay any man or woman who had a hand in taking his mate from him, any living being who didn't help her, didn't stop the sale of his mate.

And that's exactly what was happening – she was being sold in the ruse of winning her as a prize to some fucked up games.

Reaching up, Ahrkyn grabbed the rein of his horse and pulled, urging the beast to follow. They needed to get back to the Palace. He needed to speak with his father. Jhelan needed to gather the guard. They had plans to make.

"Did you see her?" Ahrkyn asked.

"Freyda?" Rhamzin asked. Ahrkyn nodded once. "They took her through the gates and forced me to stay outside. Once she was behind closed doors, several guards began to throttle me. I fought back. I bested a few of the assholes. But more men continued to arrive."

"Cowards," Ahdeben muttered.

"Once the numbers rose to ten or more, I was struggling to stay on my feet. When I heard the Princess scream..." He shuddered, and Ahrkyn swore he saw a glimmer in the massive guard's eyes before he averted them. "I tried, Prince Ahrkyn. I tried to get through the gate. I tried to get to her side."

"You were outnumbered. There was nothing you could do," Jhelan said.

He was attempting to put the guard's mind at ease, but Ahrkyn could hear the anger in his tone. Not aimed toward Rhamzin, but the situation as a whole.

Why the fuck had he let Freyda leave? He should have begged her. Reasoned with her. Negotiated with her.

Hell, he could have done as others might have and forbidden her to go. Surely, she would have forgiven him one day. He should have risked her anger. Then, he wouldn't be fearing she would be dead when he finally infiltrated the walls surrounding the Palace of Mhahzin.

The others rode atop their steeds, but kept in step with the Prince, keeping their pace slow as he led the horse carrying Rhamzin through the woods. Had the distance been shorter, he might have sprinted and pulled the horse along behind him. But they had many acres left before they would see the edge of Ahdlai proper.

He could always climb behind Rhamzin or one of the others, but all five men were large. Two men weighing over two hundred pounds each would be too much strain on the horse's back.

It was nearing midday by the time the first roof came into view over the hill.

"Get him to the healer. I must go speak with my father," Ahrkyn said, splitting from the group.

He no longer walked, but ran as fast as his legs would carry him, ignoring the looks of those working in the fields, the gardens, or tending to the livestock. The only thing in his mind, the only thing he saw before him were brown eyes lined with long, thick black lashes.

Those same eyes had haunted him, teased him, urged him into the woods to discover their meaning. Those same brown eyes had won his heart almost immediately.

And he would be damned if he never looked into those eyes again.

Freyda could barely open her eyes. Her body felt as though filled with cement. Each movement sent agony through her nerve endings.

She'd been right when she'd sat at dinner – the Emperor had not only beat her, but had ensured he had an audience.

By the time his guests arrived, she would be a bloody pulp, not much of a gift to the winner of whatever games her stepfather derived.

Attempting to roll onto her side, she cried out. The right side of her torso burned as though she'd been stuck with a red-hot iron. Broken ribs. Or in the least, severely bruised. Her stepfather had kicked her over and over when she was on the ground until he'd caused damage to her body.

And so many of the guards had watched on and laughed, they'd cheered, suggested other ways to cause her pain.

If – no, *when* – she escaped and returned to Ahrkyn, she would beg him to send every fighter in the territory to punish those who'd enjoyed her torture.

She couldn't lie here and wait for someone to find her. She wouldn't lie here and wait to see what her stepfather had in store for her.

Clenching her teeth, she choked down another scream of pain as she rolled off the side of the bed and planted her feet on the ground. Her ankle was swollen more, the bruising a deep shade of purple, outlined with black. It was harder to put weight on it than yesterday, but she still had some movement. It wasn't broken. She'd been correct in her assumption yesterday that it was merely terribly strained.

With an arm wrapped around her side, she shuffled carefully toward the bathroom, avoiding the mirror. She didn't need to see how badly she looked; she could feel every new injury the Emperor had inflicted.

Her mother was dead. She was only days away from either being beaten to death or taken away by a stranger. And surely Ahrkyn was going mad by now.

She'd continued to keep their connection through their brands closed off. Perhaps now was a good time to let him feel her, let him know she was alive and in need of assistance.

She prayed to the Mother he would keep his wits and ensure he had the numbers before infiltrating the border of Mhahzin. Doing otherwise would be certain death for her mate. And she would take her own life if he was slain. She would do it right in front of the Emperor with a smile on her face.

Staring at the shower, she pondered whether she had the strength to remain upright long enough to wash the blood and filth from her body. But lowering into a tub could make her vulnerable to any who might barge in.

Freyda figured there wasn't much difference; she would be naked and too weak and in pain to fight should someone decide to enter her sleeping quarters.

Her clothes were torn in so many places. And she truly didn't think she could raise her arms high enough above her head to remove her makeshift tunic. Instead, she gripped the sides of the ripped garment and tore it from her body, letting it drop to the ground in blood-stained tatters.

While she'd avoided glimpsing her reflection in the mirror, she was unable to avoid seeing the marks and bruising along her lower body. Obvious outlines of Ehmile's boots marred her once ivory colored skin, along with an array of other oddly shaped bruises from his fists and belt.

The faucet squeaked softly; steam filled the air as the level of water grew in the tub. When it was at a comfortable level, she stepped in gingerly, gripping the sides tightly to avoid sliding. It took far too long to lower herself until she was fully emersed in the warm water, but every move was agonizing.

Freyda used the hand of her unbattered side to splash water on her skin. The water instantly began to turn pink as her blood was washed from her flesh. Without emptying and refilling the tub, she wouldn't get fully clean, but she merely wanted to remove as much as she could before stepping out.

The towel was like sandpaper against her skin, but she pushed through, gritting her teeth against a fresh wave of pain. So many cuts. So many bruises. So many scars to come if she survived.

There was no point in attempting to drag a brush through her hair. Much of it had been cut crudely last night until the length of her formerly waist long hair now barely hung below her shoulders. She was not a vain woman. She had never been in love with her hair as it was always braided back like the Elves. But since she'd begun to search for herself, search for who she was outside of the rule of Emperor Ehmile, search for who she was as a human, she'd discovered she quite enjoyed the feeling of her hair lifting and blowing in the breeze.

It was only hair. It would grow back. There was no reason to dwell on something so small.

Then a thought occurred – would Ahrkyn still find her alluring with permanent scars along her face and body? Would he still see her as the woman he Claimed if she no longer resembled that same woman?

Yes. He would. He cared for her not for the way she looked but for the woman she was inside. He'd said she was beautiful. And she knew he meant that in every way, not merely for the way her face looked or the curves of her body.

She hadn't finished eating again last night. And she had no appetite today. Much longer of this and she might very well be lacking the curves he'd enjoyed running his hands across…days ago. Two days ago? Three?

Time was lost to her mind. Thoughts were muddled from the many injuries, from the blows to her face and head.

She needed a healer, but refused to request one. That would bring Emperor Ehmile far too much pleasure. It would show weakness. And she would not let him break her spirit.

Since he enjoyed tearing her clothing, she decided on one of the more opulent gowns in her wardrobe. It was one she wore when rulers visited or when the Emperor would host balls or parties in an attempt to win favor with one group or another.

Let him tear this frock. She cared nothing for it or any other gown in her closet. If she thought it safe, she would simply leave the room naked and let them all view the damage done to her while so many had laughed and cheered.

How many of her stepfather's employees would take it as an invitation? How many would attempt to touch her?

Not worth the risk.

Instead of pulling the dress over her head, she stepped into the neck hole and struggled to get it up over her body using one hand. So much pain. The slightest movement made her want to cry.

Once she got her arm through the first sleeve, she reached down and grabbed a handful of her blanket, sliding it between her teeth. She feared if she clamped her teeth together too hard, she might very well crack them.

Tears welled as she slid her arm on the side with the battered ribs into the hole, biting down on the blanket, until another cry of pain escaped her. She couldn't hold it in.

But she got the dress on, damn it.

Now, she had to figure out how to tie the laces up the front with one hand. Were this any normal day before she'd escaped, a servant would have been in her room the moment the sun rose. They would have chosen her outfit, forced her into a chair to wait while her hair was braided, then immediately made her bed and tidied her room.

She hadn't seen a single servant since arriving back in the Palace. At all. Where were the staff that had dutifully served Ehmile and her mother? Were they banished from the house? And for what reason?

The Emperor couldn't possibly fear one of them would help her or defend her in any way. They feared him as much as the rest of

Mhahzin. Perhaps it was so there were less witnesses to her treatment. He could merely say the *Vhtir* Elves had abused her and that the *Ihllr* had rescued her from the savages.

Oh no. That was exactly what her stepfather had planned. Why else would he banish the servants? Why risk marring her looks when he was gifting her to a stranger? This way, he would look like a hero. He had saved his sweet stepdaughter from the monsters just in time for her to find a mate.

Bull shit. Unless he cut her tongue from her mouth, she would ensure all knew the truth. Any who gave her a chance to speak would know exactly who the real monster was. They would know of her treatment at the Emperor's hands, they would know she was taken from her true mate. They would know she was Claimed and carried the brands of Prince Ahrkyn.

She could no longer square her shoulders without straining her ribs, but she sure as hell could keep her head high. Putting as much defiance as she could in her eyes, she limped to the door and pulled it open.

Two new guards stood on either side of the frame. Neither would meet her gaze.

"What does the Emperor have in store for me today?" she asked.

Neither answered.

Her nostrils flared as she inhaled deeply and forced her feet forward. Perhaps she would saunter right up to the gates, push them open, and make her way to Ahdlai. What could anyone do? Beat her more?

Yet, she knew damned well no one would allow her to get that far. She would be surprised if she would be allowed to leave the Palace and step onto the lawn.

Already she missed the fresh air of Ahdlai. She missed the sounds of children's laughter, the smiles she'd received from the residents when she passed.

She missed Ahrkyn. She missed him so badly her heart hurt.

Or was that his?

Since she'd opened their connection, she was having a hard time shutting it back down. When she wasn't solely focused on her own pain, she could feel his fear, his rage, his anxiety. She could also feel his determination.

He was planning to come for her. Her Prince was making plans to save the Princess from the tower. She was officially a character in one of her many favorite fairy tales.

Except she couldn't remember any of the Princesses being beaten unconscious. While the stepmother was cruel in Cinderella, she had never left boot shaped bruises along her ribs or abdomen.

Guards were once again spread throughout the Palace. Most would not look in her direction. Those who did glared, they leered at the exposed flesh of her breasts, or outright laughed at her injuries.

Though her vision was distorted, she tried to mentally catalogue every single asshole who looked anything less than sympathetic. They would be punished. Perhaps not at her hand, but someday, someone would punish them for what they had done to her, for what they'd allowed.

Chapter Twenty-Two

Members of the Royal guard along with residents of Ahdlai had volunteered to seek the Shape Shifters along with getting word out that the Prince sought the aid of Brizio the ogre and his witch friends.

But there was no guarantee any would be found nor was there a guarantee they would be willing to once more risk their lives for the Prince or those who held no relevance to their own survival. This wasn't their fight.

It didn't mean Ahrkyn hadn't prayed to Mother Universe fervently from the moment messengers were sent out.

He hated waiting. Hated waiting to get to his mate. The link was open, but she continuously attempted to shut him out. He'd felt her pain, though, had felt it as though it were his own.

His beautiful mate was in agony. And he planned to destroy every single person who'd had anything to do with her pain. He would cut down any fucker who'd laid a finger on her, any who'd watched on and done nothing to help her, to protect her.

The guards of Mhahzin had attempted to kill Rhamzin. He was the only person Freyda had in the southern territory, the only person who would have put himself between the Princess and danger.

And now she had no one.

A new wave of anger pierced his heart, but this wave was aimed at himself. He shouldn't have let her go. Or at least should have demanded he and a contingency of his own guard join her. It might have been seen as an act of war by the Emperor, but then his beautiful human mate wouldn't be suffering so terribly.

Human. She was human. She couldn't take the level of abuse an Elf could, wouldn't heal as quickly as Valdis had after her Clan had been attacked and she'd fought to her near death trying to protect them.

She might not survive the abuse she was enduring. Especially not if they had to wait much longer to get to her.

"Fuck!" he bellowed as he paced the living area.

The Palace and the grounds were a hive of action. Like ants scurrying about preparing for winter. Even the residents who'd had no training in battle offered their services. They'd offered to aid him in retrieving their Princess, offered their service to increase Ahdlai's numbers.

How long did they have before those who would join the twisted fucked up games set up by the Emperor arrived? How long before there were hundreds against the dozens of *Vhtir*?

They couldn't wait much longer, not if they had any chance of getting Freyda out without a large number of casualties.

Any casualty was too many, but Ahrkyn would gladly lay down his own life if it would end his mate's suffering and get her safely behind Ahdlai's walls. He knew, should he fall, his people would keep her safe, his guard would keep her safe, his father and his friends would protect her.

"You must calm yourself," the Queen said as she entered the room.

Ahrkyn glanced at her, then did a double take. "You are not joining the battle," he demanded.

She wore breeches, a tunic, and the leather battle armor worn by the guard. A sword was strapped to her back, a long dagger sheathed in a belt around her waist.

"I don't believe you're in any place to give your Queen orders," she said.

She *was* his Queen. And his adoptive mother. Both were reason enough for him to protest her presence in Mhahzin.

His father entered the room, dressed as a member of Ahdlai's guards, armed much like his mate.

"You two cannot go. If I fall, you are able to have other sons. Should either of you fall—"

"Then you and your mate shall take our place on the throne."

"The townspeople won't accept this."

The King waved off his comment with a *tsk* of his tongue. "The townspeople do not rule the land. I do. Freyda is my daughter now. And I will protect my family at all costs."

"We are both experienced fighters. We cannot ask our people to risk their own lives if we're not willing to do the same."

Ahrkyn wasn't one to cry, couldn't remember the last time emotion clogged his throat the way it did now. As tears burned his eyes, he didn't bother to stop their escape over his lashes.

These two people, the rulers and leaders of the northern region of the area, would never ask more of their people than they themselves were willing to give. He attributed his need to protect the people of Ahdlai to the way the King and Queen led their lives, to their bravery and fairness.

His mother closed the space between them and cupped her son's face in her hands.

Even dressed as a warrior, Ahrkyn was taken back by her surreal beauty. She was of mixed lineage, her father of Fae blood, her mother of both human and Elven blood. She was born in a time before the nuclear war, before the chance of non-humans breeding among themselves was made impossible by the poisons that permeated the air after the war.

Her mixed lineage would aid her in fighting as it had when she'd helped protect the people of Ahdlai who'd huddled in the basement of the Palace when they'd been attacked by the *Ihllr*.

"I don't wish to see the women fight," Ahrkyn said. "Whether they volunteer or not, most are human. They will be no match with the Elves and any others who might join."

"The human women will stay behind with the children. We have received word from the Shape Shifters. They don't wish to fight, but have volunteered to stay within our walls to keep those left behind safe should the *Ihllr* decide to attempt to divide and conquer. With your mother and I both away, we will need their help to keep our people safe."

He would prefer the numbers, but understood both the Shape Shifters' reluctance to enter a war that had nothing to do with them, as well as their desire to safeguard the innocent women and children of Ahdlai.

"How many do we have?"

"I'm awaiting to hear from Jhelan. He will have the final number," King Nhaeem said.

And then they were back to waiting.

As each minute stretched on, Ahrkyn began to wonder if the mere passage of time could drive one mad, because he felt as though he were losing his mind.

No matter how hard he tried, he couldn't block out the pain radiating from Freyda through their bond. It settled in his heart, darkened his heart, darkened his mind until all he could see was blood. All he could see was the blood he would shed the moment he crossed through the walls surrounding the Palace of Emperor Ehmile.

"Eighty-seven," Jhelan called through the house the moment he stepped through the door. "Eighty-seven guard, and forty-eight residents. Only six humans."

"The humans won't fare well," Ihsander said as he followed Jhelan inside.

"They've demanded they join. The men are strapping for humans. They're adept enough at wielding a sword and are quite talented with bow and arrow. We might use them as a second wave, or perhaps they could simply shoot arrows from a distance so they won't have to fight beings with preternatural speed and strength in hand-to-hand combat," Jhelan said.

One hundred thirty-five soldiers. One hundred thirty-seven counting his parents.

Was it enough? It had to be. Had to be enough to at least get Freyda to safety, to get her out of the clutches of the Emperor.

Whether he died trying, Ahrkyn made it his personal mission to drive his sword through the heart of the man who had caused so much suffering through the years, the man who had allowed Freyda to be beaten, the man who dared take his beautiful Princess out of his arms.

He was coming. Freyda could feel her mate, could feel Ahrkyn's determination, could practically see him pacing the living room. She focused harder, wondering if she could hear through his ears or glean his thoughts. Apparently, the bond wasn't that strong.

She had done her best to stay as far from the Emperor as possible. When she was invited to breakfast, she sat silently at the foot of the table and kept her eyes on her plate. The time for insubordination was far past. Much more of his beatings and there would be nothing for Ahrkyn to find but a bloody mess of torn flesh and broken bones.

The moment she finished her meal, she behaved as the obedient stepdaughter and asked to be excused.

That had amused Ehmile. He truly believed he'd broken her. Little did he know she was simply biding her time until her Prince arrived and carried her away from this place. She hoped to turn in the saddle and see flames licking the sky as the Palace burned to the ground. Preferably with the Emperor still inside and alive, his skin being melted and singed from his bones.

Such dark thoughts. She had never been one to relish violence, but if anyone deserved to be destroyed, it was her stepfather.

No. He was no longer her stepfather. Her mother was dead. He was merely another power-hungry tyrant. A monster in opulent clothing inside a building she once thought beautiful.

Now, she sat on the edge of her bed, the door to her sleeping quarters closed with a chair wedged below the knob while she faced the window. Should anyone truly wish to enter her private room, they could easily break through the door, but it gave her a modicum of peace knowing she would have a moment or two to seek something she could use as a weapon.

She remained dressed, having changed from the gown she'd worn to dinner into another makeshift tunic with thick tights. She didn't know when Ahrkyn would arrive, whether it would be today or the next. But she wanted to be ready, would be ready. She would sleep in her shoes if need be, as long as she was able to walk through the front doors on her.

If she continued to openly defy Ehmile, if she continued to be rebel against any order he gave, she might very well be carried out.

Part of her didn't fear the Emperor would beat her to death. After all, what could he offer as a prize in return for more power from his allies? What could he offer to entice others to bring him humans, to pay more taxes in the form of food, of livestock, of linens and other riches?

Apparently, he didn't fear her appearance would turn the competitors away.

Her ankle was the size of a large orange and blackened with bruise. It throbbed along with her heartbeat as did the many other cuts and bruises. Yet she focused her sole attention on Ahrkyn, on their bond, on the brands that allowed her to stay so closely connected to him.

She pulled strength from feeling him, pretended he was sitting beside her with an arm draped around her shoulders, pretended they were back home in the room they had only shared one night.

How had she come to care so much for someone she barely knew? Freyda was fully aware that the Bond blessed by the Mother was far more intense and far more encompassing than simple love. Not that love of any kind was simple. Far from it.

But what she felt for Ahrkyn…how she felt being separated from him…

She felt as though her heart and soul had been ripped in two, as though she wouldn't be whole again until they were together once more.

Since the Emperor didn't deem it necessary to make any information known to her, Freyda was unaware of when the visitors would arrive in Mhahzin. She prayed it would be after her family came for her. Otherwise, they could be outnumbered and overrun.

If she could get outside of the walls, she could try her best to make her way closer to the border separating the regions. That would prevent a war between the two territories; it would prevent bloodshed.

Although, she couldn't find an ounce of pity for any guard's loss of life here.

That wasn't entirely true. While no one stopped the Emperor nor aided her in her daily tasks when it was more than obvious she was in pain and struggled to lift her left arm, not all had snickered as she'd been abused. Some held sorrow in their eyes. Others even looked angry.

But they were the minority. It was a shame they, too, would die should Ahdlai round up enough to make an impact on the numbers here in Mhahzin.

Or…could there be a possibility those who fought for the Emperor merely did it out of fear for their own families, for the children they fathered, for the children being raised by *Ihllr* Elves who supported their ruler?

Hope. A fresh wave of hope touched her heart. There could be help within these very walls. The men who stood outside her door might decide against fighting with their own people and instead fight with the *Vhtir*, fight to free those they loved, those they cared for, those whom were taken from their lives and raised by strangers.

Turning her head toward the door, she wondered which guards were positioned to keep watch over her. Were they sympathizers, or were they cut from the same cloth as their leader?

The only way to find out was to cross the room and open the door. She would need an excuse for leaving her room because simply wandering was too difficult. She could barely put weight on her ankle and each step sent agony tearing through her body.

She could simply say she wanted to stretch her legs. Or she could ask for a drink. If either agreed to bring her a glass of water or wine, she would know which type of man he was.

Pushing to her feet, she held on to the furniture as she passed, using each piece for support, until she finally made her way to the door.

The knob was cool under her hand as she turned it and pulled. Neither man looked down at her, simply stared straight ahead. But they did straighten from the wall as though they'd been leaning their weight in boredom or exhaustion.

"Would it be possible for one of you to escort me to the kitchen for a drink? Though it would take much less time if it could be brought to me. I know you have all grown tired of waiting for me to hobble around."

She tried adding honey to her voice, tried to find the woman who'd resided within these walls until just over a week ago.

Neither looked at her, but the man on her left nodded once and turned on his heel, walking at a fast clip toward the kitchen.

Looking up at the man on her right, she mentally dared him to look down into her face, to see the visible proof of her abuse, to examine what his leader had done to her.

But he didn't. Wouldn't. He kept his eyes straight ahead. There was no smirk, no satisfaction on his face, no leering at her body.

Could both be sympathetic? Could both be useful when her mate finally arrived to carry her away from this place? And he would definitely have to carry her. She couldn't run on her own two feet.

Her horse. What had they done with her beautiful mare after she'd arrived? She hoped they had simply led her to the stable or released her into the fields with the rest of the horses. She refused to let her imagination run amuck, otherwise she would obsess over whether the Emperor had had her beautiful creature killed out of spite.

Freyda stayed in her doorway, patiently waiting for the guard to return with her drink. When he did, he handed her the glass and actually looked into her eyes.

She stood still, letting him examine her face, letting him run his eyes over the parts of her arms that were exposed, let his eyes trail to the foot she could not fully lower to the ground. And she saw something flash through his eyes. He did not agree with what had happened to her, with what had been done to her.

When Ahrkyn came, when Jhelan and Ihsander and Ahdeben and the rest of the warriors came, she would ensure he would not be killed. She would beg for his life, attempt to talk him into walking away from Mhahzin.

The guardsman finally peeled his eyes from Freyda, a frown forming a deep furrow between his brows, and retook his place as sentry beside the door.

"Thank you," she said quietly, stepping back into her room and closing the door softly behind her.

If nothing else, she might have at least one ally within the walls. When Ahrkyn arrived, perhaps he would help keep her safe until her mate could get to her side. Perhaps he would keep the others from rushing into her room and sweeping her away or killing her outright.

So many unknowns. So many fears. But she found herself not fearing for herself or her own life but for Ahrkyn's. His people would follow him here, they would fight by his side to get Freyda free, and they could be killed. All of them could be severely wounded or slaughtered.

Because of her. Because she was born human. Because she was born a woman. Because her mother had been given no choice but to accept the invitation to live within the Palace to ensure her daughter was housed and fed and warm every night.

Her heart began to race. Yet she was still standing near the door. She hadn't moved since closing it.

Not her heartbeat. Not *her* heart racing. Ahrkyn's. He was coming. Her mate was coming.

She had promised to return to him. And he was going to make damned sure she was able to keep that promise.

Chapter Twenty-Three

Ahrkyn glanced over his shoulder. There were men as far as he could see, their faces set in determination and anger.

He had been shocked by the willingness of so many residents to fight with the trained Royal guard. They wanted to protect their Princess. They wanted to get her home. She was part of their family now, part of Ahdlai.

The struggle to avoid jamming his heel into the ribs of the horse was overwhelming, but he stayed in pace with the others, Jhelan on his left, the King on his right.

While Ahrkyn still wasn't keen on the fact the Queen had joined the cavalry, she had at least acquiesced to his request to stay toward the middle where she was surrounded by well-trained fighters.

The humans stayed in the rear, walking behind the horses with their quivers across their backs, their bows hanging over their shoulders.

Six humans. It was far more dangerous for them, but as long as they listened to those trained in battle and avoided running headfirst into the fray, they should survive the coming battle. They could aim their arrows and let them fly, hitting the enemy from afar.

The Shape Shifters had arrived before dawn and currently surrounded the walls of Ahdlai proper, some staying inside the walls in case any should infiltrate and attempt to kill those who'd been left behind.

Never in Ahrkyn's time had the whole of the King's army been sent out at once. Never in Ahrkyn's life had the people of Ahdlai been left in such a vulnerable and precarious situation.

But none had voiced their protests. All were in support of retrieving Princess Freyda and bringing her home.

Once Ahrkyn had her in his arms, he would spend the next few months smothering her in kisses, smothering her with his love and affection. He would dote on her hand and foot, treat her like the Princess she was, give her anything her heart desired. He would do anything and everything to make her happy for the rest of her life.

If they were too late, he would strike down as many of the enemy as he could before following her into the next plane.

"How long do you think before the Emperor's scouts spot us?" Ihsander asked.

"I would be surprised if word of our approach hasn't yet reached his ears," Jhelan said.

It would have been far better if the Mhahzin army was unaware of the numbers approaching their gates. But whether the *Vhtir* was outnumbered or not, they had something the *Ihllr* did not – loyalty. They were loyal to each other. Those riding behind the Prince were loyal to the Royal family and loyal to Princess Freyda.

The guards might not have had a choice as to whether to ride into battle, but the townspeople did and had demanded they join the fight. Freyda was now one of them. She was the mate of the Prince, thus a member of the Royal family. She was a member of Ahdlai, part of *their* family now, as well.

They could get lucky. Maybe Emperor Ehmile would send some of his men out to attempt to stop them. They would be easily bested, and then there would be less to fight within the walls of Mhahzin proper.

That was the best-case scenario.

No. The best-case scenario was a complete and total surrender. The best case was getting to his mate's side with no struggle and bringing her back home where she belonged.

Yet he knew without a doubt the *Ihllr* would not lay down their swords at the sight of the *Vhtir*. They would be risking their necks if they did, although the death penalty would not come at King Nhaeem's orders. His father was a fair man and would allow any who surrendered to walk away free.

Perhaps not free. They would need to speak with Freyda first, discover which, if any, of the guards had caused the pain he still felt radiating from her through their bond.

She no longer attempted to block him out. Either she was aware he was on his way, or was too weak to achieve that particular task.

Valdis had been broken and weak when she'd come to stay with Jhelan. She had since grown stronger and was a revered member of the guard. Specifically, she was the personal guard of Queen Ahlmeda and currently rode her horse directly beside the Queen.

Ahrkyn wondered whether Valdis and Jhelan had argued about whether she should join them or not. But there was no way the Fae halfling would stay behind if her Queen was riding into battle.

Why were they moving so slowly? There was no reason they couldn't urge their horses to at least trot. Or canter. That would be so much faster; he would get to Freyda so much faster.

He knew why. Of course, he knew why – in hopes of keeping their presence secret if the scouts hadn't yet spotted them. But it didn't make it any easier or make him feel any better.

They had at least another hour before the peaks of the Palace would come into view. Another hour. Might as well have been a lifetime.

Focusing on his brands, he sought Freyda. He could practically see her location through her eyes, though it was more a feeling than true sight. She was alone in a room. Her sleeping quarters?

She was currently safe and away from the Emperor. And she was both exhilarated and scared. She knew Ahrkyn was coming for her, knew she would soon be free of Mhahzin, but she was scared.

For him? That he wouldn't arrive in time? He didn't detect any spikes in that fear, simply a steady thrum coming from her heart directly into his.

"Scout!" Ahdeben shouted, then ordered his horse forward at a full run.

Ihsander and another guard followed behind.

The scout was on foot. Foolish. Either the Mhahzin member was new to his role or the Emperor hadn't deemed him important enough to grant him a horse with which to ride away if or when he was spotted.

The scout didn't run. He merely lifted both hands into the air, showing he wasn't armed, and waited as the three *Vhtir* of Ahdlai approached.

There was some distance between where the four men spoke and Ahrkyn. He couldn't fully make out the words. But when he caught Freyda's name on the breeze, he yelled and nudged his heel into his horse's side, pushing his horse to catch up to where the men spoke.

"He claims he is here to warn us," Ihsander said.

Ahrkyn looked to his friend, waiting for confirmation. Ihsander's gift could detect lie from truth. When Ihsander nodded, the Prince turned his attention to the man.

"You would risk the wrath of your ruler to warn the enemy?" Ahrkyn asked.

"I have no enemies. Your quarrel has nothing to do with myself or my family. We simply want to live our lives."

This man was not dressed as the guard of Mhahzin. He was a resident of the town proper.

"Where is the Princess? Is she well?" Ahrkyn asked, fighting back the emotion raging through his system. He was the Prince of Ahdlai and must behave as such.

"I have not seen her since she arrived. But stories have circulated. There has been talk of abuse at the Emperor's hand. I saw her in the window this morning. She was definitely injured, but was standing on her own two feet. She still lives and is whole."

A rage he had never experienced burned through his veins. His magic swelled in a way he had never felt, seeking someone or something to punish.

Ahrkyn had only been granted minor telekinetic abilities, but at that moment he felt as though he could lift a mountain with a mere thought.

"How quickly can you return to the town?" King Nhaeem asked.

"As quickly as my feet can take me," the stranger replied.

"You should warn those whom you trust, those whom have no desire to fight beside the *Ihllr*, that war is coming. Warn them to flee into the woods or seek shelter. We have every intention of punishing any who aided in the imprisonment and abuse of my daughter."

His daughter. Not his daughter-in-law, but his daughter. She was truly part of the family after such a short amount of time. Any who met Freyda loved her as Ahrkyn did. It was hard not to love someone with such a pure, kind heart.

"A horse will make the trip faster," the townsman said, averting his eyes in respect as he spoke to the King of Ahdlai.

Ahrkyn's father looked over his shoulder and nodded his head.

A member of the guard turned and headed toward the back of the many rows of people. He would request a horse from one of the townspeople since they were the last resort and the last line of defense should any of the highly trained guard fall.

Minutes later, the guard returned, his hand wrapped around the lead, urging the horse forward to where the Mhahzin townsman waited.

"Make haste. I'm unsure of how much longer I can keep my son contained. We will give you as much a headstart as possible, but by the glow in Prince Ahrkyn's eyes, I believe we will be racing forward shortly."

There was a mixture of warning and amusement in the King's voice. Warning, because it was evident Ahrkyn was quickly losing patience. He needed to get to his mate. He needed to draw blood from the Emperor and any who aided in his mate's imprisonment. The amusement was more for the way that even the horse below the Prince was antsy, stamping its feet and snorting as it waited to be pushed forward at a full sprint.

He wasn't naïve. Ahrkyn knew the humor in his father's voice was forced, faked for the benefit of the townsman. Because whether the man knew or not, hell was riding directly toward his home and to the walls surrounding the Palace.

Freyda's heart began to race. It beat in time with Ahrkyn's. He was near. He was coming for her. And she would smile as he cut down anyone who got in his way.

She was living the nightmare version of one of her many novels and fairy tales, waiting for her Prince to save her from the abusive grip of her mother's widower, waiting to escape the future he had planned out for her.

The fear the travelers and those invited to participate in the games would arrive before her mate had caused ice to slice through her veins in the time she'd been in the Palace. How long had she been there? A day? Two? Three?

She'd lost track, and her thoughts, at times, were fuzzy. She couldn't help but fear the Emperor had done damage to her brain during the many beatings.

The moment she was back in Ahdlai she would demand her training begin immediately. She would learn to swing a sword, learn to pull the string of a bow and let an arrow fly to hit its intended target. She would learn to defend herself and to inflict enough damage to an enemy so that she could escape even the strongest non-human.

For now, all she could do was wait.

She was still dressed in something that would make it easier for her to limp outside and climb atop the back of a horse. Her shoes were strapped securely to her feet. She'd located small things she could use as weapons should anyone rush through the door at the first announcement of the *Vhtir's* approach and had them stashed in easy to reach places.

While she'd been determined to find her own style separate from the Elves, she had carefully braided her hair back, taking care to avoid pulling on the bruised and abraded spots on her scalp, so that her hair was out of her face and out of the way. Just in case.

There were so many things that could go wrong, but she needed to do what she could to aid the *Vhtir* in Freyda's escape. She couldn't fight, but she could help make her rescue a little easier by being ready in the only ways she could. And that included ensuring her clothing and hair wouldn't hinder her vision if she needed to fight for her life while waiting for help.

The two guards on the other side of her door seemed partially blind to her situation, but not fully indifferent. When the one who'd brought her water had gotten a good look at her face, obvious disapproval had been right there in his eyes.

They could be of help to her. She knew they wouldn't be able to fight more than their share of their fellow guardsmen, but perhaps they could help hold off any who would drag her away when the *Vhtir* breached the walls around the Palace.

How long must she wait? The beatings were bad, her body ached everywhere, but her heart was what was causing her the most agony.

She missed her mate. She missed Ahrkyn so badly it was hard to breathe.

They'd had one night together, one night of getting to know each other's bodies, one night of waking in each other's arms. She wanted more.

In the short time they'd been apart, she'd realized she wanted nothing more than to stay by his side night and day. She wanted to carry as many children as he wanted to raise. She wanted to feel his child growing inside of her, to look into the baby's eyes when he or she was born and look for the similarities of each parent.

All those years Freyda had rebelled against the thought of carrying an heir for an Elf and now she couldn't think of anything that would bring her more joy.

But she had to get out of Mhahzin first. Had to get far from the *Ihllr* Elves who rejoiced in the mistreatment of women, of the Emperor who treated any below him as nothing more than shit on his shoes.

Never in her life had she cursed so much, even in her own head, but being here, being treated as she had, being away from her mate was introducing herself to a sensation she didn't think she would ever feel – hate. And it was more than simple hate. There was a rage burning through her system for all who had been treated so poorly by the *Ihllr*.

Of course, just like every group of non-humans, not all the *Ihllr* Elves were sick and evil. The two on the other side of the door to her sleeping quarters had had no hand in the way she'd been treated. They didn't look at her as though she were worth no more than the number of male heirs she could bring into the world.

Another strange sensation touched her heart. There was a hope for the people of Mhahzin, a hope that perhaps those who didn't agree with the Emperor's ways would stand with the *Vhtir* of Ahdlai to overthrow the dictator.

There was a strong sense of hope that the people of Mhahzin could one day know the happiness and freedom those in Ahdlai enjoyed and could live without the fear of their daughters being dragged away, the women could live without the fear they would one day be Claimed against their will.

Freyda had never bemoaned the fact she'd been born woman or human. But today was one such day. If she had any magic, she could help in overthrowing the current government. If she had any strength or skills, she could fight beside the people to take their power back and protect their families.

But as it was, she was, indeed, both a woman and human and had never been granted permission to do anything more than simply exist. Were it not for Rhamzin, she might never have learned to read, might never have been given the simple gift of all the stories she would lose herself in every private moment she'd had.

All she was permitted before was to look and act the part of a dutiful daughter and Princess. She was trained to behave in a certain role, never given a moment of autonomy.

Until the moment she'd raced across the border into Ahdlai. Until the moment her heart had recognized Ahrkyn as her mate. Until the moment Mother Universe had forced them together, luring them into the woods at the right moment.

Shouts erupted outside. Moving closer to the window, she peered onto the lawn of the Palace and squinted, trying to see clearly through her swollen eyes.

Townspeople were running through the gates, not toward the Palace but away. If they were afraid, why would they not beg the Emperor to allow them inside? Why run toward a perceived threat?

The guard who wandered the area and those positioned below her window looked confused as they watched people snatch their kids from the ground and run, tucking the meager belongings they had present with them under their arms.

"Why do they run?" one of the guards below her window yelled to another.

She couldn't make out the words spoken back, but whatever he'd said caused the two guards to immediately look up at her window with a mixture of fear and anger.

Anger at her? Or anger that their little game was finally being ended?

Didn't matter. And she didn't care. They could be angry all they wanted. They would soon answer for their crimes. The two below her had been in the room, chuckling with glee as the Emperor dragged her through the room by her hair, as he'd punched her, as he'd kicked her in the ribs, cracking them and shortening her breath.

She planned to stand right where she was in hopes of seeing them fall. Never had she wished the death of another living being, never had she wished harm on another person, but if they had relished in her pain, what had they done to so many others? Had they abused other women the way she'd been abused? Had they laughed as they'd taken the women against their will, laughed as the women begged for help or for their freedom?

No, she had never wished harm on another and she still didn't wish harm on any innocent person. Should she warn the guards at her door? Should she beg them to leave their posts and seek shelter elsewhere?

Would they even believe her?

If they did believe her warning, there was still a chance they would stay put. They were ordered by either the Emperor himself or by the head of the guard. Abandoning their post could cause harm to them or someone for whom they cared. They were assigned a job and were *Ihllr* Elves, but that didn't necessarily make them inherently bad people.

She would wait. She would wait until her people were through the walls. She would wait to see whether the guards outside her room rushed in to protect her or followed their ruler's decree.

She would wait until she saw her mate's face. Only then would she know how the rest of her life would look, whether she would be going home…

Or whether she would end her life at her own hands.

Chapter Twenty-Four

By the time the peeks of the Palace were visible, dozens upon dozens of regular people, both human and Elf, were fleeing through the forest. Children clung to adults, some gripped the hand of whoever they could reach. But every single person who passed the large army looked terrified.

And relieved.

The people held the misconception that Ahdlai had come to liberate them. Ahrkyn's only goal was to wrap his mate in his arms and take her home where he would spend hours holding her. Perhaps days. Months.

While he hated to leave them to the rule of someone as disgustingly vile as Emperor Ehmile, it was not his job to overthrow their ruler. If they wanted a different life, they would have to do as King Nhaeem and challenge the Emperor for his position.

Through the throng of people running away from the approaching battle, members wearing black began to appear. The *Ihllr* Elves were attempting to camouflage themselves among the townspeople, hoping for the element of surprise.

Nothing would get by Ahrkyn. Nothing could get past any of the Ahdlai soldiers. All were laser focused on their mission.

Ihsander bellowed a war cry and kicked his horse hard the same moment he pulled his sword free. As Ahrkyn had thought, others of his party had begun to notice the *Ihllr* hiding among the townspeople.

As more and more black clad warriors poured through the gates, more and more *Vhtir* rushed forward to engage them in battle.

The sounds of cries of fear and dismay mixed with battle cries and the *shicks* and *tings* of metal hitting metal as the guards of the northern and southern regions clashed, their swords glinting in the afternoon light.

While the army had left just before dawn, it had taken them hours to cross the acres separating the two Palaces. Had any scouts spotted them, the Mhahzin guards would be more than prepared.

But the lack of fighters rushing the approaching army gave Ahrkyn a spark of hope that those participating in the games had yet to arrive and Mhahzin hadn't been given notice.

The *Vhtir* had the upper hand. Success was, hopefully, guaranteed.

Still, the only thing Ahrkyn cared about was getting his mate to safety. Even after she was freed from the Palace and on her way to Ahdlai, Ahrkyn would stay behind with enough fighters to ensure no one followed her.

"Close the gates," someone from inside the wall yelled.

No. It was possible to breach the walls, to add enough force or use magic to topple the wooden gates that closed in his mate, but Ahrkyn didn't want to waste that time. That was time Freyda might not have, time for Ehmile or others to drag her away while the *Vhtir* were busy fighting or distracted with the barrier between them and their goal.

With a roar, Ahrkyn pushed his horse harder than he ever had, quickly eating up ground to the gates.

It wasn't fast enough. Already there was barely enough room for the horse to move through, let alone a hundred horses.

Something in a window two stories high caught his attention. He couldn't afford the distraction but couldn't avoid glancing up.

Freyda. Her lips spread into a wide grin…but the rest of her face was colored with bruising. Her eyes were swollen much the way Valdis's had been when Ahrkyn and the others had wandered upon her in the woods.

A fresh wave of fury overcame him. His magic swelled and exploded from him, ruffling his hair and blasting the wooden doors open so hard they splintered.

He had only been gifted with minor telekinetic abilities. But seeing his beautiful mate in such a state, his veins became engorged with the sensation of magic as it sought an outlet.

Those who had rushed toward the gate were knocked from their feet and thrown several yards away. Ahrkyn hoped his magic hadn't affected his people but didn't bother looking back.

His focus was on that window.

Freyda lifted a hand, her smile still there. How full of fear she must have been, yet she stood there patiently waiting.

Until she glanced over her shoulder.

With one more look in Ahrkyn's direction, she disappeared from his sight, moving away from the window and further into the room.

Someone was there with her, in the same room. He had to hurry, had to move faster.

His sword in hand, he lashed out at any guard who rushed toward him, who looked as though they were prepared to die for their Emperor. Any who veered out of his way were spared.

For now.

Should Ahrkyn discover later that they, too, were responsible for the pain and suffering of Freyda – or any woman – he would ensure they fell at his sword or the sword of one of his men.

Blood splashed along his arm and face as his blade bit into the throat of a guard who attempted to dislodge Ahrkyn from his horse. More blood painted his exposed skin and his battle armor as more lunged at him, grabbing at the reins. If they could turn his horse's head enough, the horse would go down, taking Ahrkyn with him.

Fighting this way was taking far too long.

With another push, he thrust his magic forward, with only the briefest thought that there might still be innocent townspeople within the walls. Dozens of men were thrown from him, landing hard on their asses, their backs, some hitting trees, the wall, or even the bricks of the Palace.

The sounds of bones crunching were satisfying. It was a sound he was determined to hear come from the Emperor's body. He would punish the fucker, inflict as much damage as he'd done to Freyda. And then he would drive the tip of his sword through the fucker's heart.

Ahrkyn was now only twenty feet or so from the Palace doors. So close to his mate, so close to the other half of his heart, his soul.

Throwing a leg over his horse, he pulled on the rein to slow the beast down only enough for him to keep his balance when his feet hit the ground.

And then he ran, pushing his own legs as hard as he'd pushed his horse's. Tomorrow, his joints would ache. His muscles would burn. All he felt now was determination. Fear. Anger.

Sorrow.

He should have protected Freyda better. No matter how much the King and Jhelan had warned him, he should have joined the Princess as she'd traveled to Mhahzin. He should have demanded she be escorted by his own army.

All he could do was hope and pray to the Mother that she would forgive him. All he could do was hope and pray he got to her before whoever was in that room with her laid a finger on her.

She had wanted to train. She had wanted to learn to fight. She'd never gotten the chance.

The second she was home safe and healed up, he would demand his best fighters teach her everything they knew so she could easily best the largest Elf.

He had to get her home first.

Several Mhahzin guards poured through the doors of the Palace. Raising his sword, he skidded to a halt when three grabbed their heads and bellowed in pain. Blood poured from their noses, ears, even their eyes before they collapsed to the ground in lifeless heaps.

Ahrkyn took a second to glance over his shoulder. Ahdeben, Ihsander, and Jhelan were right on his heels. The King was with the rest of the army, fighting any who dared challenge them as they crossed onto the lawn of the Palace.

An animalist roar broke through the sounds of battle. Moments later, a group of *Ihllr* fighters were knocked to their feet as the large ogre, Brizio, used his body as a ram and knocked them over.

There were enough *Vhtir* fighters to ensure the King didn't fall. Valdis would keep the Queen safe. Brizio alone could keep the Royal couple safe with his mere size. Ahrkyn's focus could be only on Freyda, lest the distraction of fear over his parents cause him to fail her. Again.

Ihsander made it to Ahrkyn's side, swinging his sword with such ferocity and skill, the light glinting off the sharpened edge, slicing easily through *Ihllr* flesh. Both men's skin was painted with blood.

Raising a hand, Ahrkyn wiped it from his eyes, dragged a hand across his mouth to prevent the coppery liquid from passing through his lips.

When he kissed his mate, he wanted his face clean of the enemy's blood. He refused to sully her in any way, except when he crushed her body to his to ensure himself she was safe and in one piece.

She had been standing in the window. Freyda had been standing there watching him enter the gates. She'd smiled happily at him, had waved. She was whole, at least from what he could see from the waist up.

But she'd walked away unaided. No one had appeared behind her to drag or carry her away.

Ahrkyn refused to believe every single *Ihllr* Elf came from the same stock as Emperor Ehmile. He refused to believe all relished in pain and violence. And hoped, as he cut down another who attempted to stop his advance, that whoever had entered the room would treat her as well as Rhamzin had through the years. He hoped the person was friend rather than foe.

She had felt Ahrkyn long before he'd arrived, but seeing him with her own two eyes sent a wave of relief and joy coursing through Freyda. She knew he wouldn't allow this atrocity; knew he would never sit back while Ehmile attempted to sell her off.

Because he loved her. Neither had said the words, but she felt it through their brands the moment their eyes met through the glass. The moment his eyes had locked with hers, his brightened to a brilliant silver, the glow nearly as bright as the sun.

And anger reddened his face.

His lips peeled back from his teeth as he rushed forward, cutting down anyone who attempted to stop him.

As she focused on her mate below, the door behind her slammed open.

Glancing over her shoulder, she was conflicted – it was the guard who'd brought her a glass of water. She didn't know whether he would help her or not. Would he risk his own life for someone who meant nothing to him?

"The Emperor wants you moved," he stated as he stepped further into the room.

He refused to make eye contact with her, refused to look into her face.

"Moved to where?" she asked.

With one more glance at the man who held her heart, she stepped away from the window and toward one of the more effective weapons she'd stashed. It was nothing more than a heavy vase she planned to smash over the head of the first person who reached for her. It might not do much damage, but it was better than ineffectively swinging her fists at someone. She'd never raised a hand in self-defense or anger and had zero idea how to inflict enough injury with her own body to gain her own freedom.

But she sure as hell would try. She would fight for as long as needed for Ahrkyn or one of his soldiers to get to her side.

Truth was, she wasn't sure how long she could possibly hold off this guard, even if she knew how to fight. She was weak from lack of food over the past few days and her body was battered and bruised. Each breath was agonizing from her damaged ribs and she could still barely put any weight on her ankle.

Yet, she was determined to do what was necessary to buy the *Vhtir* the time they needed to get to her.

"Moved from here," the guard said, still unwilling to lift his eyes to her face.

"You know this is wrong," she said.

His eyes remained on a spot near her feet.

"You know what will happen to me if you move me. You know what will happen to me if the Emperor's wishes are granted. What if I were your daughter? Or your sister?"

That finally got his attention.

Looking her directly in the eye, a flash of light entered his irises. Not quite as bright as Ahrkyn's, but enough for her to know she'd hit a nerve. Hopefully, she'd hit the nerve that would force him to the do the right thing and not the nerve that angered him into harming her.

"You know nothing of my family," he said, his voice deep and menacing.

Well, damn. It appeared she'd angered him. But she could still attempt to use his emotions to benefit her.

"You're right. I don't. But you don't appear to be the kind of person who would stand by while someone you loved was beaten and raped."

"The Emperor raped you?" he asked, his brows slamming together.

"No. But if he forces me to allow another man to Claim me, what do you think will happen?" She held up her arm, showing him the marks that would appear as silver lines to him. "I have a Fated Mate, someone the Mother sent to me. I am already Claimed. My mate has my heart and soul. I would never willingly lie with another man. Do you really think my protests would be heard? Do you really think whoever the Emperor gifts me to will accept my reluctance and give me the freedom I deserve?"

He said nothing but a muscle ticked in his cheek. His eyes darted from her face to the window where the sounds of an ongoing battle raged on.

"He'll send others. If I walk away, he'll send other guards. He's already prepared to kill you rather than allow the *Vhtir* to take you again."

That piece of news squeezed her heart. The man who had been the closest thing to a father her whole life would rather her dead than with someone he deemed the enemy. If she hadn't known true hate before, she sure as hell did now.

"Are there others in the hall?" she whispered.

If they were close enough, they would still hear her due to their preternatural hearing. But she had to do something. She couldn't stand there and either let one of the Emperor's minions drag her away or kill her.

He nodded once.

"How many?" she whispered again.

He glanced over his shoulder than back at her. "Too many."

Damn it. Time. She needed time. Just enough to allow Ahrkyn and his soldiers to breach the Palace doors and make it to her room.

But what if there weren't enough with him? What if there weren't enough *Vhtir* warriors to defeat the *Ihllr?* She'd seen a large group of people trying to get through the gates but had no idea how many were here in Mhahzin. Nothing was ever revealed to her when she lived within the territory, and they sure as hell wouldn't tell her now that she was mated to the Prince of Ahdlai.

Too many. In other words, too many for this lone man to fight to protect her. And all she had in the form of weapons were things like the vase, an umbrella, and other useless items.

Again, she couldn't do *nothing*. They would win if she tried to fight them. She was fully aware of that. But she would rather die trying than lie down and curl into the fetal position.

"I won't go," she said, taking a step closer to the vase.

This man had done nothing to her, not directly, but if he was willing to stand by and allow another to brutalize her, he was just as much her enemy, just as bad as the others. Silence and obedience to a dictator was as bad as the actions taken by the guard who enjoyed making others suffer.

That muscle jumped in his cheek again. Glancing over his shoulder, he turned and studied her for a few more moments. Then seemed to make up his mind.

Crossing the room, he quickly closed the door and began to move furniture in front of it. That would only slow the other *Ihllr* guards for so long.

"Does the bathroom lock?" he asked.

She shook her head, unable to form words. He was going to help her. And he would probably be killed as a result of his actions.

Perhaps she had hit a raw nerve when she'd mentioned something like this happening to his mother or sister. Perhaps he'd had no choice but to stand by idly as some asshole Claimed his sister against her will, forced her to carry his heir, then ripped the child from her arms to be raised by strangers.

Whatever his reasoning, she was thankful she had at least one ally within these walls.

Heavy thuds rattled the door. Freyda grabbed the vase and held it in both hands like a sword.

"What do you plan to do with that?" the guard asked, his lips twitching at the corners.

At least *he* could find a little humor in the moment because she sure as hell couldn't find any.

"Smash it over someone's head," she said, raising it high above her head and pretending she was hitting someone.

He shook his head then leaned his weight against the heavy dresser as the door began to rattle and move with each loud thud. Reaching down, he pulled a dagger from its sheath and held out his arm.

When she didn't move, he turned his attention to her. "Take it. It'll do a lot more damage than the vase."

Staring wide-eyed at the sharp knife, she shook her head side to side slowly. "I don't know how to use it."

The guard thrust his arm forward. "Use the pointy end to stick the closest person to you. Steer clear of the ribs; you'll end up hitting bone and cutting yourself. Aim for the throat or stomach."

Bile churned in her stomach and rose up her throat at the thought of actually stabbing someone. Of killing someone.

But if she had to wield it to defend herself, that meant the person on the other end meant her harm. They weren't some innocent victim. She wouldn't be doing as so many *Ihllr* had and slaughtering an innocent person.

Squaring her shoulders, she limped to where the guard physically held the door shut, and took the proffered weapon.

She had to ignore the pain in her ribs. Freyda refused to allow the pain in any part of her body to hinder her from staying right here in this room and alive long enough for Ahrkyn and the *Vhtir* to make it to her.

"Should I stay here?" she asked, standing only feet from the guard.

"The bathroom would be better. Is there something in there you can use to block the door?"

Freyda pictured the bathroom in her mind. There was a chair she used to a sit at the vanity where she used to wait as the servants braided her hair, but didn't think it was tall enough to wedge under the knob and definitely wasn't heavy enough to create any form of a barrier.

"I don't think so," she said.

Nerves began to burn her stomach. It felt as though hours had passed since she'd looked through the window and spotted her mate. She was ready for this day to come to an end. She was ready to be in her new home, wrapped in Ahrkyn's arms, her head against his chest.

She'd been in Ahdlai barely a few days over a week. Not even a full two weeks. Yet the northern territory and the Palace felt more like home than Mhahzin ever had. The King and Queen felt more like parents to her than her now deceased mother and stepfather ever had.

A new wave of sorrow warred with the already tumultuous emotions singeing her nerves. Her mother was dead. They'd been able to say goodbye, she'd been able to finally discover why her mother had pretended Freyda hadn't existed all those years.

It was because she was doing her best to make her daughter invisible to the Emperor. She had taken beating after beating in her daughter's place, allowed him to break her body and spirit so that her daughter wouldn't have to go through the same pains.

And now she was gone.

Backing toward the bathroom, she started hard when something heavy slammed into the door hard enough to budge the guard doing his best to hold it closed.

She didn't even know his name. He was putting his life on the line for her and she didn't know his name.

Freyda opened her mouth to ask, but screeched when another crash to the door shoved the guard and the dresser a few inches.

And then screams of pain and anger erupted outside the door.

The guard used the moment of distraction – hopefully the distraction being the *Vhtir* making their way inside the Palace – to push the dresser back against the wooden door.

Could she make it into the bathroom before whoever was on the other side managed to crash through? Every step was difficult and she couldn't exactly run. She could barely shuffle.

But nothing else slammed against the door.

"What's your name?" she blurted. She might not have another chance to ask him before one or both of them were killed.

He frowned at her, then dipped his head. "Mhalaki, Your Highness."

A giggle burst from her lips. For some reason, the formality in his slight bow along with her title seemed absurd in the moment.

His frown deepened in confusion, but he said nothing else.

"Thank you, Mhalaki," she said, wiping the smile from her face. "Thank you for trying."

"Are you giving up?" he asked.

No. Not yet. There were sounds of a battle on the other side, meaning the *Ihllr* were fighting her people, her family. It wasn't too late. Not yet. She had to continue to hold on to hope that her mate would make it to her, that he and his friends would survive the fight, that all the Ahdlai people who'd risked their lives to come for her would return home and to their families.

No. She wasn't ready to give up.

Turning to face the door head on, she gripped the knife in one hand while using the other to brace herself against the dresser. She wouldn't hide in the bathroom. She wouldn't cower while Mhalaki was cut down trying to protect a Princess to which he should no longer be loyal.

She would fight by his side if need be. And she would go down fighting.

Pushing everything she hadn't had the chance to say through her bond to Ahrkyn, she prayed he could feel the love she held in her heart for him.

She prayed harder she would have the chance to say the words to his face while looking into his beautiful blue eyes.

Chapter Twenty-Five

She was right on the other side of that door. Ahrkyn could feel her, could feel his brands leading him to her, could practically see her waiting for him.

Someone was in there with her, though. Someone was barring the door. As he and his friends had rounded the corner, they'd spotted three guards taking turns slamming their bodies against the wood, doing their best to gain entry into the room.

With nothing more than a thought, Ahrkyn used his magic to push them away from the door. There was no way they would walk away without a fight and he would rather not be so distracted that one of them was able to get past him, Ahdeben, Ihsander, and Jhelan and get to Freyda.

Ahdeben didn't hesitate, simply lunged at the first fucker who'd regained his feet. With a look, the guard's brains were scrambled in his head.

Jhelan was engaged in battle with another who'd been thrown across the room but had never fallen. Ihsander shoved past Ahrkyn to engage another.

"Get the Princess," Ihsander barked out.

Turning to reach for the door, white-hot pain shot through his side as a sword bit into his flesh.

Ahrkyn turned, slamming his arm down to lock the blade in place, and swung his own weapon. The guard who'd snuck up behind him dodged his blow and yanked his sword free of Ahrkyn's body.

And then the room was filled with the sounds of metal hitting metal, the grunts of pain, and curses.

Fuck. He needed this to end. He needed to get to his mate. He needed to kill whoever was holding her in that room, lift her into his arms, and take her home. The damage he'd seen to her face would need the healer's attention. How much more damage had her body taken in the short time she'd been in the Emperor's clutches?

"Kill them all! Start with the Prince and my stepdaughter. I don't want a single member of that family alive!" the Emperor bellowed.

That was all he needed to hear.

Ahrkyn swung his sword with so much force his foe's head was detached from his neck. The head hit the floor with a dull thud and rolled until it stopped at the Emperor's feet.

His friends were faring fine. So Ahrkyn made it his official mission to end the rule of this dictator for good.

He should get Freyda to safety first, should get her home, but she would never truly be safe as long as this man and men like him walked the planet.

Stalking toward Emperor Ehmile, Ahrkyn let the rage filled smile stretch across his face as the ruler backed away, terror written all over his face.

He no longer had anyone at his back, no one protecting him, no one to stop Ahrkyn.

"You took my mate," Ahrkyn growled as he continued to stalk forward. "You hurt her."

"It wasn't me," Emperor Ehmile said, a look of feigned innocence on his face. "She is my daughter. I love her. I've only ever tried to protect her."

"You took her from me. You hurt her. You would sell her to the first person who offered you enough power."

Ehmile looked behind him as though seeking an escape route. He could easily turn and run through the halls, maybe dart into a room and barricade himself inside. But that wouldn't stop Ahrkyn. He would burn the fucking Palace down with Ehmile inside, as long as he didn't take another breath once the day was over.

The Emperor lowered his chin and glared at Ahrkyn. For a brief moment, Ahrkyn was unable to move, unable to take a step in the Emperor's direction. But then the words Rhamzin had spoken about hearing Freyda's cry of pain returned to his ears. This fucker had caused the Princess pain. He had intentionally hurt her, tried to break her, tried to make her pliable to his demands.

Ahrkyn pushed through the magic swelling around him and took another menacing step toward the Emperor, then another.

"What is it that you want? You want the Princess? I can give her to you."

That halted Ahrkyn's feet. "Give her to me?"

"Yes. Is that what you seek? I can give her to you. You may both leave with my blessing."

"*Give* her to me? She is not a fucking possession, you piece of shit."

Without warning, Ahrkyn used his magic to thrust the Emperor back, causing him to lift from the ground, fly a good ten feet where he smashed into a door frame.

Ahrkyn lunged at him, sword drawn, ready to cut his throat and watch him bleed out.

No one stopped him. No one warned him. No one urged him to spare Ehmile's life.

"Get my mate," Ahrkyn barked.

When he heard no movement behind him, he glanced over his shoulder. The guards his friends had been fighting were either down or completely neutralized. His friends watched him, breathing heavily from their fight.

"Get my fucking mate out of that room."

He would leave the decision as to whether the Emperor lived or died in her hands. It might not have been fair to make her choose, but he needed to know whether she wanted her stepfather dead. He wouldn't be seen as a monster in his beloved's eyes.

There were thumps and thuds.

"Freyda!" Jhelan yelled. "If you're blocking the door, move the item. It's Jhelan. Ahrkyn is with me. He requests your presence."

"Jhelan?" Ahrkyn heard his mate question.

Her voice sounded different, off somehow. Muddled.

"Yes. Ahrkyn is with me. You're safe. Remove the block from the door."

The point of Ahrkyn's sword pressed directly against Ehmile's throat, Ahrkyn looked over his shoulder, his heart racing as he waited to catch a glimpse of Freyda.

A man stepped out first, his chin raised, his sword sheathed and hands held high.

"He's not a threat," Freyda stated quickly. "Don't kill him. He was protecting me."

He'd heard her voice, but it was a few more moments before she stepped through the door. She walked with a heavy limp. The parts of her arms that were exposed were covered in varying shades and sizes of bruising.

She favored her right side, keeping her arm close to her side while clenching her left fist around a dagger.

Her eyes scanned the room, widening when they landed on Ahrkyn standing over the Emperor.

"Ahrkyn," she breathed with nothing short of relief.

When she attempted to hobble to his side, Ihsander lifted her, cradling her carefully against his chest, and carried her to where Ahrkyn waited. Any other time, the sight of a man touching his woman would send a possessive rage through his system. But now, all he felt was gratitude. Ihsander hated to see any woman in pain, and it would have hurt him worse being someone he knew and the mate of his friend and Prince.

Using his free arm, he dragged her to his body the moment Ihsander put her on her feet, holding her tight…

Until she cried out in pain.

Ahrkyn released her immediately and did a visual inventory of every injury on her body, at least what wasn't covered by her clothing.

"Who did this to you?" he asked, although he knew the answer.

Though her face was swollen and bruised, though her eyes were nearly swollen shut, though her lips were cracked and her speech was slurred from the damage, she raised her head, jutting her chin in defiance, and looked at the Emperor.

"Ehmile did this to me." She didn't use his formal title, didn't refer to him as her stepfather.

It was such a beautiful display of defiance and disrespect.

"Do you wish for me to spare his life?" Ahrkyn asked. "Or would you prefer I end it now?"

Freyda stared into the Emperor's eyes. "You killed my mother," she said as tears welled. "You made my life hell. You made so many lives hell. You treated everyone below you as though their very existence annoyed you. You starved the people you were meant to lead. You punished any who spoke against you."

Ehmile's lips moved, but nothing came out as he cowered against the wall, the tip of Ahrkyn's sword still pressed firmly against his flesh.

Turning her face up to Ahrkyn, she nodded and said, "Kill him," then turned her back and began to limp away.

Freyda wanted Ehmile dead, but that didn't mean she wanted to witness it. Even with everything she'd been put through, she still didn't relish the idea of violence.

Ihsander stepped forward as he had before and lifted her into his arms. He followed Jhelan through the house, Ahdeben closely behind her.

"Rhamzin?" she asked.

She hadn't seen him since she'd been brought there and feared he was dead. The other guards had insinuated as much.

"He's in Ahdlai. He will need time to heal, but he'll survive," Ihsander informed her.

Her heart was a touch lighter. He had been against her return to Mhahzin but refused to allow her to travel on her own. And had almost paid for her mistake with his life.

"Where are the King and Queen? Are they okay? What about Valdis?"

"All are well. The King is guarding those who surrendered as we speak," Ihsander said.

"Alone?"

Ahdeben snorted. "Of course not. The rest of our remaining guard is with him, as well as the ogre."

Remaining guard. They had suffered losses. They had lost members of their guard, their friends, because they came to her aid.

Guilt would remain her constant companion long after her physical wounds were healed.

Valdis glanced at the party of four as they approached, then did a double take. She said something to the Queen, who looked toward Freyda and nodded.

Valdis slid her sword into its leather sheath and ran toward Freyda. "Oh my gosh. Are you alright?"

"Yes," Freyda said at the same time Ihsander said, "no."

"They're just bumps and bruises."

"Is that why you can't walk without a limp and are favoring your right side?" Ihsander asked. There was anger evident in his voice.

He had been careful both times he'd lifted her to avoid touching her right side, instead, keeping his arms under her shoulders and under her legs.

There was no point in arguing. She was beyond the point where she could fake a lack of injuries. Besides, the moment Ahrkyn saw her undressed, he would spot the excessive swelling and bruising along her right side and know her ribs were cracked if not fully broken.

"You can put me down," she told Ihsander.

"Place her on a horse. I don't want her putting weight on that ankle," the Queen said as she led her horse to where they stood.

Not just any horse. The Queen of Ahdlai was offering her own horse for Freyda to rest. Complete opposite of Emperor Ehmile in every way. He would have never offered his horse or seat for someone in need. He barely offered enough food for those he ruled to survive.

"I couldn't possibly–"

The Queen waved her hand in the air, cutting off Freyda's protests.

"You can and you will. I can order you if it would make you feel better."

There was a slight uptick of Queen Ahlmeda's lips. Of course she would never order Freyda to do something as small as sitting atop her horse. But the slight humor lightened the tension filling the air.

That light moment lasted a mere moment.

As Ihsander hoisted Freyda onto the saddle, Ahrkyn stepped through the front door of the Palace. His skin and clothing were saturated in blood. She had no idea how much was his and how much was the enemy's. His clothing was torn in some places, indicating injuries, but, like her, she wouldn't know until they were undressed and cleaned up after the battle.

His eyes scanned the crowd, searching for Freyda. When his gaze settled on her, she was once again struck with awe at the brilliant beauty of his bright silver eyes. Even now that the fight was over, his fury hadn't waned.

Jogging down the stairs, his long legs ate the space between them. In his fist was the Emperor's ridiculously large golden crown.

"Is he dead?" she asked when he was near.

"He will never harm you again, *khaere*," he said, placing his free hand over his heart and bowing his head.

Tears she had fought for days welled in her eyes unbidden and spilled over lashes to streak in hot streams down her cheeks. They were tears of pain, tears of residual fear, tears of relief.

Her mother's murderer was dead. The man who had tortured her was gone. The man who had terrorized and imprisoned an entire region was no longer breathing the same air as Princess Freyda.

"Long live Emperor Ahrkyn!" someone shouted.

Ahrkyn's brows slammed together as he sought the owner of the voice.

A guard dressed in black with the emblem of Mhahzin knelt onto one knee, slammed a fist over his chest, and bowed his head.

One by one, those who had surrendered followed suit.

"I am not your Emperor," Ahrkyn said.

"You killed their leader, son. You now own the throne," King Nhaeem said.

Freyda's tears continued. She would have to remain within Mhahzin, live in the same Palace she had for years? If her mate took the position of leader, of the new Emperor, she would remain at his side. That was her choice. But the thought of sleeping in the same room as her mother or Ehmile…

Ahrkyn turned a questioning look up to Freyda. He was silently asking her opinion, asking her to speak, asking her to help him choose.

Like he would never force anything on her, she would likewise never make a choice for him.

"You could make a difference here," Freyda whispered. "These people, they're good people. The residents of Mhahzin were never given choices over their own lives. They were forced to pay their taxes in the form of the food they grew and the livestock they raised to the point of near starvation."

Ahrkyn looked to Jhelan, Ihsander, and Ahdeben. Jhelan was the head guard of Ahdlai. He couldn't leave that territory. But the other two…

"You may choose any of our guard to stay with you until you learn who within Mhahzin can be trusted," the King said.

"I'll stay with Emperor Ahrkyn," Ahdeben said, stepping forward.

Ahrkyn shot him a look that let his friend know exactly how he felt about being called Emperor.

"I will stay," Ihsander said.

Others began to volunteer, as well, until there were enough Ahdlai warriors to protect Freyda and Ahrkyn from any Mhahzin soldiers still loyal to Ehmile.

"Can Rhamzin return?" Freyda asked.

"Of course, Your Highness," King Nhaeem said with a bow of his head. "I always knew I would spoil any daughter I was blessed with to no ends. Your request will be granted the moment he is well enough to travel. In the meantime, is there a healer here who can tend to your wounds?"

Freyda listened as plans were made to move Ahrkyn's things to the Palace, listened as the remaining guard of Mhahzin instructed others to seek the healer, listened as each pledged their loyalty to Emperor Ahrkyn and Empress Freyda.

But she barely heard any of it.

She was now the Empress of Mhahzin. She had taken her mother's position, Ahrkyn had taken her stepfather's. But unlike the time of their rule, the people residing within Mhahzin proper and the surrounding towns would be treated with dignity and respect.

The stress of what was to come took her breath, but so did the look of hope on the people's eyes as they moved closer, as they listened to the plans of change being made by Ahrkyn and his men.

They truly could do some real good here. They could change lives. They could free so many and ensure other women weren't treated the way her or her mother had been.

And she couldn't think of a better way for the day to end. Her aches and pains no longer mattered. The time she would have to rest while her injuries, the bumps and bruises, the cuts and broken bones healed no longer mattered.

These were her people. She had two families, though she would have to reacquaint herself with the people of Mhahzin after being kept away from them her whole life.

Two families. Two regions who would work together.

No longer did she regret coming to say goodbye to her mother. This one trip would end up saving thousands, if not millions, of lives.

Chapter Twenty-Six

"You don't need to do that," Ahrkyn said as he approached.

Freyda's hands were currently wrist deep in dirt as she helped plant the cold weather crop to hold them over until spring.

Since Ahrkyn had taken over the region of Mhahzin, he had implemented the same rules and laws as Ahdlai – the entire area was to come together to care for each other. Each town grew the food or raised the livestock they would need to survive. They would use trade, bartering services from each other such as blacksmith, seamstress, and so on.

Ahrkyn's was not a dictatorship. And he hated the term Emperor. He didn't even want to be called King.

But the residents refused to refer to him in an informal manner, thus Emperor Ahrkyn was the official title.

"I don't *need* to, but *want* to. I like this. I like working the garden," she said, taking his hand when he offered it and pushed to her feet.

Pulling her close, he set a hand gingerly on her swollen belly. "You should be resting."

"I have a few more months before this little one makes her arrival. I want to work while I can. After that, my days and nights will be consumed with caring for and nursing her."

"Her? Could be a him," he said, wrapping his arms around her shoulders and hugging her close.

"Her *or* him," she corrected with a smile.

She knew he hoped for a boy, but they both agreed they would be happy with either as long as their child was healthy.

There was no doubt their child would be loved. Since she refused to allow anyone else to raise her baby, one of the first changes Ahrkyn had made – after outlawing Claiming a woman against her will – was that any woman may choose to remain with the offspring if she so choose. And just like in Ahdlai, if she chose, instead, to return to her Clan or town without the child, she would still be cared for in terms of extra protection, extra help with their crops, or food if their yields weren't enough to sustain the town.

"So much work can't be good for your body," he said. "You should rest. The townspeople would understand."

"Women have been having babies for thousands upon thousands of years, my love. And rarely did they have the luxury of lying around and having their every need met by someone else. Besides," she said, resting her cheek against his chest, "I like it out here. I like knowing I'm helping care for our people."

The first few months of Ahrkyn's rule hadn't been easy. There had been several guards who'd surrendered who had refused to obey. Some had been banished, while those who had reveled in the violence Freyda and others had endured had been executed.

But the townspeople had accepted Ahrkyn as their new leader without a single protest. Freyda had lived in the region her whole life, but was only now beginning to get to know them, to truly know the people who lived only yards away from her.

Valdis had suggested they build a second wall around the town, similar to the one they had in Ahdlai. So, while the people worked on that, women were invited to stay inside the Palace if they felt unsafe outside the current wall.

Only two young women had accepted the invitation. The others struggled with the change and were unsure whether they could truly trust the guards who stayed within the Palace.

Rhamzin was one of those guards who lived within the Palace walls, and had become Freyda's personal guard. Of course, taking turns with Mhalaki who remained loyal to Freyda and had learned to respect his new Emperor as well as the reinstated head of Mhahzin's guard.

"I've begged her to go inside more times than I can count," Rhamzin said. "It's too hot for her out here. Her stubborn streak has only grown stronger since she became Empress."

Freyda looked over her shoulder at her first friend. "I'm not stubborn. I'm just always right."

The large guard rolled his eyes and shook his head, but she caught the twitch of his lips as he turned away.

He had been the closest thing to a friend and a father her whole life. Until she'd joined Ahrkyn's family. Now, both Queen Ahlmeda and King Nhaeem treated her as though she were their blood rather than married into their family.

Pulling away from Ahrkyn, she lowered to her knees and returned to her gardening. "Exercise is good for the baby. And the sunshine is good for me. I like it out here."

Since she'd been so restricted her whole life, doing something as simple as working in the dirt with the townspeople brought her a sense of joy, a sense of peace. She would work alongside her people for as long as her back and feet could take it.

Then, after her first child was born, she would immediately begin to teach him or her everything she was forbidden to know. She would make sure the child had choices about their own life, would make sure they knew they were loved unconditionally.

And if she happened to have a little girl, she would make sure her daughter learned to fight from the moment she could walk. She would hire every tutor possible to teach her to read, to teach her mathematics, to teach her strategies of war.

And then, if her daughter decided her life's dream was to find a mate, she would encourage her to follow her heart and not to mate with someone for power or status. Freyda wouldn't even mind if her daughter fell for an outlier, someone who chose to live outside the towns, someone who lived in the woods or caves. As long as the man was good to her and made her happy, she would support her decision.

Her father, Freyda knew, would probably have a lot more to say about who he allowed his daughter to choose. But, in the end, Freyda knew she would win that argument. After all, she had fallen for the enemy of her home territory, the son of her stepfather's enemy.

They had found each other, had been brought together by Mother Universe. He had taught her love and trust and respect. They had fallen in love over such a short time and loved each other more than Freyda thought was worldly possible.

Though they'd endured tragedy and pain and loss, they had found so much more. They had liberated the people of Mhahzin. They were building a community. They were protecting the women of their territory.

And they were building a family of their very own.

No. She could never find an ounce of regret of her first attempt at running away. Because that one ill-planned day had earned her enough happiness to last her three lifetimes.

Thank you for reading **Throne of Ash and Dust**. I hope you loved Ahrkyn and Freyda as much as I do!
If you liked this book, please consider leaving a review. Your support will help other readers find this book!

Thank you!

ABOUT THE AUTHOR

Lynn Howard lives in Cedar Hill, MO, where all her sexy Shifters exist. She lives and breathes hot Alpha males and sassy, brassy females. She feels the most at home knee deep in mud and chicken muck and prefers to be outside under the stars, cuddled up under a blanket in front of a bonfire.

When not typing away or feeding her chickens, you can find her fantasizing about hot country boys for her next book or wandering the woods in search of wildlife. She loves all animals and insects…except spiders. Her favorite foot accessory is barefoot and she owns at least thirty sets of salt-n-pepper shakers, yet only uses one.